HARRY
Saves the World
AGAIN

HARRY
Saves the World
AGAIN

GARY ALEXANDER

Encircle Publications, LLC
Farmington, Maine U.S.A.

Editor: Cynthia Brackett-Vincent
Book design: Eddie Vincent
Cover design: Deirdre Wait, High Pines Creative
Cover images © Getty Images

Published by: Encircle Publications, LLC
PO Box 187
Farmington, ME 04938

Visit: http://encirclepub.com

Printed in U.S.A.

CHAPTER 1

Bremerton, Washington.
Sunday, December 7, 1930.

Cold drafts came straight through the cracks in the wall like icicles. Diana didn't mind the freezing wind. It drowned out the sound of the rats between the wall and the outside boards, running and crawling and fighting. Anyway, she was so sore tonight, she barely felt the cold.

This time, her latest step-daddy had been so rough he may have broken one of her teeth when she fought him. She could feel it with her tongue, a molar, loose and jagged. She tasted blood.

This one, he was the worst of the lot. It wasn't doing it to her that got him excited, she knew. It was hurting her. He was twice her size and smelled like a rotten gym sock and a toilet backup.

Diana sat up on her bunk, wrapped in the only blanket she had. The stove wasn't going. Either they'd forgotten to fill it or their coal delivery was cut off for nonpayment. Again.

Today was her 16th birthday. Sweet Sixteen. No presents or cake anywhere in the cabin for her, but that was no big surprise.

She thought about what she was going to do. Should she go ahead and do what she wanted more than anything she had ever, ever, ever wanted to do?

Diana's father had left when she was a baby, and an older brother ran off five years ago. Her dad had been killed in a bar fight in a

1

California speakeasy, so she'd heard, and her brother had joined the Navy, off to see the world, anywhere but here. Diana had nobody.

She remembered the last time she complained to Mama about the step-daddies. She had picked a rare time when Mama was sober, thinking she'd listen to reason. Mama slapped Diana in the face and said that men had their needs and for her to stop leading them on.

"I don't, Mama. Honest."

"You're telling me you don't know how you look at them? The hell you don't."

"Scared to death is how I look at them, Mama. They're animals."

Which earned her another slap from a woman whose mind was rotted from too much bad liquor.

Diana had dropped out of school last year and worked as a waitress in downtown eateries where they turned a blind eye if a customer had a flask in his pocket. They all liked her, and the ones that pinched her butt left the biggest tips.

Bremerton was a sleepy Navy town with a permanent population of around 10,000. The Great War was long over, but the Great Depression wasn't. The town's biggest employer, the Puget Sound Naval Shipyard (PSNS), had few openings at any given time. You made a buck where you could, how you could. There was nothing here for her except misery.

She had saved as much as she could from her waitressing jobs, hiding the money inside a lamp base. Otherwise Mama and her step-daddy, whoever he was at the time, would take it and go out drinking. The current one worked day labor when there was work, and when he felt like working. She was never sure what Mama did, but whatever it was, it bought her drink and new step-daddies. Cleaned hotel rooms and homes of the city's few rich, Diana thought.

Diana made up her mind. Out of bed quietly, she dressed in double layers, most every piece of clothing she owned, and packed everything else in a cloth bag. A ratty cloth bag with handles, so pathetically small, with ample room for her few belongings. A comb, pocket mirror, toothbrush, undies, not much else.

Carefully, she flung her remaining belongings all over the cubbyhole of a room, then her pillow against a wall and her mattress half off the bunk. As if a fight had taken place.

She pulled aside the peekaboo curtain that served as her bedroom door. All quiet.

She tiptoed into the kitchen and took the sharpest knife out of the drawer. Into Mama's bedroom she went. It was a paring knife—the one that this step-daddy had held to her neck from behind when he first bent her over the kitchen sink and yanked down her panties. Diana's vocabulary was good; she knew what "ironic" meant.

She went into their bedroom. They were passed out. Snoring like buzz saws.

On step-daddy's side, she gently lifted their blankets up. He was bare-ass naked, fat, hairy and stinky. She hesitated, thinking that nobody would *ever* help her. Calling the police—her word against theirs—would earn her an especially-rough beating. Her mouth and head throbbed from last night's, and she continued to ache between her legs, but that was nothing compared to what'd be in store if she complained to the police.

Before quitting school—a truant with bad grades—she was written off by teachers. The principal and teachers were exasperated with her. In testing that was given to the students, her IQ was 133. They had talked to her mother, who was no dummy herself when she was sober. She had sold them a bill of goods: uncontrollable at home, a compulsive liar, a thief, a nymphomaniac, et cetera. She told the school that she'd teach the girl the three R's at home if she could.

Ha ha.

Their cabin was out by Kitsap Lake, deep in the woods, at the end of a dirt road. Too far to be seen or heard by neighbors.

Nobody would help her.

It was so tempting to first go between his legs with the knife. Cut off the thing that he so often made her take in her mouth. Let him see it before the end.

But no. Eventually, it would hurt her as much as it hurt him. They'd hunt her down like a rabid dog.

Using all her strength, she bent at the waist and stabbed his neck, digging in and sawing through his carotid artery. She'd read about it in biology class, what the consequences of a severed carotid were.

Step-daddy sat half-upright, howling. He slapped his neck as if he was bit by an insect.

Diana stood where he could see her. This was important.

He looked at his hand, then at her. Fists clenched, gurgling, he came off the bed.

Blood spurting as if from a pump, he dropped to a knee, then fell over on one side. Then the neck-pumping stopped. Diana stared at him, atop his own shiny red puddle. She had no idea a human body contained that much blood.

She kept staring until she was certain he was dead.

She felt absolutely nothing.

Diana went to the sink, washed off the knife, and began to put it back in the drawer. She dropped it into her cloth bag instead. Who knows when it would come in handy? Then she went through her mother's purse and her stepdad's wallet, taking the few dollars they had.

On her way out, she stopped at their bedroom door. Her mother was still snoring, sleeping the sleep of the dead-drunk.

Diana blew her a kiss and said, "Sorry about the mess, Mama."

They had a junk car, a Model T as old as her. Diana didn't know how to drive, even if she did know how to use the hand crank they stuck in the front to make the car start.

Their cabin was a good three miles from downtown Bremerton, too far to walk on shoes ready to fall apart. Diana made it to the highway, fingers crossed that the buses ran this early. Her feet were so cold that she couldn't feel her toes.

After a half hour of shivering, one came. It was so early that there were just a scattering of other passengers. They were half asleep and hopefully would not remember her. Diana rode the bus all the way in to the ferry terminal and bought a ticket to Seattle, an hour's ride across Puget Sound.

She didn't know what she was going to do next, but it wouldn't be in Bremerton. It'd be in the big city, a city she had visited a few times on school field trips. Seattle, a gigantic place with skyscrapers that made her dizzy when she stood beside them and looked upward.

She took a seat one row away from a man who kept looking at her, a man who had barely keep his eyes off her from the time they boarded. He was an old man, at least in his forties. He was dressed in expensive clothes and had a nice haircut, not a home shearing like she got from Mama every once in a while.

This Depression that was throwing everybody out of work and into soup lines sure didn't seem to bother him, she thought. Him and his business suit and wool overcoat.

The boys at school who tried to do to Diana what her step-daddies did told her she was beautiful. She knew it wasn't entirely a line to talk her out of her panties. If she only had decent hair, like a Marcel, and makeup. Stylish clothes, too. So she didn't look like a ragamuffin.

The man's name was Hubert Hennshaw, age forty-four. He had a double chin and the pursed lips of the righteous and the wronged. He was a Bremerton attorney who had been forced by the Depression to close his office. He was commuting now to Seattle and his employment at a large firm where he worked essentially as a law clerk, at a commensurate salary. *Take it or leave it*, they'd said, *there's a long line of out-of-work lawyers right behind you.*

He was going in on a Sunday to review briefs that one of the partners needed for court tomorrow. A partner six years younger than himself and arrogant to boot. If all this wasn't humiliating enough, Lizzie, his battle-axe wife, was quick to remind him how far he had fallen.

Hubert Hennshaw was raising his eyebrows now and smiling at

Diana. Like a predator to a waif, he knew. The girl was a diamond in the rough. Her upper lip was either the result of a blow or evidence of an overbite. So sexy, either way.

Diana smiled back, sheepishly. A fierce storm had begun as she had stepped onto the boat. She could hear the rain against the windows and the ferry was rocking.

Hubert Hennshaw took a deep breath and stood up. He had never done anything like this before, anything just for *him* whether anybody else liked it or not. She had to be a virgin, too. Lizzie sure as hell wasn't when he married the shrew.

Diana kept her eyes on the old man as he stood up. She had seen Pola Negri movies. She knew what a vamp and a femme fatale were. As the old man moved out of his row, she knew what she'd do. She knew what she had to do, not only to survive, but to prosper.

Diana read his nervousness, his discomfort. What he'd do when the ferry landed in Seattle, she thought, he'd drape his topcoat over her shoulders, a daddy protecting his daughter from the elements, protecting himself from prying eyes.

By the end of the day, the police would be at the cabin, Mama hysterical. The daughter missing.

Two and two being put together. Diana, either a fugitive killer or the other victim of a murder-kidnapping. She was counting on the detectives noticing her cubbyhole in disarray and presuming the latter. Step-daddy killed by the marauder as he heroically rushed to her aid.

She needed concealment and protection. Money, too. Diana made up her mind then and there to get all the money in the world.

No man would ever touch her again without her permission. Which they wouldn't receive unless there was something in it for her.

She smiled bashfully at him.

A Sweet Sixteen smile.

Awkwardly, the old man sat down across from her.

CHAPTER 2

Paris, France.
Monday, June 17, 1940.

"You are certain you can accomplish this?"said the German, a man of immense power who had once been, among other things, a failed chicken farmer.

"Yes, Herr Reichsführer."

"The individual you will be reporting to was persistent at our consulate in San Francisco, and is the originator of this proposal."

"Yes sir, so I am given to understand. I will obey all orders."

"Our diplomats on their western coast have been persecuted and deported, singled out for our friendship with Japan, who America baits and taunts without cause. Soon, I feel, our American embassy and consulates will be closed altogether."

"I am discreet," the man said. "I will obey and serve the Führer in any way imaginable."

"You were so convincing that your upcoming steamship passage and lodging in this hotel room has been paid for by us."

The man glanced at the room's window and its view of the alley. The hotel wasn't a fleabag, but it was out-of-the-way. The Reichsführer-SS was dressed immaculately in double-breasted pinstripes. The SS officers who brought him here were in uniform, waiting outside in the hallway.

He had trouble holding eye contact with his host. The man was soft with an undefined chin. The sides of his head were shaved, the top allowed to grow, and slicked down. He had a hint of a mustache, a faint copy of his Führer's.

"I am grateful, sir, and devoted to your cause. The Jewish Communist international banking conspiracy is a worldwide enemy."

"I must say that the Führer is skeptical, but enthusiastic if the plan works. He has given me a free hand in this matter, pending his final approval."

"I am honored that you agreed to meet with me."

"You have not been to America, nor have I."

"No sir. I look forward to it."

"I think of you as a chameleon, able to blend into any society. You speak several languages without an accent. This is commendable and useful."

"Yes sir. Thank you."

The United States of America, the Reichsführer-SS thought. A vast and rich land weakened by their increasing mongrelization and their diminishing resolve. Their pioneers had been of sturdy Aryan stock. As they moved westward, they killed the aborigines with guns and disease. Later, due to easy prosperity, they softened. But in a brilliant move, their government contrived to have the Custer soldiers eradicated to the last man by the savages.

This generated an outrage that put an end to the nuisance; the sub-humans that were not eradicated were placed in camps they euphemistically called reservations. As the Third Reich was doing now for all the same exemplary reasons.

The Americans may have endless resources, the German thought, but their Aryan purity was contaminated by Orientals and Negros and Mexicans and, worst of all, the Jews. After Europe was fully in German hands, who next? The Americans or the Bolsheviks? Or both? The Führer's imagination had no bounds.

The German reached into his jacket pocket and took out a picture postcard. The foreground was a bridge crossing the Seine, the rear the sprawling city of Paris.

"Gay Paree," he said with a trace of a smile. "We are defining what gaiety is for these French. If their soldiers had not been inept cowards, we would not have prevailed so easily. We shall mold them like putty."

"I have the greatest confidence that you shall, Herr Reichsführer."

"When I leave this room, I am posting this to my mummy, with my warm greetings, wishing her well," he said. "She loves these. I send them from all the cities I visit."

The man who had been summoned smiled and nodded, wondering where this was headed. The German loved his mother and he despised millions of others. Without doubt, a complex individual.

"The Führer will be visiting Paris next week in his private train. He is excited at all we have accomplished in such a short time. Think of this. A mere twenty years ago, in 1920, the German Worker's Party met for the first time in Munich to adopt its platform. I am constantly dazzled at what we have become in two short decades. It is thrilling to think of where we will be in 1950, the conclusion of the third decade since our beginning. Will there be a person on the planet who does not bow to Adolf Hitler?"

"I cannot believe there will be a single one, Herr Reichsführer."

"Our American ally who brought forth this proposal believes as we do. A pragmatist, not an ideologue, this individual knows who will win the war. I strongly believe that one who serves us for personal gain, for greed alone, is far more trustworthy than one who salutes a flag."

"As do I," said the man, whose sole allegiance was to himself.

"England is scheduled next. Operation Sea Lion. Reichsmarschall Göring has assured the Führer that his Luftwaffe will cleanse the skies of the Royal Air Force, making a landing possible, the first successful invasion of England since 1066. Can you conceive the importance?"

What the Reichsführer didn't say was that Göring had the Führer's ear in every important matter. It drove him crazy that Göring—the morphine-addicted pig who could barely pull himself away from the dinner table to waddle to a mirror and award himself another medal—had more influence than he himself had.

"I can, sir. England must fall. But in case it isn't successful —"

The Reichsführer could not control his contempt for Göring. He interrupted with a raised hand and said, "In strict confidence, the Führer and I and others have doubts about Sea Lion. The Luftwaffe should have wiped out the rescue fleet of leaky rowboats at Dunkirk, but they did not."

"No. No, they didn't."

"A third of a million men escaped to fight another day, and the Royal Navy controls the English Channel, so the proposition is sound. Delivery of the bombers to Britain must cease."

"Yes sir. It must and it will end."

"America will enter the war at some point," the German said. "Then the bombers sent to England will no longer be a stream. It will be a flood. This is why I have brought you here."

"I am honored to serve."

"Secrecy is essential. You are not to associate with the Bund or any other organizations in America sympathetic to our goals."

"Of course not. I would not think of it."

"Good. Their hearts are in the right place, but the German-American Bund is noisy. It is fading, too, hounded since the Führer was compelled to react against Poland's aggression toward us. Every single member is known to the police and FBI. When your Jew-loving, Communist President Roosevelt declares war against the Reich, the Bund membership will be scattered and arrested."

"I am in total agreement, Herr Reichsführer."

"You stated that you already have plans to make contact with like-minded friends employed at the Boeing Airplane Company in Seattle, Washington, that manufactures the majority of the B-17 bombers that menace us."

The "chameleon" nodded proudly. "They work on the production lines in different areas. If one is singled out, the others will not be implicated. They will be told what will happen if they talk."

"We have consulted with our scientists. They have developed a reagent that can speed the corrosion of aluminum. I am not a chemist or a metallurgist, so I know nothing more than that it has been tested and that it works beautifully. A vital part on the airplanes will snap in midair or when under other stresses, far away from the Boeing plant. Different parts at different times. It will appear accidental and stall production as engineers pour over blueprints for a redesign solution to the problem without even knowing the true cause of the failures. We can get this material to you and funding for its use, too. If the Führer is convinced, a cornucopia of money will pour forth."

"I am excited. I cannot wait to begin."

"Speak to me once again of motivation. Yours and the other people you will focus on."

"They are different and the same, sir."

"The same?"

"They all resent being drawn into an unjust war. The United States should stay neutral."

"The difference?"

"Each of them for different reasons that are, by and large, selfish. They have combat experience, which has gone unappreciated. They have been poor all their lives. Money overrules patriotism or political dissent."

"Excellent. The reagent is already awaiting you there. Application can be made with an eyedropper or a small sponge. It will dry immediately. It has to be applied on bare metal before a protective coating is sprayed on."

"Zinc chromate."

"Exactly. The aluminum structures beneath are all alloys containing silicon, copper, magnesium and other metals, whether they be forgings, castings or stampings. Beyond that, I am ignorant of the chemistry. I only know that the reagent works as an accelerated corrosive."

TECHNICAL NOTE: Zinc Chromate, ZnCrO4, was used extensively on aircraft during the 1930s and 1940s, most often utilized in landing gear assemblies and other parts exposed to the elements.

"Again, you will be funded generously. Initially, ten thousand dollars for you and for disbursal to those who are cooperating with us. This, at your discretion. Your commander has already rented a post office box for your compensation and has received the sum to establish a base of operations.

"Our people in place have the communications equipment readied and have been schooled on the messages that will be passed along to them by telegraph symbols. The transmissions, when decoded, will provide orders on procedures. Procedures to be followed implicitly."

"Ten thousand dollars. That is very generous, sir."

HISTORICAL NOTE: That was indeed generous. A 1940 dollar was the 2020 equivalent of $19, a nice chunk of change. In 1940, you could drive off the lot in a new Ford or Plymouth for $850. A snazzy Cadillac started at $1350.

"You have studied the dossier we have prepared for you, your identity, and the list of possible persons in American intelligence you are to insinuate yourself with?"

He was insulted by the question. He had memorized every word, every syllable, every letter, and had narrowed down who he would approach and how. For them to look over his shoulder was to treat him as if he were a child. "Yes sir."

"You are a ladies' man, I am told."

Spoken as if an insult? The man blushed.

"If you say so, Herr Reichsführer."

"Select a woman close to an American intelligence agent. This might prove helpful in gathering information from which you can discern what the enemy's countermeasures may be."

Before he could reply, the German stood and extended his hand. "You will be driven to the airport now. From Lisbon, you will proceed to New York."

As he took the Reichsführer's soft, sweaty hand, the man had no choice but to face him directly, not so easy to do. Behind round, rimless glasses, he stared at and through Heinrich Himmler's blank, beady eyes.

The eyes led to the central plaza of Hell.

He was at once terrified and thrilled.

HISTORICAL NOTE: *The central plaza of Hell was a place where Reichsführer-SS Heinrich Luitpold Himmler was right at home. As overseer of the Final Solution and mass murderer extraordinaire, a case could be made that Himmler was the most vicious monster in history. Some would argue that Hitler or Joseph (Uncle Joe) Stalin was number one, but it couldn't be denied that Himmler qualified in the top three.*

Himmler watched as the SS guards escorted the man out of the room. This operative, carefully chosen, *was* a chameleon, molded to fit the Fatherland's requirements.

Himmler thought fondly of something he had *not* disclosed: Ztrvn gas.

Not how the aluminum-corroding reagent was merely a gateway, a decoy, not the mission *in toto*.

On October 14, 1918 at a battlefield near Ypres, Belgium, young Corporal Adolf Hitler had been temporary blinded by a British mustard gas attack. For that reason, and the fear that the enemy would retaliate in kind, he banned the use of deadly gas in this war.

HISTORICAL NOTE: Zyklon B, the brand name for hydrogen cyanide (HCN) was being considered for implementation in concentration camps. In September 1941, it went into use. It is unknown whether the psychopathic Führer appreciated the irony.

Whichever, Hitler made an exception for the virtually-unpronounceable Ztrvn, for this one time only. It was as full of benefits as it was consonants. Ztrvn made Zyklon-B like the scent of roses in comparison. It killed and then clung to surfaces.

The Führer was difficult to amuse, but a Ztrvn joke had him laughing out loud: *Two minutes after exposure and you'll be unable to pronounce anything ever again.*

CHAPTER 3

Havana, Cuba.
Monday, September 2, 1940.

As Americans at home celebrated Labor Day, Horatio Alger (Harry) Antonelli celebrated the absence of broken bones.

Harry was flat on his ass on a narrow rocky beach, having been lifted and dumped over Havana's Malecón wall by a couple of goons, two out of the five still conscious after dragging him out of the Hotel InterPresidential's casino.

They had accused him of card counting at the blackjack tables. Maybe, theoretically, he was memorizing face cards and aces. As they dragged him away, he tried to explain that he wasn't cheating, no cards hidden up his sleeve or anything.

They replied by dragging and shoving harder. All five in the entourage outweighed Harry by twenty to thirty pounds each. It was in the alley behind the casino that Harry claimed his rights were being violated.

Of course, this was ridiculous: he was in Havana, Cuba, not Seattle, Washington, USA. Touristy Havana was the property of President Fulgencio Batista, his cronies, and American gangsters. Harry Antonelli had no rights whatsoever.

But that was no reason for them to slap his face and laugh at him.

Harry grabbed the slapper's forearm as it came around, pulled him near and dear, and head-butted him in the nose, crushing cartilage.

15

Harry's opposite elbow to the temple dropped him for the count.

Three of the four were motionless, stunned. The fourth was slipping on brass knuckles. No such thing as playing dirty now, Harry thought, as he launched a foot at his crotch. It was every man for himself.

Harry Antonelli had been a star halfback as well as the placekicker for the University of Washington Huskies, class of 1938, routinely booting 30-yarders between the goal posts. The guy he kicked fell to his knees and keeled over, out for the remainder of the game.

The other three tore into him. Harry responded with feet, elbows and fists. After a knee-ligament snap and a howl, it was down to two-to-one, but they were wearing him down with body and head blows.

Harry could swear he heard a woman's voice in broken English, *stop, do not kill him, stop it.*

Could be because his ears were ringing and he was hearing what he wanted to hear, but they did stop and stumbled along, hauling him, heels dragging, like an ox cart with a seized axle.

Over the Malecón's waist-high wall Harry had gone, where he sat uncomfortably on a pile of slimy rocks. After ruling out broken bones, he felt and twisted for torn joints. Okay, good.

He tried to stand. *Not* so good. Wobbling, he slammed his hands against the wall. He was freezing cold. Yeah, the ocean here was the Caribbean and tropical, but having it lap over you in the middle of the night—

"Are you all right?"

That same woman's voice.

Harry looked upward at twin angels with long hair and fluffy white dresses.

"Never better," he said. "How about you, girls? Thanks for calling off those jackals."

"Girls? I am alone."

Harry didn't reply. Was he awake or dreaming?

"Do you know why they were so rough on you?"

"I don't. I wasn't doing anything wrong," Harry said.

"It wasn't because you were card-counting."

"I wasn't," Harry lied. "I was concentrating."

She laughed. "You were too, but you are not very good at it. You were winning very small sums."

Harry took a deep breath. His double vision was going away. There was just one of her now, even more beautiful than when she was twins. He had seen her in the casino. But where?

"Yeah, I know. My memory's not as good as I thought it was."

"It was because you were disrespectful to that man before you went to the blackjack table."

"The little guy?"

"He is little like a coral snake is little," she said.

"He's a chain smoker," Harry said. "I guess that's what stunted his growth."

"What did he say to you?"

"He told me that card-counting wasn't allowed."

"What did you say to him?"

"I told him to mind his own business," Harry said, omitting the adjective he used before *business*. "The flashy shows with famous bands and chorus girls, a square mile of slot machines and gaming tables—all the money in the world—there's no call for him to pick me out of the crowd."

"That casino *is* his business. His and President Batista's and my father's and others. I know all this because I work for my father as a hostess for high rollers who are new at the InterPresidential, showing them around."

"Yeah? Who is that midget?"

"Meyer Lansky. He ordered those thugs to teach you a lesson."

"Never heard of him."

"Meyer Lansky is an American gangster."

"Oh. Uh-oh."

"Mr. Lansky is at the very top of their organization."

"I've heard of Al Capone and Lucky Luciano."

"They are in prison. Lansky is not. He handles Luciano's business for him. They say he is a genius with numbers."

"Who's your father?"

"An important army general."

"Oh. Well, that shrimp Lansky, he oughta cut down on the smoking. It'll hurt his lungs and cut down on his wind, too."

HISTORICAL NOTE: Unknowingly, Harry had made a good point. Meyer Lansky (1902-1983), known as the Mob's accountant, had beaten all odds to survive what befell most mobsters of his high rank: assassination or long-term incarceration. His only conviction was for illegal gambling. Lansky died of lung cancer at the age of eighty.

"I am Gabrielle," she said.

"Pleased to meet you. I'm Harry."

"You should get you out of there, Harry. When high tide comes, you will drown."

"That's a swell idea, Gabrielle. I don't swim too well."

Harry hoisted himself up onto the walkway.

He stood, brushed himself off and said, "Gabrielle, I appreciate what you did. If you hadn't, they'd still be pounding away on me."

"You fought them like an expert," she said. "Did you have training as a fighter?"

"You might say so. I played college football."

"I do not understand. If you fight in soccer, the referee shows you a red card and sends you off."

"No, football, not soccer. Fighting is against the rules too, but plenty of stuff happens in piles when you're going after a fumble."

"I do not understand what you are saying. Soccer is football, *fútbol*."

"No," Harry said. "Soccer is soccer. Football is football."

Gabrielle sighed. "Very well."

"Actually, I really had to learn to fight after college. In Europe, where I was for a couple of years before coming to Havana, I got into scrapes that weren't my fault."

"These scrapes, they were not?"

"Nope. It was a language barrier. People got the wrong idea."

They began to walk.

"Tell me your story," she said. "When did you first come to Cuba and why?"

"Well, that's a *long* story, Gabrielle."

"The night is pleasant and the Malecón is long."

"Okay. I owe you."

Harry spoke slowly and cautiously, as his story required careful editing.

"After college graduation in thirty-eight, I went to Europe for the summer. Everybody's plan for me was to come home in the fall, teach high school history and coach the football—not soccer, nobody plays soccer where I come from—team, settle down, get married, raise a family, keep doing that until I got old, and retired, and died in my rocking chair.

"Well, I realized that everybody's plan for me wasn't *my* plan for me—even though I didn't know what my plan for me *was*—and now that I think of it, still don't know my plan for me. I moved around in Europe, had some differences of opinion with people, mostly Nazis, who helped me refine my skills as a fighter. Only because I had to, language barriers and Nazis, you know, acting like evil Nazis.

"I wound up in Lisbon, where some old friends from home asked me to help them out putting the skids on a Nazi scheme to poison millions of people with radioactive uranium."

"Goodness," she said, unsure if her English was good enough to understand all he said, or whether he was telling tall tales or not.

Harry shrugged and said, "It worked out for us, but I had other troubles that weren't my fault."

This was where the very careful editing kicked in. There were three deaths in Lisbon, two of which were murder, the third an apparent accidental fall. Harry, at the moment, was doubtlessly being investigated for the murders, which he did not commit.

There probably wasn't any official interest in the accidental fall, which wasn't accidental, but rather a murder Harry *did* commit. It could be convincingly argued, however, that the accidental fall/murder was justified, as well as the murders he didn't commit, since the all of victims were Nazis or Nazi stooges.

Whichever, Horatio Alger (Harry) Antonelli wasn't sticking around Lisbon for any of it, as language barriers and overzealous police wouldn't be in his best interests.

"Before anybody could make me a patsy for things I didn't do, I hired on to the first tramp steamer that'd take me out of Portugal. Havana was the first stop. I hopped off here around a month and a half ago. I had a little money, enough to rent a room a half mile from here. It's in a slum. You have a lot of poor people in Havana, you know."

"Just between you and I, Harry, I do know," Gabrielle said. "President Batista pretends that poor people do not exist."

"They sure do exist, Gabrielle," Harry said. "They're nice people, making the best out of what they have, living in scrap-wood shacks without electricity or running water. Some don't know where their next meal is coming from and that's a damned shame."

Harry had the pigeon-toed gait of a natural athlete, but now he was crabbing slightly to starboard. Something was out of kilter. A good night's sleep or two will fix me, he thought. Maybe.

Harry Antonelli was the first in his family to attend college. He had majored in history and coeds and football, where he was a star halfback, playing both offense and defense. He had given out punishment and taken it, too. Guys he'd clobbered had been carried off on stretchers. He'd taken some hits that sent him off the field the same way.

At 5' 9½" and 180 pounds, Harry was no shrimp, but the linemen he had to run through were gorillas, getting bigger and bigger, some tipping the scales at 210, 220, even 230. The goons he'd taken on earlier tonight were in that range, At age twenty-four, he wondered if he was getting too old to give and receive so much abuse.

He could smell his rescuing angel's perfume as they walked. Gabrielle had olive skin and a classic Latin profile. She was cute—elegant, even—but no Miss America. He knew he was a fine one to talk. Of Scottish-Italian persuasion, Harry's nose had been broken too many times to count, sometimes due to football, sometimes to other forms of contact.

Harry Antonelli's face fit in a category between ruggedly handsome and disfigured. Too much football, too many brawls. Have to get this schnoz fixed someday, Harry thought. If only people would stop busting it.

Gabrielle found Harry masculine and exciting. She thought of him as a wounded bird, too, but didn't say so. A bird that should be nurtured in many ways.

"You should not stay in a place like that. It is not good for your health. We have a spare room at our home. You can stay there until you recover from your injuries."

"You're sure you have enough rooms to spare one for me?"

Gabrielle's home contained *ten* spare rooms, plus the servants' quarters over a five-car garage.

"Yes, I am sure. We are shorthanded. A handyman went away to his home village to visit and never came back. Are you handy with tools?"

Unlike his father and brother who ran the family's auto body shop, Harry didn't know one end of a wrench from another.

"I can fix anything," he said.

"The handyman room is over the garage, but it is very nice."

Harry didn't know what "nice" meant, but it had to be nicer than what might be his next home, one with an underwater view while wearing concrete boots. He doubted if the casino gangsters would settle for just another beating, not after what he'd done to their goons.

21

This might be a real job, one he could learn from while working at it. Like an apprenticeship. Harry knew that he was running out of time to blame everything on others and his own post-adolescence.

"What are we waiting for?" he said.

CHAPTER 4

Miscellaneous locales.
Tuesday, September 3, 1940 to Sunday, December 7, 1941.

Heinrich Himmler's operative was now in Seattle, Washington State, USA, doing as he had been ordered, carefully establishing himself with his superior and his mission. He had ample money too, aware that he was on the verge of righting personal wrongs, and also on the cusp of making history. He would be rewarded in so many ways.

*****

Heinrich Himmler was in Berlin at his office on Prinz-Albrecht Strasse, secretly gloating. Thanks to Göring's ineptitude, the Luftwaffe was losing the Battle of Britain to the tenacious Royal Air Force, to fighter pilots scarcely out of their teens flying Spitfire and Hurricane fighter planes, thus compelling the Führer to indefinitely postpone Operation Sea Lion, the invasion of England. The fat man's influence was waning, propelling Himmler himself into Germany's second in command.

The man he had sent to America had played right into his hands, too. Yes, if he and his small band of mercenary loyalists didn't bungle it, they would do a significant measure of damage, distracting American intelligence officers from the true objective. A handful of

B-17 Flying Fortresses crashing while en route to England was nice, but hardly pivotal. The best was yet to come.

It was a glorious time to be Heinrich Himmler.

On June 22, 1941, when Germany invaded the Soviet Union, it took the Russians completely by surprise and seemed like another masterstroke by the Führer.

But then on December 7, when Japan attacked Pearl Harbor, bringing the United States into the war, the Wehrmacht was stalled within sight of Moscow, bogged down by Soviet resistance and the worst Russian winter in memory.

Himmler was beginning to have second thoughts about his future, and of Adolf Hitler's judgment. If victory on the Eastern Front was becoming dubious, their hegemony in the West had to be maintained.

He idly spun a pencil on his desk.

The bombing of the Reich had to stop at all costs, he knew. His imperative at the Boeing Airplane Company in Seattle had to get off the ground before the flood of B-17s did.

*****

Horatio Alger (Harry) Antonelli was in Havana, Cuba.

Gabrielle's home was feeling more and more like a jailhouse, where it soon became apparent that he had the handyman skills of a chimpanzee.

Gabrielle's father despised Harry and Harry knew it. The man had the leathery, bronzed skin of the cane cutter he had once been before joining the army and coming up through the ranks by using his machete on other than sugar cane.

Gabrielle had her daddy wrapped around her little finger though, and wrangled Harry a job at the Hotel InterPresidential, where he worked as an "executive security concierge," a stupid title for what he actually did: escort well-heeled Americans around the casino, making certain they weren't robbed or cheated by anyone except the house. As often as not, the women were bejeweled, the men loud and drunken. Harry was expected to do anything for them but clean up their vomit.

The worst were the rich old men with the young blondes. Gabrielle kept a close eye on Harry, checking that he didn't keep too close an eye on the blondes. Just as she did when his eye wandered to the showgirls on stage or the swarms of hookers.

It was even worse at Gabrielle's, an estate or plantation or mansion or hacienda or palace... whatever you wanted to call it. Harry stayed in the spare room over the garage, staying alone for only three days, before Gabrielle began visiting when she could, unseen by her parents.

Gabrielle was an only child, and her parents lived on the other end of the mansion. It was as if they lived in a different time zone. They had a family meal on Sundays, a long-standing custom. Harry was invited, too. Everyone was civil, but quiet and wary.

Gabrielle's mother was dropping leaden hints to Gabrielle about advancing age and grandchildren, her little girl the ripe old age of twenty-three, an old maid in waiting. Gabrielle was dropping hints, too, by not shushing her mother.

Her father, the general and casino potentate, had no obvious interest in Harry as a son-in-law. He kept a close eye on him though, wherever Harry was, whether he was actually watching him or not. Harry could count the number of times the general had spoken to him on one hand.

At work on the casino floor, when he saw Meyer Lansky or any of his gangster friends, Harry remembered Gabrielle's coral snake remark, and steered clear. He knew Lansky was keeping a close eye on him even when he was around the corner.

Harry was bored to tears, jumpy, suffocating, ill at ease, paranoid, insecure...

And homesick.

*****

In that period of time, The Killer Klown Gang—so named by the press—had robbed sixteen Seattle banks. An ongoing dragnet produced nothing. The Killer Klown himself usually did his stick-ups on Fridays; out of fifty-nine Fridays in that period, he had robbed on fourteen. The gang's wheelman waited outside in a freshly-stolen car, always a souped-up coupe. They considered days before holidays, too, just to mix things up, as the banks always carried plenty of dough then.

On Friday, December 5, 1941, the bank robber who thought Dillinger, Willie Sutton, Baby Face Nelson, and others were pikers compared to him, stepped out of a 1937 Ford that had been modified with two carburetors. He nodded to his driver, slipped on his clown mask, and entered his bank of choice. It was a branch on Broadway Street, a concrete and stone building dating to the 1910s. For some reason, he believed that the old, ornate banks contained more money than the others.

Inside, he waved his Colt .45 automatic and yelled semi-intelligibly through the mask. The employees and customers did not require a translation. They knew who he was and coughed up the dough fast.

The Killer Klown had wounded two and killed two during the gang's spree.

CHAPTER 5

Havana.
Wednesday. December 10, 1941.

Monday's *Miami Herald* and other big-city dailies confirm what has been all over the radio since Sunday afternoon.: the Japs attacked a U.S. Navy base in Honolulu, Hawaii, named Pearl Harbor. The Americans were caught with their pants down and lost a number of ships and had thousands of casualties. The radio announcers were outraged that it had been a sneak attack.

Harry Antonelli agrees that it was a lousy thing to do, but as far as a sneak attack went, what were the little guys supposed to do, send out engraved invitations? *Yankee devil, we cordially invite you to look up in the sky at 0800.*

Harry keeps that thought to himself.

There is a Seattle paper in the stack too, a rarity. Possibly a rich Seattleite, fearing a Jap invasion of the West Coast, hopped on an airliner and made the two-day trip to Miami.

Studying the front page of the December 8 *Seattle Post-Intelligencer*, Harry has to admit, the headlines are pretty scary:

WAR EXTRA! WAR EXTRA!
JAPS BOMBING MANILA, HAWAII.
Pearl Harbor Base Blasted by Enemy Craft. Navy Men
Ordered to Posts as News Of Attack Comes In.

Page 2 is just as bad:

MANILA AND PEARL HARBOR
UNDER ATTACK BY JAPAN.
Big Blast Rocks City of Honolulu.
Second Wave of Bombers Makes Attack.

In a lower corner of the page, Harry sees the start of a story:

THE KILLER KLOWN GANG Strikes Again.
Bank #16. Fortunately No Gun-play This Time
by the Mad Dog Killers.

Guns and clowns. Harry shivers and returns to the less frightening war stories, one speculating how the Pacific Coast may be the next Jap target, bombing with an invasion to follow.

Harry worries about his best friend, Saburo (Chuck) Shimizu. Chuck is a loyal American of Japanese descent, born and raised in Seattle, as loyal as can be, not a sneaky bomber pilot. A great guy, brilliant in school, and a damn hard worker, now in medical school at the University of Washington. Will Chuck still be regarded that way, not as the enemy? Harry sure as hell hopes so.

It is a ritual of his to get a copy of the *Miami Herald* and other papers when they come in on the Miami-Havana steamship. It's an overnight trip of 220 miles, and it doesn't come in every day.

The papers are always a day or two late, but no problem. Until now, Harry has read them mostly for the funnies. Harry likes the daily funny papers and *loves* the Sunday funnies, a separate section in color.

Flash Gordon, Batman, Superman, Captain Marvel, Dick Tracy, The Phantom, Buck Rogers. Harry loves those guys.

A couple of gals, too. There's Little Orphan Annie and her dog, Sandy, that says "Arf, arf." And the guys around her, the inscrutable

Asp, Daddy Warbucks, and gigantic Punjab. None of them seem like child molesters, but the story lines are strange.

The other gal is Wonder Woman, a hot dame wearing patriotic tights of blue with white stars. Her top is red, and doesn't leave much to the imagination.

She's as tough and talented as any male superhero—Captain Marvel—or any of them, except maybe Superman. Wonder Woman has bracelets that deflect bullets—a good kind of jewelry to have— and an invisible airplane at her disposal. It looks faster than a Messerschmitt or Spitfire, or anything else in the air for that matter.

She carries a magic lasso, too. When she ropes you and pulls you in close and questions you, you've got no choice but to tell the truth. Her and me and that polygraph lariat, Harry thinks, we'd never hit it off.

HISTORICAL NOTE: Wonder Woman wasn't introduced until December 1941, but red-blooded Harry needs to welcome a female superhero into his fantasy world earlier than that. Buck Rogers' Wilma Deering and Flash Gordon's Dale Arden are already spoken for, and he suspects that the sexual preference of Dick Tracy's Tess Trueheart is unclear, too complex or lurid for the comic pages.

Wonder Woman doesn't have a favorite fella; her relationship with Colonel Steve Trevor is platonic, although Steve wishes it weren't. Harry likes nothing more than a great figure and a challenge.

Harry has gone in to the InterPresidential early to read the papers in the lobby. The general does not allow American newspapers in his home. The only papers permitted are the Havana rags, propaganda sheets that stop just short of deifying Batista.

Harry can't concentrate on the funnies today. He keeps turning back to the Pearl Harbor stories. Since the first radio broadcasts, he's been thinking about doing his part.

Before that, actually. He's been a crummy son, barely keeping in contact by letter and postcard with his mother who adores and frets over him. In the last year, she has written of "war clouds on the horizon," as she put it, naming friends of his who already signed up for the Army, Navy and Marines.

It's been in the back of his mind for some time. Go home and do his duty, not to mention escaping from Havana. His druthers would be the Army Air Corps. Go through fighter-pilot training and head for the Pacific. Join the Flying Tigers or anybody who'd have him. Shoot Jap Zeros out of the sky until there were none left, that, or on to England to bag Messerschmitts. He almost dropped a hint that he was thinking about it in his postcard to her last week, but didn't, keeping it neutral and the picture on it scenic.

He will have to work it out carefully. Get his steamship tickets secretly. Break the news gently to Gabrielle, beginning with patriotism and how he'll always love her. Anything to keep her from crying on her daddy's epaulets.

Harry has sensed that the old man has been waiting for a misstep, any sign that he's hurting his little girl. An excuse to take him on a midnight swim.

Lost in thought, Harry doesn't notice the man until he's directly in front of him: polished boots, creased slacks, and cigar in hand.

He looks up from the paper and sees the general in full uniform.

"You and I should talk," Gabrielle's father says. "We should do this immediately."

More words spoken to him than in the past fifteen months combined.

"Uh, sure," Harry says, rising to his feet. "Yes sir."

"Let us go outside and enjoy the fresh air."

Outside they go and to the Malecón. Harry is smelling the fresh sea air, not a comforting fragrance at the moment.

"Your nation is at war," the general says.

"Yes sir, I know."

"How Cuba will respond to the hostilities, I cannot say. It will be up to President Batista's great and wise judgment."

"I know he'll do the right thing, sir," Harry lies. Batista will sell his nation's allegiance to the highest bidder.

"And you? Americans are known for their patriotism and their willingness to fight for their freedom. This since that Boston Tea Party, a wonderful legacy."

A trap?

"I want to do the right thing, sir."

"Serving your country with all the America-loving young men, yes?"

"Well—"

The general stops and looks Harry in the eye. "You are going to do the right thing. I know you are. I can see it in your face, how you desire to kill and defeat—how is it you say?—the Yellow Peril. Gabrielle will be sad for the time being, and we will miss you, too. My wife and I have looked upon you as a son."

"Uh-huh."

As Harry tries to answer, he hears a boat. An outboard motor launch pulls up. It's high tide and fairly calm. A man jumps out with a rope and stands on the rocks, serving as a human anchor.

"I know you are anxious to do your patriotic duty to your nation as soon as you possibly can, so you will be taken to Miami on my speedboat here. You will not have to wait for the steamship, yes? Your belongings will be sent ahead to your home city in the Province of Washington."

Harry knows of the general's speedboat. He has seen it several times at night when, so the rumors go, he smuggles drugs to his gangster friends in Miami and Tampa.

The man/anchor extends a hand for Harry, who obediently climbs over the Malecón wall and into the boat.

As the launch pulls away, the general salutes and says, "God bless you, my boy."

When the boat is out of sight, the general puffs on his cigar, and thinks: *good riddance*. He despises this Antonelli gigolo. Gabrielle knows this, a large part of her attraction to him, the primary reason he has remained silent. He knew if he obeyed his initial instinct and threw the gold-digging gigolo out of his home, Gabrielle would leave too and probably elope with him. Girls these days, there is no comprehending them.

The general cares not what Antonelli does when he reaches American soil. He can enlist or not. The war is not his concern. Now he can tell his little girl that Antonelli ran out on her. She will have no way to prove otherwise.

For a year and three months, he has suppressed a molten-hot fury. If not for his beloved child and his idiotic wife and her obsession with grandchildren, he would have disposed of the gigolo long ago, instead of giving him a home and a job at the InterPresidential.

Have him disappeared or have him arrested for *anything* and put before a firing squad.

The general walks toward the InterPresidential, thinking that Meyer Lansky is due in later this week. He will talk to Meyer about the gigolo, how he has no respect for a lady. Meyer knows people in Los Angeles who can go up north to Seattle and teach Antonelli a lesson, and give the general the vengeance he richly deserves.

Benny Siegel runs the operation out in Los Angeles, California. Benny is not all the way normal in the head, the general has been told, and this is good. Benny will know what to do with the gigolo and he will not be delicate about it.

CHAPTER 6

Seattle.
Saturday, December 13, 1941.

Rocco Antonelli walks in the front door after work to see his wife Joanne holding a postcard, smiling from ear to ear, like it's already Christmas.

He takes it from her and sits in his easy chair. They live in south Seattle in a tidy neighborhood where everybody knows everybody else, which in his opinion can be good *and* bad. It's a one-story home with a full basement made into a bedroom for the boys, a weedless lawn, and siding that Rocco faithfully repaints every three years.

Out the window, across the street, at the end of the block, he can see the Booth home. Of similar architecture, it's twice the size of theirs. A nice man and a dentist, Dr. Booth doesn't lord it over anyone. Dorothy, their daughter, and Harry were once longtime boyfriend and girlfriend.

Last year, Dorothy and her egghead brother, David, had gone to Lisbon to see Harry, a trip they've keep mum on ever since.

"I'll wager a week's income it's from Harry."

Joanne Antonelli's smile widens. "You win."

It's a picture postcard airmailed from Havana, Cuba, half the photo of quaint buildings in town, the other half of happy peasants in a field, cutting sugar cane.

Rocco doubts if the cane cutters are really happy. He sure as hell wouldn't be, bent over all day in that heat, being paid peanuts. He reads the papers and knows that Batista, dictator of Cuba, is a trigger-happy crook who's as mean as a basket full of snakes.

"Harry says he's well and hopes we are. As usual, he says nothing. I guess he's still a bouncer at some gangster casino in Havana."

Joanne is a pleasant-looking woman in her late-forties, turning slightly plump. She quickly says, "Stop it. He has an important security job of some sort at that casino. We can pray that the war hasn't changed things down there."

Rocco, string-bean lean, with the profile of a hawk, doesn't pray about anything. He says, "Cuba doesn't care about us or the Japs."

"I lost my brother Fred in the Great War, you know," Joanne says. "The whole world is a powder keg. Those Germans and that crazy bug-eyed Hitler of theirs, they follow him like sheep. The Nazis have their U-boat submarines all along the East Coast, don't forget."

Rocco steps out of his coveralls. Antonelli Body and Paint on Empire Way, a mile from home, is a three-stall shop: just Lou, their other son, another body man, and a painter. Rocco can't sit in the office in a coat and tie like some big-shot executive swell. He works on the line when there's a lot to do and there aren't any visitors pestering him. If there is work piling up, like now, he goes in on Saturdays, him and Lou both.

It's a comfort to Rocco that Lou has no high-falutin' ideas in his head. Lou's a year younger than Harry and a century more mature. He's living downstairs in the basement where the boys did while growing up, saving money for a ring so he can pop the question to Julia, a really sweet little gal he's been going steady with since the 8th grade. She does typing and stenography for a major insurance company downtown, bringing in a little money, too.

The shop will be in good hands when it's time for Rocco to call it quits, and Joanne will get the grandchildren she's so eager for. Harry and Lou. Damned good boys in their own different ways, he has to admit.

Joanne takes the coveralls from him and says, "You have fresh slacks and a shirt on the bed."

Joanne keeps a tidy house. She has doilies and trifles in the living room, lamps and knickknacks where they should be, everything just so, not a speck of dust anywhere. She looks at a silver-framed picture of Harry on the mantle in his college football uniform, a snarling smile inside his leather helmet as he clutches a football.

Rocco likes football, but doesn't understand why his son wanted to get the daylights knocked out of him every autumn Saturday. That didn't stop Rocco and Joanne from attending at least half the home games, and listening to the others and to all the road games on the radio. On the edge of their seats.

He has never understood the boy at all. In the back of his mind, he thought that it all started with Joanne putting her foot down that he be called Horatio Alger instead of a good Italian name like Carmine or Silvio. Horatio Alger, the name of some writer who wrote about poor boys who made it to the top with diligence and hard work.

She said she'd carried him around for nine months, the last three in the heat of the summer, so she ought to have the final word.

He couldn't argue with that.

After he bathes, Rocco sits in the living room while Joanne finishes fixing dinner. He's poured himself a generous glassful of his own dago red from a laundry bleach bottle with a ring handle. He'd begun making wine during Prohibition in an attic above the shop, and is known throughout the area as the best vintner around.

After the powers that be came to their senses and repealed the stupid Volstead Act that handed the country over to mobsters, Rocco saw no reason to stop. His red is as good as any the grocery store crooks want an arm and a leg for. Add a quart bottle of it to a bag of flour and a dozen eggs, and you're out three bucks.

Rocco has the Philco console on, a big handsome machine made of polished hardwood, with a dial set in the upper center. Benny Goodman is turned down low.

That goddamn cat of Harry's is staring at him. It's like an African voodoo stare. The goddamn thing's perched on a chair that's been passed down on Joanne's side of the family since Christ was a corporal. High-backed with old-timey cloth, they saw some just like it in *Gone with the Wind*, which Joanne dragged him downtown to see the year before last. No one's permitted to sit in the antique chair except guests and that goddamned cat. It's like she's substituted the goddamn thing for Harry.

Rocco and the cat have a mutual hatred, worsened by the fact that Rocco can't lift a finger against it, and the goddamn cat knows it. How he'd love to take it for a one-way ride into the woods where it can attack wolves and bears instead of neighborhood cats and dogs. Rocco is sick and tired of apologizing and paying vet bills.

When Harry was a kid, Rocco had wondered about him and his love of cats instead of dogs, but he came to realize that there wasn't anything wrong with the boy after all. Not in that regard.

He saw his son carry two would-be tacklers into the end zone in a game against Oregon State. He'd seen helmets go flying, Harry's and the guys he'd hit, some of them real bruisers. They were in the stands when a star UCLA halfback had to be taken off in a stretcher, thanks to Harry's open-field tackle that lifted him off his feet and planted him on the ground flatter than a pancake.

There was one thing about the boy, among many, that had Rocco scratching his head. When Harry was a squirt, Rocco had paid a day's income for circus tickets, front-row seats. The kid loved it, the elephants, the fire-eater, the nut case shot out of a cannon, everything. Then a couple of clowns on unicycles came by so close you could touch them. Maybe it was the booze on their breath or the paint on their faces, down-turning their lips like they were frowning, that made Harry go hysterical. Rocco didn't know why, but he'd had to take Harry out of there. They never talked about it, then or since.

The goddamn cat keeps staring. A stray that showed up eight or nine years ago, it has a whole lot of Harry in him and vice versa. If trouble doesn't come to them, they'll go out looking for it.

Tabby—the gray-striped thing's name—tires of the staring contest, yawns, and begins licking its privates. Rocco mutters a curse and drinks his wine, thinking again of Harry wasting four years of book learning at the University of Washington, studying history, stuff that already happened.

The boy should've taken a cue from Chuck Shimizu, his best chum, who's going to be a doctor and make some real dough. Harry and Chuck were high school track stars, about all they have in common. The Shimizus, all of them, are nice folks. Not everyone thinks so; just because the Japs over there in Japan are sneaky, vicious bastards. It'll get a helluva lot worse for the Shimizus before it gets better, he knows. There's talk of shipping them off to live in camps like they're zoo animals.

Rocco is damn worried about them. The night after Pearl Harbor, a couple of their front windows were broken out by rocks.

Rocco gets up, studies the postcard, thinks of Harry's postcards from Lisbon, and yells into the kitchen. "Dorothy's too good for him."

"What brought that on?" she yells back.

"I don't know. The Lisbon postcards, I guess."

"You and I know that Dorothy Booth is too good for him. If she could only corral him for good and lead him to the altar, she could change him."

Rocco laughs and says, "Give it up, kiddo."

"You pooh-pooh me, but I know she can straighten him out if she has half a chance."

Rocco smiles and drinks his wine. He says nothing; no point to. He thinks of Harry, thinking that he's too dreamy for his own good. He'd spend half of every Sunday reading and rereading the funny papers. Spending the day in outer space with Buck Rogers and Flash Gordon. Or zooming around down on earth like Superman.

Rocco Antonelli hadn't gone far in school, but he knows that all women believe they can change their men, and none of them ever do.

Why even try?

Why the hell hook up with someone in the first place if he needs changing?

Rocco finishes his glass. If he was a praying man, he'd say one for Harry, that he'll for once keep his nose out of trouble. The boy goes through life like he played football, lowering his head and smashing his way through. All over Europe, then Cuba. Where next?

The doorbell rings.

Rocco goes to the door.

One man stands, facing the other.

They fall into each other's arms, crying.

CHAPTER 7

Seattle.
Sunday, December 14, 1941.

S unday dinner at the Antonelli's, aka a Norman Rockwell painting.
The Antonellis are lapsed Catholics who rarely attend Mass,
even on obligatory Christmas and Easter. Nor were the boys ever
required to attend parochial schools. So the meal begins without
anyone saying grace.

Plates and bowls are passed around: ham, scalloped potatoes,
mixed vegetables cooked to within an inch of their lives.

At the table: Rocco, Joanne, Harry, Lou and Lou's fiancée, Julia
Wilson.

Harry's belongings haven't been sent ahead by the general, and he
doesn't expect them to be. He imagines them being ceremoniously
burned. A demon exorcised.

Lou is an inch shorter than him and his waistline an inch or two
wider, but a pair of borrowed corduroys and a sweater fit well enough.
His mother hasn't decided whether to launder or burn the clothes he
wore for three days straight.

"Rocco," Joanne coaxes.

A jug of his red occupies a place of honor in the center of the table
with the ham. Water glasses have been filled with it.

Rocco raises his. "To Harry. Enemy fighter pilots oughta be losing
sleep."

"When are you signing up, Harry?" Julia asks.

"I'm thinking tomorrow, for the Army Air Corps. I think they'll need all the fighter pilots they can get."

Lou says, "You flew some in college, didn't you?"

"A little time in a Piper Cub. Not the same thing as a Warhawk or a Wildcat, but maybe they'll take that into consideration."

What Harry hopes the army brass won't take into consideration is that, while a member of ROTC, taking flying lessons in a Piper J-3 Cub and looking ahead to an Army Air Corps future even then, he was drummed out for insubordination. After being chided during a morning inspection for scuffed shoes and a wrinkled uniform after a long night out, he told the West Point captain to "Sir, go fuck yourself. Sir." This was considered bad form. Disobedient and un-military.

Joanne says, "Don't be bashful about seconds on the ham. Mark my words. Rationing of everything imaginable is going to happen soon. It'll be mass confusion."

HISTORICAL NOTE: Joanne Antonelli is correct. In the spring of 1942, the Food Rationing Program will be set in motion. Every family will be issued a War Ration Book full of stamps. Some items will require a blue stamp, some a red stamp, some none at all. Further complicating it will be a point system that would challenge an accountant. Grocers will tear their hair out, trying to label everything correctly. A black market will flourish.

Joanne breaks the silence with, "Harry, As far as I know, Dorothy's still teaching at the high school."

As far as she knows.

"Oh, well, good."

"Dr. and Mrs. Booth are on holiday in Palm Springs. I was tempted to invite Dorothy for dinner today."

Harry knows he's expected to ask why she didn't. She stares at him until he does.

"Why didn't you?" he asks.

"She may have a new beau. Not that I know for sure, of course."

"Oh," Harry says.

"He's rich and handsome and has a fancy car. From what I hear."

Harry doesn't bite. He shrugs and slices his ham. Dinner finishes quietly.

While Lou drives Julia home, Joanne is dying to probe him about his intentions when he returns. When will Lou pop the question? Will he be drafted if they tie the knot? She doesn't, though, in the faint hope that he'll voluntarily open up to his parents.

Rocco wonders about Lou, too, and the others at the shop. Will they enlist or be drafted as well? If he's on his own, will it matter? He probably won't be able to get parts anyway. The steel in the Studebaker fender he can't get will be made into a section of tank armor.

Harry worries about his best friend, Saburo (Chuck) Shimizu. Mom and Dad have told him about the vandalism. Lou has seen a sign on a window at the barber shop where they went as kids for their haircuts: FREE SHAVES FOR JAPS.

First thing tomorrow, on his way to the recruiting office, Harry will pay Chuck a visit.

The Antonellis savor their dessert of ice cream and coffee.

Everybody is reading the paper closely, while listening to news broadcasts on the Philco. The Japs are like locusts, Rocco is thinking, overrunning countries that produce sugar and coffee and many other things that are taken for granted.

What will happen to our boys?

*****

In the basement in their childhood room, it's like a reunion. They have always been close, up and through high school, where they played football, Lou on the line blocking for Harry, who ran around and through their opponents, making all-state in his junior and senior years. From there, they went their separate ways, Harry to college to study history, football and girls, and Lou to Antonelli Body and Paint.

Tonight, it's their childhood revisited. One big difference. Their father has reminded them to keep their shades pulled down. The whole West Coast is under black-out orders, so Japs attacking from the air won't have easy targets.

The dressers, the tiny table, and bunk beds are there, nothing has changed. They know Mom wants it kept that way. Harry, the older, always claimed the lower bunk. Now they flip a coin and Lou wins.

Sitting side by side on the lower bunk, drinking bottles of Olympia beer, Lou says. "Can you keep a secret?"

"That's an insult," Harry says, smiling.

Lou smiles back. "Yeah. Sorry."

Harry clinks his bottle against Lou's. "Mum's the word."

"Julia made me promise to ask after I promised I wouldn't say anything, and I think she knows I will anyway."

"Go ahead. Fire away."

Lou draws a deep breath and says, "I want to join the Marines. Mom and Dad don't know."

"How about Julia?"

"She knows and she's dead-set against it."

"She's thinking ahead to a June wedding, huh?"

"Yeah, kind of, but not like Mom is. Mom's dropped only like about five million hints, you know."

Harry laughs. "I know, I remember."

"Julia and me, we've talked about it, you know. A lot," Lou says. "I'll be drafted by June even if I don't join up. Even if I am married."

"Yeah," Harry says after a long pull on the Oly. "The way things are going, you will be."

"Unless," Lou says.

Harry looks at him.

"Unless, you know, we *gotta* get married."

Harry likes Julia, a sweet kid, blonde and a little chubby. Green eyes, rosy cheeks, nice bust and gams. After three kids, she'll be as big as a house, but Lou won't care.

He shrugs. "How do you feel?"

"Well, we've talked about, you know, doing it anyway. Just to see if, I don't know—"

Lou is blushing so hard that he's purple. That confirms what Harry has suspected all along, that they're both virgins. They'd been going together for what seems to Harry like centuries, neither one with anybody else on the side. This, despite Harry's unwanted advice to Lou to play the field before snapping on the ball and chain.

Lou wants his advice now. Considering Harry's extensive and dubious experience with women, he knows he's the last person who Lou should be asking. Harry's background with the fairer sex dated back to grade school, when he'd beat up bullies who picked on shrimps. He learned early on that all bullies were cowards, so they were easy to take. Girls loved him for it. They'd walk him around the corner of the schoolhouse and lift up their dresses to show him their panties. Some even had pink ones.

Harry was tempted to say something like, "Lou, if you go to a car dealer, you're not gonna buy until you take a test drive, are you? Sample the merchandise before you sign on the dotted line?

"And don't behave like your older brother, by any means, but there are girls out there who'll do what you want them to do if you buy them a burger and a malt." But, no, it's far, *far* too late for that. Lou and Julia are bound and determined to walk down the aisle.

Harry looks more like Dad with the hawk profile, his gotten secondhand by brawls and goal line stands. Lou looks more like Mom than Dad, and is more like both of them than Harry in a lot of ways, how he thinks and does things. Lou thinks things out before acting, where Harry thinks things out later, often to his regret.

Harry chickens out and tells Lou to do what he and Julia feel at the moment. Don't plan it out. Just do what you feel and forget about the Marines for a day or two. "They can still win the war if you're late joining in."

That seems to satisfy Lou, who then says, "Like Mom said, there is a guy wooing Dorothy. For sure."

Harry studies his beer, pretending to be nonchalant. "Yeah?"

"Yeah. They say he's handsome and rich, but I've never seen him."

Harry shrugs. "When I was in Lisbon and Dorothy was there with her brother, she said she had a boyfriend in the RAF who flew Spitfires. She said it so I'd lay off and keep my paws to myself. Later on, she admitted she was lying, but still made me keep my distance."

He shakes his head and says, "Girls."

"Yeah, this guy, it's probably all baloney," Lou says.

"It was, then. Could be now, too." Harry says, unconvinced.

"Julia and me, we think Dorothy's carrying a torch for you."

Harry shrugs, not explaining that in Lisbon, Dorothy had once smelled another woman's perfume on him and then gave him the bum's rush when he tried to get extra-friendly with her. So close to the promised land and he botched it. Double-botched it, to be accurate. Because then the Lisbon gal whose perfume was on him, she smelled Dorothy's perfume on him when he tried to make his move on her.

"Don't ever try to figure out a dame, Lou. It's too complicated. All you'll do is give yourself a headache."

Enough talk about girls. They open more beers and just like the good old days, they have a belching contest.

Tabby is curled up on the lower bunk, opening his eyes as he listens to them, impatient for the nonsense to end so he can get a good night's sleep.

CHAPTER 8

Seattle.
Monday, December 15, 1941.

Saburo (Chuck) Shimizu, Harry's best friend throughout school, is somebody else he has lost touch with—also his fault.

Chuck was their high-school class valedictorian and the only guy in the all-city track meet who was faster than Harry in the 100-yard dash, 10.1 seconds to Harry's 10.2. Chuck didn't gloat, and Harry wasn't crestfallen. They were just happy that they were first and second, in whichever order.

Chuck is in his second year at the University of Washington medical school, passing with flying colors. But what's gonna happen to him now? He didn't rape Nanking or sink the U.S.S. *Arizona*. He's not sneaky and he doesn't bayonet Chinese babies. Just the opposite. He wants to specialize as a pediatrician.

His dad teaches biological science at the UW, and his mom is a housewife. Chuck has a younger sister, a high school junior or senior, who gets straight As. An upstanding family by any measure, Harry thinks, as he jaywalks across Rainier Avenue. Solid people doing no harm to anybody. Jacket zipped up against the chill, he wonders what's in store for them.

Their home is two blocks past Rainier and a half-block to the left. Before Harry makes the last turn, he notices a ruckus. There are police cars and army MPs in front of the Shimizu home, standing beside a bus. It's like a school bus, but painted olive drab, the Army's favorite color. Harry sees Japanese people inside it.

The Shimizus' two front windows that were broken have been replaced, but one on the side is busted out. Harry would dearly love to catch somebody in the act. After he got done with him, the son of a bitch wouldn't be able to toss a marshmallow five feet, let alone a rock through a window.

Chuck's kid sister is walking down the steps, tears streaking her cheeks, carrying books and a childhood doll. Neighbors are watching. From a distance.

Harry asks a cop, "What the hell's going on?"

The cop is looking at the activity, not at Harry, a nuisance. "Nothing that's any of your business, boy."

"They're my friends. It is my business."

The cop is heavy and florid, stomach overlapping his belt buckle. "I'll tell you again, it's none of your business, kid. Butt out."

Harry says, "And I'll tell you again, fatso. It *is* my business."

The cop faces Harry, a step closer. "Who're you calling fatso, punk?"

Before Harry can tell him to look in a mirror, an MP steps between them and says, "The President just signed an order to get all enemy aliens off the West Coast so they can't help out if the Japs invade. So like the officer said, go mind your own business."

HISTORICAL INACCURACY: Executive Order 9066, issued by President Roosevelt on February 19, 1942, gave broad powers to military leaders to exclude both Japanese aliens and citizens from western parts of the country including Washington; 300 people, mostly men, were immediately removed.

An editorial decision was made by the author to move the order up to December 1941, in order to give Harry a chance to obey his instincts and advance the story.

"This is bullshit," Harry says. "These people are great Americans. You should've done half of what they have. They aren't 'Japs'."

Another MP flattens his eyes with his index fingers and says, "Better get yourself some glasses, boy, if you can't tell one from the other."

"Who're you calling fatso?" the fat cop persists.

Chuck comes outside, laboring with two overstuffed suitcases, held shut with ropes.

"Chuck!" Harry yells.

"Harry. Please don't interfere. There's nothing you can do except get yourself in trouble."

Chuck hasn't changed a bit, lean, wiry, and handsome by any standard. He's obviously frightened. Harry can't remember the last time he saw him scared.

Harry tries to move forward, but the MPs block him. "Better listen to him, boy. They got twenty more minutes before we move on to the next nest of Nips."

The fat cop has gotten behind Harry and has him by a shoulder, squeezing hard. "Who are you calling fatso?"

Harry's had all he can take from these birds, who are acting just like the Nazis he encountered in Europe. He rotates, setting a back foot, and drives a fist into the fat cop's gut. The cop makes a whooshing sound, and drops to his knees, gagging.

They're all over him, billy clubs swinging. Harry ducks the hardest blows, pivots, breaks loose, and drops the MP on his left with a right cross to the temple.

"Harry, please, no!" Chuck screams from the porch.

Harry grabs a billy club with his right hand as it lands hard on his left, sidearms it to his right, and hits something solid—ribs or a skull?

They have him now, more hands on him than he can count, dragging and pounding on him.

The fat cop is back on his feet and in Harry's face. His breath smells like raw sewage, and he sounds like a ventriloquist with asthma. "You fuckin' cocksuckin' punk, I can't wait till we get you in our jailhouse. Pretty young thing like you, you better have your Nip friends bring you a jar of goose grease for your be-hind. The pre-vert homos we got locked up, by the time you're out, your be-hind will be big enough for the 20th Century Limited to tunnel on through."

Harry has just enough energy and range of motion to head butt the fat cop, so he does.

The satisfying sound and feel of crushed nose cartilage is the last thing he remembers.

CHAPTER 9

Seattle.
Wednesday, December 17, 1941.

Horatio Alger (Harry) Antonelli knows that he's in the Seattle city jail, but not much else. He didn't see the outside of the building as he was yanked out of the police car, his head lolling downward from the beating. Booked and printed at some desk, nothing done gently. Then tossed into a large cell he now shares with vomiting drunks, a 300-pounder with runny, beady eyes who makes lip-smacking sounds as he stares at him, and an assortment of petty crooks with greasy hair and tattoos. He knows European jails firsthand, and this one is no improvement. The pervert wears filthy bib overalls and looks like something that should've gone extinct during the last Ice Age, so Harry keeps one eye on him.

The punks and hustlers try to one-up each other with tales of derring-do, talking like they're Dillinger. Harry doesn't know for sure what they're in for, but he seriously doubts if any of them could break into a parking meter.

There are twenty-some prisoners and a dozen bunks, but Harry doesn't compete for one. Though still recovering from the beating, he could take any two of his cellmates at the same time, but chooses to sit on the floor, against a wall, asleep or awake, so his back is covered.

He's made a friend who sits beside him, an older gent named

Herbie Barnwell. Herbie is scrawny, with rounded shoulders, gray whiskers, and a nose redder than Rudolph's.

"Stick with me, kid," Herbie Barnwell tells Harry. "They think I'm a crazy drunk, and nobody messes with crazy people. Even that overstuffed degenerate who been making goo-goo eyes at you."

"*Are* you a crazy drunk?" Harry asks.

"Nah. I'm a drunk, but I ain't crazy. Mr. Jack Daniels, he cuddles up with me and keeps me sane and helps me sleep at night. Sure could use a taste of Mr. Jack right about now. Yes sir, I could."

Harry has noticed Herbie Barnwell holding his hands together to control the trembling.

"What are you in for, Herbie?"

"Indecent exposure. They say I was taking a leak against a lamppost on the corner of Second and Marion. It's three blocks from here, so it was an easy trip for them to haul me here to the hoosegow."

"Were you?"

"Can't rightly say. They say I did, so I guess I did. My memory ain't as good as it was before the war."

"What war's that?"

"The Spanish Civil War. I was with the Abraham Lincoln Brigade. We fought with the Republicans against Franco."

Harry says, "I was in Lisbon last year and all over Europe before that, so I heard plenty of sad stories about it."

"Real life is goldurn likely worse than any of them stories. We were in the Battle of Jarama, which isn't too far from Madrid. We held off Franco's gang for a long while, but they outnumbered us in every manner. Men and firepower and Condor Legion planes bombing us. When the Nationalists crossed the river, we got chewed up bad. Them too, as we were a tough lot. All that got accomplished was blood and guts all over the place.

"Tell you one thing, though, you didn't want to get taken prisoner by them fascists. Francisco Franco, he's a mean, sick little bastard.

What he's done in Spain, killing off anyone who speaks up against him? You can take my word for it, he ain't hardly got started."

Harry says, "Lisbon was hair-trigger. Still is. Everyone there is worried sick that if Franco joins Hitler, Portugal will fall in a week."

"Damn right it would. Still might."

Harry says, "The war for you was bad, huh?"

"Badder'n bad. I hear cannons and screaming at night, asleep *and* awake. Mr. Jack Daniels, he helps quiet them down. Mr. Jack, he hushes in my ear, singing me lullabies. What're you in for, Harry? I gotta say, your head, the way it's all swole up, it looks like it was target practice for bumblebees."

Harry tells him.

"How many cops and MPs?"

"Eight or nine. I lost count," says Harry, who is given to exaggeration. As he was three years earlier in Berlin...

Which he tells Herbie in formal language, as he had done numerous times before:

"November 9, 1938, the first of two days of Kristallnacht. Meaning Crystal Night or the Night of Broken Glass. A scene out of Dante's Inferno. A nation of juvenile delinquents, including the police, who instead of guarding and protecting, joined in the fun.

"Had I been able to understand German, I would have known that in Paris, on November 7th, a seventeen-year-old Polish Jew had shot to death a German diplomat. This was regarded by the Nazis as an organized political assassination, a Hebrew conspiracy, a pretext for a Kristallnacht rampage that burned 267 synagogues, vandalized 7500 Jewish businesses, killed as many as 100 Jews, and rounded up 30,000 Jewish males for shipment to concentration camps.

"I should've known better and scrammed right out of town the day I arrived, a week earlier. I couldn't remember any tyrant coaxing his subjects to behave so badly, like deranged animals. Genghis Khan, Caligula, Ivan the Terrible, none of them. Hitler is one of a kind, a new depth of evil. I know my history, Herbie. I studied it in college.

"Frenzied mobs were breaking faces as well as windows. You couldn't walk down the street without crunching on glass or tripping over a human being, either unconscious or worse. I was all set to hustle into an alley for the night, sleep in a doorway to save money, and hop the first train out of town in the morning.

"Before I could, I was set upon by a pack of thugs who decided that an American of Scottish-Italian persuasion whose nose had been broken playing college football appeared Jewish. They had demanded that I thrust the Nazi salute. Frankly, not one to ever exercise common sense or back down, I obliged, modifying it with a middle finger, thinking as they came at me that I sure could use Buck Rogers' ray gun.

"In preparation for such an occasion in Europe's growingly-uncomfortable environment, I had been uncharacteristically moderate in food and drink. When they tore into me, I created enough emergency dental work to keep a clinic happy. The leader, a soft-looking fella with a weak chin, came at me first with a lead pipe.

"I'm not bragging when I tell you I'd been a placekicker as well as a halfback for the University of Washington Huskies. Imagining a 50-yarder straight through the uprights, I made the lead-pipe boy eligible for the Vienna Boys Choir with my 10-DDD, an act that unfortunately would follow me to Lisbon, as he turned out to be the son of a Nazi general. But that's a whole other story.

"They prevailed in numbers. Next morning, I looked like I'd bobbed for apples in a hornet's nest, a whole lot worse than I do right now. Having worn out my welcome in a country the Nazis had turned into an insane asylum, I used documents I'd stolen from one of my attackers and crossed into Austria, six months after the Anschluss or German annexation, jumping from the fire into the frying pan."

As he ends his tale, Harry is slipping into a Sunday-comics fantasy. Superman smashing through the concrete walls of this jailhouse as if they're butter. *Up, up and away!*

Herbie Barnwell pats his shoulder and says, "You know, that's a grand story, Harry. It's like you're one of us in the Brigade. We had all sorts of nationalities fighting for the same cause. Same with what got you in here. A Jap isn't in every case a Jap. You got your Nazis right here in town, you know."

"The German-American Bund?"

"Nah. Not them dimwits. They ain't anything but goose-stepping idiots who're being rounded up as enemy agents. Since that Hawaii bombing and war declaration, they're out of business for good, scattering like cockroaches do when the light is turned on. I don't travel in what you call your fancy-pants circles, but down low with lowlifes, where I hear scuttlebutt. Guys I knew from the Brigade, they hear things they pass along. The more dangerous breed of roaches are out there, looking for a chance to help out Hitler."

"That's not right."

"Don't worry. Federal agents will take care of them."

"I hope so. Herbie, how come I can't make a phone call to let people know where I am? The guards say the line's tied up because of the holiday season. And they won't tell me what I'm charged with."

Herbie says, "They can do what they want to. I wanna call Reverend Snell down at the mission. They know me there. The reverend knows a lawyer who volunteers for them and he can maybe spring me, but they tell me the same lies about the phone."

"That'll be swell if you can get through to Reverend Snell, but in the meantime, don't we have *some* rights? Any at all?"

HISTORICAL NOTE: *If Harry did have rights of any sort, they weren't read to him, informing him that he had the right to remain silent and the right to be represented by an attorney. Nor that if he can't afford an attorney, one will be provided for him. Miranda v. Arizona wasn't ruled on until 1966, twenty-five years too late for Harry.*

"At this point it's best to keep your yap shut and let them make the next move, Harry. Don't talk to the jailers or prosecutors or none of them. They'll only twist your words. I know. I been there."

Harry has remained silent, counting all the offenses he might be charged with, coming up with three.

The 300-pounder has been staring at Harry again. He grins and licks his lips. And squeezes his groin to make his intentions clear.

Harry has had enough. He stares back, flexing his fists, daring him to make a move. He'll be able to sleep better if the pig is in a heap, spitting out his teeth.

The pervert looks away, scanning for easier prey.

Three charges against me, Harry thinks?

Three isn't the half of it.

CHAPTER 10

Seattle.
Thursday, December 18, 1941.

"Horatio A. Antonelli?" a guard yells.

Harry raises his hand. "I didn't do it, whatever it is."

"Shut the fuck up, Antonelli. Off your ass and on your feet."

Harry obeys. The guard opens the cell.

Herbie Barnwell says, "Farewell, my friend."

Harry shakes his hand and says, "Behave yourself, Herbie."

Herbie smiles. "There are no guarantees in this life."

"Move it," the guard says. "I ain't got all day."

Harry moves it, following the guard down the hallway that smells of toilets and alcohol disinfectant that doesn't do the job. He finds it odd that the guard is alone and in front of him. He's been half-expecting to be treated like Public Enemy Number One. In shackles and chains, surrounded by bulls with shotguns.

The hall leads to a corridor, another corridor, and then a large room where he can see a door and daylight beyond. David Booth is standing by a counter, unsmiling, arms folded.

David (Don't Call Me Dave) Booth became *David* Booth in the third grade, a year ahead of Harry in school, when he brought home a report card filled with stick-on gold stars. Harry hadn't seen it, but he can imagine Booth looking at himself in the mirror holding up the card. I am so special. I am *David*, not Dave.

David's hand shot up first to answer every question while Harry was in the second-grade classroom slipping notes back and forth with girls.

Dave/David Booth had zoomed through high school, college, and grad school lickety-split, brainier than most of the teachers and professors, leaving a thick shiny glow of gold stars trailing from his Phi Beta Kappa key like moondust.

With a chin out to there and Dorothy's intelligent eyes, David Booth is neither pretty nor handsome. David is, Harry thinks, *aristocratic*. Has been since the third grade and that constellation of gold stars, maybe even emerging from the womb with a jutting jaw.

"Retrieve your belongings, Harry," David says, gesturing at the counter.

Harry does so, pocketing a wallet and change, counting every penny, and then saying, "You bailed me out?"

David picks up the briefcase he'd laid on the counter. "We shall talk about that later."

"Uh, thanks."

"You are welcome," David says coldly.

Outside, Harry says, "Where are we?"

"Third and James in downtown Seattle. You just exited the Public Safety Building. If I had an ounce of common sense, in the interest of public safety, I would have left you there."

Exactly where Herbie said they were, but Herbie and his Mr. Jack, they could've been on the dark side of the moon for all Harry knew.

"Hey, David, have you had lunch yet? I'm buying."

"They didn't feed you in there?"

"They do, but you don't want to know the fine details of the cuisine."

"Well, it is lunchtime."

They go into the first diner they come to and take a booth in the rear. Both order hot beef sandwiches that come with mashed potatoes, gravy, and canned corn.

"What *did* they feed you, Harry?"

"You can't believe the chow in there. Macaroni and cheese that glows in the dark and S.O.S."

"What's that? SOS is a distress signal."

"'Shit on a shingle,' which is creamed chipped something on toast. You're distressed after you eat it."

"Think about that when you are again tempted to misbehave, Harry."

"Misbehave? I was only—"

David lifted a hand. "We eat, then we talk."

"Okay, but once again, thanks for bailing me out. However much it is, I doubt if I'll ever be able to repay you."

"I didn't bail you out. I arranged to have the charges dropped."

"Jesus. All three charges?"

"Three?" David laughs.

"Four?" Harry says.

"All six and possibly more to come."

"Six?"

"Ultimately, I venture to say, seven or eight. The locals and the Federals want to throw the book at you. Assault against two local police officers, one of whom had surgery yesterday on his nose. Another had a cracked rib wrapped."

"The fat cop lunged at me. I lowered my head to protect myself."

"Assault against two federal employees, the military police. Two or more violations of federal law, interfering with the issuance of a federal order."

"It wasn't right, what they were doing."

"If convicted on all charges, Harry, you could be pounding rocks at Leavenworth for thirty years. A Sisyphean punishment they delight in. Finish your lunch so we can talk."

David belongs to a federal agency so secret that he will not even divulge its name to Harry. An agency he claims isn't an agency. According to him, his non-agency is nonexistent. He and his non-agency got things done in neutral Lisbon that Harry thought were impossible. To Harry, it's right out of the Sunday funnies.

Now this. Payback isn't gonna be simple and easy. Picking up the lunch check won't do it. When their plates are taken away and the tabletop is cleaned, David unzips his briefcase and removes a folder.

"Have you heard about the accidents the B-17 Flying Fortress bombers are having?" David says.

"I remember something about it in the paper. An airplane snapped apart in midair."

"Well, that was just one out of too many. The majority of the crashes have been kept out of the news. There are others that we believe aren't accidents. Read this. A recent incident, from a recorded pilot conversation, distilled into this narrative."

Harry opens the folder and reads:

Saturday, November 15, 1941. *Near Gander, last refueling stop before crossing the Atlantic, the B-17 ferry pilots talk about what's top-secret, but all the ferry crews know that the crash of a B-17 last month wasn't pilot error. Yeah, Gene liked to whet his whistle, but he had 5000 hours and could fly one of these buggies blindfolded, same with Jim in the right seat. Witnesses out of Toronto said they heard a funny noise and then it nosing in, a corkscrew, missing a wing, like it'd been hit by Nazi ack-ack. A kid in a field who saw the most was written off as a pipsqueak with a wild imagination.*

Then their outboard starboard engine starts vibrating like crazy. A piece of the engine nacelle flies off, but they got it shut down just in time; if it'd broken off, it'd be curtains.

Mayday to the tower who gives them a straight-in to Runway 03, wind NNW 15 knots. They land as the port landing gear collapses and the engine snaps off and skips across the infield like a child's top. Fire trucks on hand to put out fires. They were lucky, but others won't be.

"How many of these do you think?" Harry says.

David shrugs. "No fewer than eight over a twelve-month period."

Harry whistles. "How?"

"We think vital parts, major load-bearing parts, are somehow being weakened in the factory. Different parts at different times over different assembly points. What wreckage that has been recovered indicates breakage due to metal fatigue you customarily see in an aircraft twenty years old, with thousands of hours in the air. Wing spars, control surface hinges, landing-gear boxes..."

"Why are you telling me all this, Dave?" Harry says, the *Dave* thrown in to coax a smidgen of anger and a straight answer.

David Booth doesn't bite. "Harry, you did your nation and the nations of democracy a great service in Lisbon by helping trace the location of the factory where Nazis were enriching uranium to drop over London. To kill millions with radiation poisoning. With my sister's help, of course."

"You said I saved the world. An overstatement and then some."

"Perhaps, but who knows what would have transpired if Hitler had succeeded? The Germans could have invaded Britain with little resistance. A disaster of incredible proportions. So many people owe you and Dorothy a debt of gratitude."

Harry is curious where this flattery is headed, but keeps his mouth shut. Curiosity ain't gonna kill this hepcat.

"There is a parallel. England is safe from invasion. But the Nazi bombing campaign is doing horrific damage. If we cannot supply bombers to the RAF and now to our own air forces, we can't retaliate and destroy German factories. It is a vicious cycle."

Where do I come in to this conversation? Harry doesn't ask.

"Where do you come in to this conversation?" David says.

"Good question," Harry says with a laugh.

"Quid pro quo."

"Quid pro quo," Harry says. "That's Latin for 'all charges reinstated' if I don't agree?"

David Booth smiles. "Indeed it is."

"I know, I know. I owe you the sun and the moon."

"Indeed you do."

Harry doesn't reply.

"Dorothy."

Harry raises both hands to his chest. "I know, I know. Don't come within five miles of her or else."

"She has a suitor," David says. "A serious one."

"A little birdie told me that," Harry says. "He's good-looking and rich. Drives a fancy car."

"Unfortunately, all true."

"I promise, I won't get in the way of true love," Harry lies.

David leans forward and says, "I *want* you to get in the way, Harry. I want you to court her."

CHAPTER 11

They leave and walk around the corner to David's car, where he complains how bad traffic and parking is getting to be in downtown Seattle, how he had to plug *two* nickels in the meter so he wouldn't be ticketed while he was retrieving his prisoner. Harry whistles, admiring his car, a 1939 Hudson coupe, the deluxe model with 8-cylinder engine, heater, and white sidewall tires.

As they pull away, Harry has recovered from shock sufficiently to speak. "This sure is a snazzy jalopy for a secret agent drawing a government paycheck, working at—where did you say?"

"Give it up, Harry. I will only say that I am being kept in Seattle, on special assignment to be near the Boeing Airplane Company."

David is slow and polite behind the wheel, Harry thinks. Like an old lady, not a dashing secret agent. He isn't paying much attention to his driving either. Also an old lady trait, and dangerous. Maybe someday they'll put safety belts in cars like they do in airplanes.

Harry says, "Does this buggy have a rumble seat?"

"We can talk freely now. People in the restaurant were looking at you."

"Me?"

"They remember you from the days when you were a football star for the University of Washington. How you looked after the games

61

when your photo was in the Sunday paper."

"Yeah. I should've been wearing my helmet when I went to Chuck's." Harry looks at David. "Dorothy and me... when you said what you said back there, I thought I was gonna faint. You've always said that she's too good for me."

David honks his horn at the car ahead that's slow to move along after their light turns green, and says, "She is *much* too good for you."

Harry shrugs and looks out his window at the Christmas lights in store windows and sidewalks filled with shoppers, bundled up because of the chill.

"This individual she's infatuated with," David says, leaving it that.

"I hear he's slick-looking and has dough coming out of his ears."

"His name is Dewey Concannon the Fourth."

"A rich-boy name."

"Yes it is. Dewey Concannon I, 1828-1879. Dewey II, 1850-1894. Dewey, III. 1877-1930. Dewey IV was born in 1900," David says, ticking them off on his fingers. "The first three were a succession of a family dynasty that makes iron castings for multiple industries. To hear Dorothy tell it, they own half of Pittsburgh.

"Dorothy's Dewey claims he rebelled and joined the Army reserve when he believed war was imminent. After the family cut him off without a cent, he moved out here with his meager savings and his car. He's now a captain, awaiting assignment. That is his story."

"Jeez, Dave, how'm I supposed to compete with Mr. Wonderful? When I did my part in Lisbon against the Nazis, it was mostly Dorothy doing my part. Half the time, *I* was the damsel in distress."

"As well as you having a girlfriend on the side. As I recall, a Lisbon café singer."

Whose perfume Dorothy had smelled on him.

Harry points ahead. "The fourth red light in a row. Not your lucky day."

"We are not changing the subject. I thoroughly researched Mr. Concannon, Harry, and have found no evidence that he exists or that his forebears existed."

"Dorothy has more sense than that. She's smarter than you and me combined."

"Agreed, but this is infatuation. Nothing more, I hope."

"What's his angle, do you know?"

"I have a theory. You've known how frustrated Dorothy has been in her high-school teaching job."

Harry does, recalling almost word-for-word what she said when she popped in on him in Lisbon:

"Harry, I've just finished teaching a year at Jefferson High. One long, long, long year of home ec. I wanted to teach chemistry and physics. I'm good at science, a lot better than most of the boys. I majored in both physical sciences in college, with a minor in metallurgy. Half the time I was the only girl in my classes. There was one opening to teach those classes at Jefferson, and it was given to a man. I could run circles around him in quantitative analysis, but chem and physics were quote-unquote unladylike. If I wanted a job there, I had to teach the other opening, home economics, teaching girls how to cook and sew, things they should be learning at home from their mothers. I was forced to be the advisor for the Homemaking Club too, which was more of the same, preparing them to be good little housewives. And to substitute in a girl's health class. I'd teach them about washing their hands and things, but not the stuff they really need to know, if you catch my drift."

"She's still at Jefferson, stuck in home ec?"

David says, "She is. The straw that broke the camel's back is that the nincompoop who took the job she should have had is going in the service. To replace him, the school is calling a teacher out of retirement."

"Nincompoop emeritus?"

"Well put. Dorothy says he can barely light a Bunsen burner without setting himself on fire."

"She deserves to be treated right," Harry says.

"She surely does. About that time, our Mr. Concannon the Fourth came into her life."

"How did he?"

"I'm unclear on that. Dorothy was vague, too. I gather it was a tea social of some kind given by Boeing to recruit professional ladies such as herself who are adroit at math and science."

"Hmm. Boeing. What are her work plans? Is she staying at Jefferson?"

David says, "This is where it becomes very confidential. She took a test and passed, finishing ahead of time with the highest score."

"What kind of test?"

"It's so secret, she won't even tell me, except that she took the test at Boeing Airplane Company Headquarters, and it has to do with numbers. Numbers only, bunches of numbers."

"Like code?"

"Quite possibly."

Harry thinks of decoder rings like you send away for with cereal box tops and a dollar. Flash Gordon used secret codes to foil Emperor Ming the Merciless from the Planet Mongo. Wisely, Harry doesn't share that insight.

"I think this may have to do with the B-17 crashes," David continues.

"You don't know for sure?"

"It's only a theory we're tossing around. We are not one hundred percent certain. Your guess is as good as mine, but the pieces do fit. This is where we need you and the need is urgent."

"It's like making a cut with the football, tacklers are on each side?"

"You analogy has *some* merit. After Pearl Harbor, all West Coast eyes are on the Pacific Ocean. Japanese invasion is believed to be a real possibility as there are hundreds of miles of unprotected coastline. My people are dubious. The enemy is stretched very thin with their so-called 'Greater East Asia Co-Prosperity Sphere' and the supply lines from Tokyo to Seattle are impossibly long. Nevertheless. Boeing and the War Department will soon cover Plant Two with a cloth tent with a Potemkin village atop it to confuse Japanese bombers. Some B-17 production will be moved to California, but the majority of the work will remain here."

HISTORICAL NOTE: In fact, they did erect a cloth cover, concealing Plant Two under the world's largest tent. A Hollywood set designer was in charge of the twenty-six acre assemblage of Plywood, cloth, netting and other material.

"This Dewey phony..." Harry says, leaving it at that.

"Without doubt, he is worming his way into her life with nefarious motives."

"I am to get her away from this guy by romancing her?"

"Precisely."

"I'll do it, with a couple of conditions."

David sighs and downshifts as the light ahead turns yellow. "*You* have conditions?"

"I know, I know. You got me out of a tough spot and I'm grateful. I am short on cash. I can't be positive, but I think the cops may have helped themselves when they frisked me and took my belongings. After paying for lunch, I'm tapped out. I'll have to shell out for flowers and candy if I court her the way courting *should* be done. Some new duds, too. I must look like a hobo."

And smell like a hobo too, David thinks. He digs a wad of money out of his pocket that he had been issued for this occasion.

"A trench coat and snap-brim fedora, too?"

"We are not in the movies." David rolls his eyes. "Your other condition?"

"Do I get a secret-agent badge?"

"Harry."

"I'm kidding, Dave. You really need to work on developing a

sense of humor."

"Your *other* condition?"

"Where did they take Chuck and his family?"

"Minidoka."

"Where the hell is that?"

"It's in Idaho. A camp. Essentially in the middle of nowhere."

Red-faced, Harry slams a fist into a palm. "A concentration camp like the Nazis send the Jews to?"

David hesitates. "It will not be luxurious."

"Me joining the Army Air Corps—I guess you're putting the kibosh on that, huh?"

"With loads of help from you, yourself when you attacked the police and MPs."

"I'll play along, but I want you to have your boys, whoever they are, swing by the Shimizus' home from time to time, to be sure nobody's breaking in and helping themselves or making a mess for the fun of it. There's another broken window."

"I can do that. If you do your job, when the assignment is completed, your criminal record will be expunged and your military enlistment will not be impeded."

"This is about Dorothy and it isn't about her personally?"

"Whatever you said, yes. It is about her personal well-being and about what this Dewey individual can glean by manipulating her."

"How do I follow this Dewey the Fourth bird? I don't have a car and have no intention of buying one. Even if I had the dough."

"You can borrow our parents' car. They drove their new forty-one Chrysler Royal to Palm Springs."

"They still have the old Airflow?"

"They do," David says, digging the key out of his vest pocket.

Harry is reminded of the back seat of that 1934 Chrysler Airflow, in his college freshman year and her high-school senior year, doors open, his oxford-clad feet hanging out, armrests killing his ankles, slacks bunched at his ankles, her saddle shoes around him, panties dangling from one. The Airflow was a design failure and a big loss of Chrysler's money, as well as the loss of their virginity. A bargain, Harry thinks.

"You got a picture of this Dewey who isn't Dewey?"

"No. I'd take one, but it would be too obvious. He does bear a superficial resemblance to Cary Grant."

"Ah, swell. What kind of car does he drive?"

"He never parks out front, making an excuse that he wishes to leave the spot for others, but I understand that it is a new Lincoln."

"You haven't given me much to go on, David."

"I'm sorry. That's all I have. You are resourceful, Harry. You can do it."

"Resourceful," Harry says. "You make it sound like an insult."

David smiles.

Harry thinks: *I'll be playing Dick Tracy without a wrist radio.*

He says, "Hey, what're we waiting for?"

CHAPTER 12

Seattle.
Thursday, December 18, 1941.

Fresh from shopping, carrying a bag of new clothing, Harry walks in the door with a sheepish smile and a scraped and bumpy face. He kisses Mom on the cheek as Tabby rubs against his ankles. Joanne Antonelli gives him a raised-eyebrows *look what the cat dragged in* stare, but says nothing. Her boy picks up his cat and heads downstairs.

This is a ritual repeated much too often since Harry was in junior high. Whatever happened, Joanne Antonelli does *not* want to know. She is just happy to have her little boy home more or less in one piece. She has heard rumors of a large ruckus the other day at the Shimizus, law enforcement people involved, but nobody will give her a straight answer. It's not in the papers either. If there was a hoopla, it was hush-hushed by the bigwigs.

Harry is so much like his kitty, out at all hours, brawling and tomcatting. No wonder Tabby and him are so close. Gone only three days this time, instead of two years in Europe. She'll count her blessings wherever she can find them.

Harry slips upstairs while Mom is in the kitchen, bathes and shaves, then considerately scrubs off the ring he's left in the tub. He changes into new slacks and his Washington letterman sweater, purple with a gold "W," going for a wholesome, collegiate look.

On this dry, brisk day where Harry sees his breath, he quicksteps to Rainier Avenue and a florist shop, where he buys a mixed bouquet and a box of Whitman's Sampler.

He counts on Dorothy being home. Home *alone*. Dr. and Mrs. Booth are in Palm Springs, and David's car is gone, making the coast clear for him. If the phony Dewey guy is there, he'll have to dream up something on the spot. A knuckle sandwich comes to mind.

Dorothy Booth answers the door. The sight of her takes Harry's breath away.

Green eyes and the smoothest, milkiest complexion. Her permanent wave is right out of the beauty salon. Inside her white blouse and dark pleated skirt that shows nary a wrinkle is her classy chassis. What she's doing to him, it's not like his feelings for Gabrielle. It's something deeper, whatever it is.

"Harry. I was going out to do some Christmas shopping. I haven't much time."

"Doesn't school start again after the first of the year?"

Dorothy doesn't answer. Harry in the collegiate duds, the all-American boy who happens to be as bruised and scraped as a down-and-out prizefighter. He's up to something fishy, she knows.

"Uh, here. These are, you know, for you."

Puzzled, Dorothy takes the gifts and says, "This is a nice surprise, Harry. You're blushing."

"It's the cold," he says, rubbing his hands together. "I'm used to the tropics."

She steps aside. "Come on in before you catch pneumonia."

They go into the living room. She takes the flowers into the kitchen and puts them in a vase. Dorothy recalls high-school formal dances, the one time she was invited to one, by a boy whose name she doesn't recall. He and most of the other boys in tuxes, bearing gifts and dressed like penguins. She does remember that Harry, who could have had his pick of cheerleaders or any other girl, never attended one. He hated being dressed up and forced to behave.

"Harry, these are lovely. Did you pick them out?"

The florist had recommended the iris and some others; he's forgotten the names.

"The florist and I, we put our heads together on it. Took a while. The iris was my first choice."

She opens the Whitman's Sampler and offers him one. He accepts two and she takes one. Harry seems different to her. This visit isn't Harry's definition of romance, an attempt to lure her into the bedroom. Harry is on a mission.

They sit opposite each other on wing chairs. The Booths have decorated more expensively than Harry's folks, because they can he supposes, but they aren't showing off. At right angles to them is the stuffed love seat where Dorothy and him smooched in the tenth grade, when he first tried to get his hand inside her blouse. Calling him an animal, but not resisting. Memories.

"It's been ages, Harry, since our adventure in Lisbon. Where on earth have you been? Your mother said something about Havana."

"Yep. Fun and sunshine."

Without bluntly mentioning his damaged face, she says, "I heard what happened at the Shimizus. Weren't you hauled off to jail?"

"The charges were dropped. They realized it was all hooey."

"Hooey? I have to ask. You're covered with bumps and bruises. Didn't you fight with the Seattle police and military police too, and hurt one badly? There are rumors going around."

"The bastards, they had no right. Chuck and his family aren't enemies. They were acting no different than the goddamn Nazi and their—"

"Harry, please calm down. I completely agree with you, but it's the law. The law you broke. You didn't escape from jail, did you?"

David hasn't told her what he did, Harry thinks. He used to confide in her, but with that fifth columnist in her life—

"It took a few days, but they came to their senses and sprang me, realizing I acted in self-defense. That fat cop's the one behind them trying to frame me. My head was shoved forward into his nose."

Dorothy looks at him.

He adds, "Anyway, it's complicated."

"I'm happy to see you, but…"

"But?"

"Harry, there have been changes in my life, too. I'm seeing somebody."

"Gee, you are? Anybody I know?"

So *that's* what this is about, Dorothy realizes. David's handiwork. Verification that he put Harry up to the flowers and candy.

"No. He's new in town."

"Is it serious?"

"To answer your next question, Dewey is real, not someone I dreamed up, like my fictitious British fighter pilot."

"I wish he was a made-up guy, although I wish you and him the best, Dorothy."

Dorothy smiles. "I know you don't, but thank you just the same."

Harry says nothing.

"I thought David might have broken the news to you."

"I haven't seen big brother. How is he?"

"He's fine," she says, intrigued by his little game, happy to play along to see where it leads.

"David still with that secret, secret, top secret agency?"

"He is. And no, I'm not telling you what it is. Also, I'm leaving teaching."

Harry touches his neck with a flattened palm. "I'm not surprised. In Lisbon, you said you had had it up to here with teaching girls how to cook and sew."

Dorothy nods. "The guy who teaches physics and chemistry is going into the service and they're giving his job to—somebody else."

"That's rotten, as brainy as you are in math and science. In high school, I was the top athlete, and you were the smartest girl."

Dorothy glares. "I was valedictorian, the smartest boy *or* girl."

Harry clears his throat. This formal courtship business is gonna be harder than he thought. He wonders if there's a book on it he can study. By Emily Post or one of those gals.

Dorothy enjoys seeing Harry squirm. Whatever the flowers and candy are about, she presumes that David financed the purchase. Him and his aversion to Dewey. David is so subtle in his line of work, but when it comes to boy-girl, he's as clumsy in his own way as Harry.

"I have to confess this to somebody, Harry. I'm going to be fired at the school. I'm anticipating a phone call any time."

"Why?"

"Well, I firmly believe that teaching health to girls should include the birds and the bees. They let me do it so I'd pipe down about being cheated out of teaching math and science. As long as I wasn't too blunt."

"I remember that."

"With war clouds on the horizon, I decided last year that dancing around the topic wasn't enough."

"I don't blame you. You and me, we didn't dance around—"

"Harry."

"Okay, okay."

"Egg whites."

"Huh."

"A comparison for inexperienced girls, which I do hope many are. I told them that egg whites are the consistency of semen. I believe it's a vital part of their knowledge with their beaus going off to war. They have to insist that the boys be responsible and wear rubbers."

"Good thinking, Dorothy."

"One girl told her parents."

"Oops."

"Yes, oops. Her father is on the school board."

"Oops and oops."

She smiles and says, "It's all right. I'm going to work at Boeing. That's why I'm in a rush. No more long school holidays for me."

Harry says innocently, "That's a shock. Doing what?"

"I'm going to be a Rosie the Riveter, building B-17s. It pays better than teaching, and I get to roll up my sleeves and do important work."

HISTORICAL INACCURACY: The term "Rosie the Riveter" didn't come into use until the release of the popular song by the same name in February 1943. But that doesn't prevent Dorothy Booth from becoming one.

If David had told him the truth about her passing a bunch-of-numbers tests at Boeing for a job even too secret for him to learn, she's lying through her teeth as she looks him in the eye. Lying even better than he does. Very disturbing.

"Congratulations. When do you start?"

"Soon, after some paperwork is done. After Christmas sometime, if not sooner. What are your plans?"

"The Army Air Corps, to become a fighter pilot."

"That's great, Harry. When?"

"Soon. Same as you, after the paperwork is done. Probably right after the first of the year."

Dorothy says, "I can't help thinking about the night before David and I left Lisbon, what became of that horrid Horst Wessel, the top Nazi in Portugal, the attaché who was up to his ears in the uranium plot. You stole David's car—"

"*Borrowed* it."

"Borrowed without permission. We know that you chased after Wessel in it."

"Never found him."

In fact, Harry did find him, and after a skirmish at the battlements of the Castle of Saint George (*Castelo de São Jorge*) that overlooks Lisbon, he prevailed, holding Wessel over the edge by the ankles. He remembers every word:

"Hey, Wessel, I'll pull you up if you tell me what your real moniker is, before you had it changed."

"Is that a promise?"

"Scout's honor."

"Does that mean the truth, a promise?"

"I swear on a stack of Bibles that it's the honest-to-God truth."

"Fritz Hansnegle."

"Really?"

"It is. Do as you vowed and pull me up."

Harry released him.

And listened to fading German obscenities.

"Never did find him," Harry lies, recalling his one and only murder, the deed highly justifiable. The lunatic had legally changed his name to Horst Wessel, a Nazi thug who had his face blown off in a dispute. He was martyred by them, "The Horst Wessel Song" becoming the Nazis' top dance number. In Harry's view, both Wessels were pure evil and should've been stillborn.

"In any event, I'm happy you're back home in one piece," she says, standing.

Harry stands, too. "Well, I guess I've worn out my welcome."

"No you haven't, silly, but I have so much to do before Christmas," she says.

"Sure," Harry says at the door, accepting her handshake.

"Before you go into the service, drop by."

"I will, Dorothy," he says, gently pulling her closer.

I want you to get in the way, Harry. I want you to court her.

"Harry."

"A peck on the cheek."

She doesn't resist.

Dorothy thinks of Dewey sweeping her off her feet at the tea social. A perfect gentleman ever since. Unlike Harry, whose notion of sweeping a girl off her feet is to rotate her to the horizontal.

Back outside in the cold, the tiny kiss wasn't like them thrashing around in the back seat of a car, but it's a start.

So he hopes. So he hopes *she* hopes.

She watches him, wondering if he swallowed her lie. Her almost shoving him out the door was really because she had a date with Dewey.

Harry walks back to his house without seeing the 1941 Lincoln Zephyr coupe parked around the corner.

CHAPTER 13

Seattle.
Thursday evening, December 18, 1941.

Joanne Antonelli swears by Italian olive oil. She cooks with it and drizzles it on salads. A family favorite is her homemade pasta, olive oil, and shredded Parmesan atop it. Since the war started, she's been unable to find Italian oil or Parmigiano Reggiano, so she gets by with local cheese and California oil.

As Harry makes popcorn in a cast-iron pot using California oil, he thinks that if you blindfolded Mom, she couldn't tell the difference between it and the finest Italian extra-virgin oil. He keeps his opinion to himself, unwilling to step into that minefield.

An old Antonelli family tradition, handed down from Rocco to Harry when he was in the 10th grade: making perfect popcorn with olive oil in a cast-iron pot, to enjoy while gathered around the Philco. Tonight, they listen to Red Skelton and Jack Benny.

The topics of conversation at the dinner table are the war and rationing, not a word spoken of Harry's three-day absence or his damaged face. Conversation on how strict limits will soon be placed on rubber, gasoline, coffee, sugar, meat, butter.

Rocco says, "I'm saving all our scrap metal at the shop. Somebody will be by for it twice a week."

Joanne says, "I read where we're supposed to save our nylons. The Navy wants them for gunpowder bags."

"Don't forget the newspapers. I've cleared a spot on the back porch for them," Rocco says, adding as he looks at Harry, "The Sunday funnies, too."

Joanne says, "I'm putting in a vegetable garden this spring. So much of the food grown on farms will be canned and sent off to the boys overseas."

HISTORICAL NOTE: *Joanne Antonelli is right. By 1943, 20.5 million home gardens produced ⅓ of all the fresh vegetables consumed in the country.*

Harry says little about his Army Air Corps intention, and Lou says nothing about the U.S. Marines. No sense in upsetting Mom about things largely out of their control.

Harry is fidgety, restless. He's up during the commercials that are selling Lucky Strikes and Ovaltine, in and out of the kitchen. From one window, he can press his face against the glass, cock his head, and see the Booth house. He's on the lookout for strange cars in front. Dewey Concannon the Zero.

He smells Dorothy's perfume, even though he knows he doesn't.

*****

Dorothy Booth has received a telephone call from Dewey Concannon IV, apologizing for not dropping by like he said he would. There is background noise, traffic and horns honking, so she thinks he's in a phone booth. Dewey says he's been called into Army Reserve Headquarters to go over his assignment. Very confidential.

Dorothy says she understands perfectly and hangs up. Oddly, she's not disappointed. Nor is she curious about this Headquarters of his and why it's so confidential. If that *is* the truth. He was due to pick her up within minutes of Harry's drop-by and is very punctual. Could he have seen Harry with his bouquet and box of chocolates?

There are some things about Dewey she doesn't understand. He's a dreamboat. Considerate, mannerly, a complete gentleman. *Too* much of a gentleman in some ways, downright Victorian when they're alone. Male chastity makes her feel unattractive. At least he could *try*.

She's fidgety, thinking about Harry, who is impossible to visualize as a complete or *in*complete gentleman. *Goddamn you*, red-blooded, promiscuous Horatio Alger Antonelli!

Dorothy goes upstairs, into her bedroom and locks the door. She slides her cedar chest over until an end is inside her closet. She stands on it, lifts a lid, and removes paper-clipped sheets of paper she has hidden in the attic.

Just then, David comes in the front door and hurries upstairs, to his room down the hall. They exchange yelled hellos, and she gets to work, beginning with the practice sheet on top. She looks at her watch and starts:

56812 44825 90536 41514 96296 44994 21569 85294 77336 31753

She scribbles possible combinations of the first two 5-digit sets on a notepad, knowing that if she finds a commonality, the other sets can also be broken down. She spots it quickly, converts the sets to letters. The answer: MARY HAS A LITTLE LAMB.

Dorothy looks at her watch, records the elapsed time by her answer, and smiles.

*****

David Booth sits at his desk, drumming on it with a pencil. He is meticulous regarding most things. He has thought and thought about Harry and how he's invited him into the project. Antonelli is impulsive, immature, and violent. Antonelli is also sharp as a tack, courageous, and loyal to family and friends. The very best and very worst traits imaginable.

In Lisbon, if Harry didn't save the world, he certainly risked life and limb to save London from a horrific attack. He is unpredictable and—according to Dorothy from a confession obtained from Harry in a weak moment while they were in Lisbon—afraid of only two things in the whole wide world: guns and clowns.

David shakes his head at the incongruity. He doesn't want to know the specifics of that "weak moment," but smiles at the thought of additional leverage to use on Antonelli if he doesn't toe the line. He can always call Harry off. He has the power to have the assault charges reinstated, and Harry knows it.

David has made up his mind. He composes a message he will take to the office tomorrow for transmission to Headquarters:

18 DEC 41

SUBJECT: H. A. ANTONELLI

CLASSIFICATION: TOP SECRET

ABOVE SUBJECT HAS BEEN GIVEN MINIMUM INFORMATION. WILL PROCEED WITH SUBJECT UNDER CLOSE SUPERVISION.

CHAPTER 14

Seattle.
Friday, December 19, 1941.

It's cold and a few sprinkles don't help. Compared to Cuba, Seattle is the North Pole.

Harry scampers around the house, astounding his mother by doing chores he had promised to do while in high school. He digs under and around furniture in his and Lou's room, removing cat-sized dust kittens. He lubricates hinges and rails on windows throughout the home that need it and on some that don't.

Joanne Antonelli tells him that she's planning a big, big Christmas dinner, and that he is welcome to invite a guest, a special guest or guests. Hint, hint.

Harry smiles noncommittally.

Time for outside chores. Mom watches to make sure he's bundled up properly and says she'll have some chicken soup ready before the end of the afternoon.

Harry hugs her, then heads out to get what he needs from the backyard shed. He carries a ladder out, and works his way around the house, sweeping moss off shingles and cleaning leaves from gutters. All the while watching the Booth house.

He spots a pretty boy going to the Booth's front door. Gotta be Dorothy's phony whoever and whatever-he-is. The guy's no Cary Grant, but looking much sharper right now than Harry is in a pair of coveralls borrowed from Lou. In his early thirties, too, an older man, a man of the world. Gotta be her new beau.

Harry can feel the phony's perfect white teeth against his fist. Down the ladder he goes, two steps at a time. At the bottom he sees Dorothy leaving with him, walking around the corner to his car.

Can't change clothes or they'll be long gone. He races around the opposite corner of the house, the last forty feet on his hands and knees to the Chrysler Airflow.

He stands up and stops just short of the corner. The guy's a perfect gentleman, opening the passenger door on his Lincoln coupe for Dorothy. Harry will keep that it mind as part of the courtship rites mandated by David. That Lincoln, you've spent $1000 if you spent a penny for one of those buggies, too rich for Harry's blood.

Off they go and Harry trails discreetly in the Airflow, keeping two blocks back. Fancy cars like the Lincoln have mirrors on both sides and one above the dashboard too, so he has to keep his distance.

The phony Dewey the Fourth takes Rainier Avenue northbound, straight into town. He's talking to Dorothy a mile a minute, looking at her as much as he's watching the road, so Harry thinks he could smash into the Lincoln's rear-end before he'd notice.

Harry watches them pull up in front of a swanky downtown hotel. A doorman dressed like a general from some old war when they rode horses and swung swords opens their doors for them.

Harry swerves into a parking spot, beating out a guy in a Packard who is backing up to parallel-park. The guy's out of his car, shaking a fist at Harry, who shrugs an insincere apology as he runs by. As the doorman begins to move the Lincoln, Harry is close enough to read its license number.

He goes to the nearest phone booth and calls David with the number he was given, thinking that it's probably his secret-agent office.

"Booth."

"Is this Secret Agent G-Man Dave Booth?"

"What is it, Harry?"

Harry tells David about trailing the Lincoln and gives him the license number, adding, "If they're in that hotel more than thirty minutes, I'm gonna find that car and slash its fuckin' tires."

"Good job, Harry, but please don't do that, and please don't shout and curse."

"I'm not shouting," Harry shouts.

"Harry, they have a restaurant in there, too. A good one. And it's lunchtime."

Harry looks around and sees people looking at him and his filthy coveralls and filthier mouth, giving him plenty of room.

"Okay, okay. Can you trace the plates and let me know?"

"I will. Give me your phone number and fifteen minutes."

"That's all?"

"It is. *Please* give me the phone number there, and try to be inconspicuous. I'll call you right back."

Harry goes into a drug store that's directly behind the phone booth. He buys a pack of gum and chews a stick, thinking impure thoughts about the Doublemint Twins.

The phone rings in ten minutes. Harry rushes out and answers.

"It's registered to Dewey Concannon. Post office box one-thirty-seven. Seattle one, Washington. That is the main branch not far from you."

"No room in one of those boxes for bed, bath, and closet, I guess."

"No, so he must live somewhere close by. You know what you have to do, Harry."

He does, but playing dumb, he says, "I do? What?"

David doesn't bite. He hangs up on him.

Harry sticks around, window-shopping, but really studying the reflection of the hotel entrance, a secret agent trick. Dorothy and Dewey walk out and wait for the doorman to bring the Lincoln.

It's been forty or forty-five minutes, time for lunch but not for a quickie. Harry's relieved. Hunched inside the coveralls, he walks fast to the Airflow.

The timing is perfect. Harry pulls out and stays four car lengths behind the Lincoln. They're headed south on Rainier Avenue, a good sign. They slow at Bayview, the cross street at the north side of Sicks Stadium, where the Seattle Rainiers of the Pacific Coast League play baseball.

Then Dewey gooses it, runs the red light, goes three blocks and turns right on Winthrop. The light's green and Harry takes it slow, eyes swiveling right. No sign of the Lincoln.

On to home, Harry banging fists on the steering wheel as his blood boils. Three blocks away, there Dewey is, letting Dorothy out of the car where he'd let her in. Opening her door. *Of course*, he's a perfect gentleman.

Therefore informing Harry that he knows he was being followed.

****

Meanwhile—seventeen blocks away, east and north of Harry, Dorothy, and Dewey—the boss of The Killer Klown Gang strikes again, their seventeenth stick-up.

It's a small branch of a large bank with a stately old edifice. Yelling orders, waving his .45 automatic. He's in and out in ninety seconds, burning rubber in a stolen '39 Mercury coupe.

The bank is $1135 poorer, but thankfully, nobody is harmed this time.

*****

Meanwhile, nineteen blocks west and many feet higher, Diana Doe is far richer than $1135, and the money continues to arrive from overseas.

The money is big money by any measure, but no amount of money will ever be enough.

Diana's suite is big, but *big* is never big enough. Her suite is a salon and a suite, temporary and permanent.

In her suite, for amusement and research, she has collected clippings on the Boeing B-17 Flying Fortress bomber.

It is a lovely, silvery bird that costs $200,000 each to produce. It has a 103' 9" wingspan, is 74' 9" long, and weighs 65,000 pounds. Powered by four Wright radial air-cooled engines, the B-17 has a 9,600 pound bomb load.

Its top speed is 287 MPH, but its cruising speed is only 150 MPH, making a trip from England to Germany and back very long and potentially lethal.

It has thirteen .50-caliber machine guns, aimed every which way, a lethal porcupine of firepower. Crew members in the unpressurized aircraft must wear fleece-lined uniforms because high-altitude temperatures are as low as -40 degrees Fahrenheit.

Diana slices one of the clippings with her paring knife, testing its thickness. She obsessively sharpens the knife, so it cuts through the paper as if it were butter.

Diana Doe tosses the clippings aside and smiles. When Pearl Harbor was attacked, only 200 Flying Fortresses were in service. Production is gearing up to increase that number significantly.

She is being paid a small fortune to ensure that doesn't happen.

Any fortune is too small a fortune.

It is not within her to stop, to ever be satisfied.

CHAPTER 15

Los Angeles and Seattle.
Saturday, December 20, 1941.

The house is close by in Hollywood, white stucco with a red tile roof. It has five bedrooms and seven and one-half bathrooms. It sits on 1.84 acres, and has a sixty-foot-high living room, an oak-paneled library, a movie screening room, a gym with pool and spa, formal rose gardens, and a tennis court.

The thug who brings the homeowner a letter has a nose even more misshapen than Harry Antonelli's. "Message from the boys in Tampa, boss."

The homeowner's nose isn't misshapen. He is handsome, and can be charming. He hobnobs with Hollywood actors and socialites, segueing easily from their company to that of psychopathic killers.

In his drawing room, the thug smells perfume and hears water running in the shower. Benjamin Siegel is dressed in a silk robe and smoking a cigar. He takes the letter and tears it open. "Could've saved days if it'd been safe for Meyer and them to call me, but the goddamn Feds, those motherfuckers, I know they got my line tapped. They piss all over my Constitutional rights, is what they do."

"It's from Mr. Lansky?"

Siegel ignores him, reading, then says, "Meyer wants me to do him a favor. You ever hear of a guy called Harry Antonelli?"

"Nah."

"Me neither. He's some nobody who disrespected a friend of Meyer's down in Havana, this army general who looks after a casino of his. This Antonelli guy, he moved into their home, fucked his daughter regular-like, mooched off them, eating their food at their table. The general chased him out of town right after Pearl Harbor."

"He's rid of the guy, yeah?"

"Yeah, but he still gotta be taught a lesson. This Antonelli, he treated the general's daughter like a common whore. A gigolo is what Meyer calls the motherfucker. You don't treat a classy dame that way. Meyer says he lives up in Seattle. Meyer has an address for him here."

"Hey, ain't that where this bandit with the clown mask is, the one we been reading about in the papers? The Klown Killer. He clipped some people in the banks he robbed. He don't fuck around."

"Yeah, this guy, he's going to town like Willie Sutton and them, except he's never been in the pen doing hard-time like Willie's been, as far as we're aware."

"You know who he is?"

"I think I do. When he started making the papers, I asked around out of curiosity. This joker, the word is that he walked off an honor farm down south somewhere around Turpentine Springs, Arkansas, some hick place like that. He was doing a few months for stealing chickens."

"These stick-ups, would be quite a jump for him, boss. From chickens, I mean."

"Yeah, the guy, he's a seventh grade dropout, never wore shoes till he was fifteen. He's done pretty good for himself, came up in the world. All the way up in Seattle, they'll never connect him with who he really is. You'll never guess what his name is."

The thug shakes his head.

"Joe Bobby Banks. He goes by Rob Banks."

"No."

"Yeah. He has some guy named Leamy-something as a driver. They did time together down there, this Leamy guy for stealing cars."

"You want me to go on up there, Bennie, on this Antonelli thing for Mr. Lansky?"

Siegel thinks for a minute. "Nah. It's something I gotta handle myself on account of it's personal from Meyer."

"How far's this lesson you're gonna teach him, you know, go?"

"Meyer's leaving it up to me. I think he is, but it's not clear in the letter. Go get on the phone and arrange a flight up there for me and whoever we got in that hick town."

"On an airplane?"

"No, goddammit, on a fucking submarine!"

The thug backs out of the room, thinking that the boss, he got a temper like a stick of dynamite. They call him Bugsy for a reason.

*****

As Bugsy Siegel burns, Harry Antonelli shivers in a light, icy rain.

He rode a bus downtown in the morning, and is now walking figure eights around the blocks adjacent to Seattle's main post office on the corner of Third and Union Streets. Normally closed on weekends, the post office is open this Saturday to accommodate shoppers who are mailing Christmas gifts and receiving them at the counter. People in the long lines seem either happy and festive, or grumpy and impatient.

Harry hasn't given or received a Christmas gift since 1937. His pathetic excuse is that in the summer of 1938, he went to Europe, was in hot water throughout, until scramming from Lisbon in July 1940. Havana was just as tenuous. Being home is present enough for him.

As Harry walks and walks, searching for Dewey Concannon, he looks south on Third toward Skid Row, thinking of Herbie Barnwell, wondering if he's out of the can yet. He thinks of Herbie's Reverend Snell, whoever he is, who tries to keep Herbie and others like Herbie on the straight and narrow, and off the sauce.

Harry is wearing a pea-coat and knit cap pulled down low, each borrowed from Lou, trying to look like a merchant seaman.

This is a long shot, Harry knows, waiting for the phony Dewey Concannon to pick up his mail at PO Box 137. If he doesn't see him today, he'll try Monday, then Tuesday, then... It's his only chance.

At 3 PM, in the chilly gloom, Harry catches a break. There Dewey is on foot in a wool topcoat, entering the post office, slipping past the line. Meaning, he has nothing to mail. He's there to check on his own.

Out he comes a moment later, walking at a brisk clip northbound on Third, a thick manila envelope tucked under his arm like a football. If he goes into a parking lot to his car, Harry knows he may be screwed; Dewey gets his mail here, but could live in Timbuktu.

Harry gets lucky again. Moving even faster, Dewey heads north on Third, a block or so past where you'd turn left to go to the Public Market, still in the heart of downtown. Then a right turn, a couple of blocks, and into the entrance of the Dorrinsen Arms Hotel. It's as ritzy as where the pretty-boy and Dorothy had lunch. Lots of brick and marble and brass and a nineteenth century doorman. The odds are good that he lives there, but where? He counts eleven floors including the lobby. It's likely got 200 rooms, a palace for visiting moneybags.

If he waltzes in there looking like he looks, he'll get tossed out on his ear. There are ways around anything, Harry knows. He'll dope that out after he warms up.

He rewards himself with a tall cup of hot chocolate in a diner across the street, taking a stool facing the Dorrinsen Arms. Laid out on the table is the comic section of the Sunday paper that somebody left. They publish a Saturday edition that contains filler such as the funnies and Rotogravure. Harry habitually reads the comics before any other section, even the sports. He likens this to having his dessert first.

Superman is a shocker. The Man of Steel takes his draft physical and is ruled 4-F. He fails the eye test because of his X-ray vision. Unknowingly, he looked through the wall at an eye chart in the next room. The letters he called out rule him as blind as a bat.

Donald Duck is right below Superman. His nephews—Huey,

Dewey and Louie—are giving Donald fits. Henceforth, when he thinks of Dewey the Fourth, he'll think of Donald's irritating nephew.

Harry takes his cup to the counter for a refill and notices a poster of Wonder Woman on the wall behind the cash register. Hands on hips, sexy as can be, she's asking, "Are you a girl with a Star-Spangled heart? JOIN THE WOMAN'S ARMY AUXILIARY CORPS. UNITED STATES ARMY."

Harry sits back down, knowing that the right thing to do is call David immediately. But instead, he'll do the right thing for Harry Antonelli now, and drop by the Booths later. He'll fill David in face-to-face, and maybe accidentally-on-purpose run into Dorothy.

EDITORIAL NOTE: Albert Einstein once said that time exists so everything doesn't happen at once. Superman's failed draft physical didn't take place until later in the war, nor was the Wonder Woman poster out then. Donald Duck in that Sunday's paper? Who knows? In this small way, Einstein's assertion is corroborated.

*****

Dewey Concannon IV is now in one of the Dorrinsen Arms Hotel's top-floor suites. He is standing in a spacious drawing room filled with Victorian furniture. Normally, others on the team are there receiving tomorrow's orders, but not now. This makes him ill at ease.

He dumps the contents of the manila envelope on a table — packets of $100 bills, Ben Franklin's arrogant gaze centering the obverse side.

"You didn't take long?" she says. "How?"

"I went right to my box."

"There were long lines, weren't there? 'Tis the season."

"Just to mail and pick up?"

"Nobody was annoyed at you?"

"I don't think so."

"You don't *think* so?"

He doesn't reply.

She looks at her watch. "Even so, you walked to and from quickly. Did you attract attention?"

"No, no. People were keeping up a good pace. The cold and the rain, you know."

"No, I don't know. Could you have been followed?"

"I doubt it. I'm very careful."

"You *doubt* it." She sighs. "Your lady friend's former beau has taken an interest in you."

"He's a bumbling idiot. As a matter of fact, I contacted a former classmate of his that will divert his attention."

"Antonelli wasn't surveying you today?"

"I'm pretty sure I would've noticed."

She sighs again. "*Pretty* sure. But not positive."

Dewey studies his feet. Beautiful as she is, he cannot look her in the eye when she's like this.

"The Booth woman, what about her?"

"She's taking a job at Boeing, claiming to be a Rosie the Riveter."

"With her education, I don't believe it any more than you do."

"No, I don't."

"You're a big lover boy. Find out more."

"I'll try."

She takes the paring knife out of a pocket and touches his chin with it.

"You were boasted to me as a chameleon. You are demonstrating the intelligence of that creature. You will do better than *try.*"

His sphincter tightens.

"Yes, yes I will."

CHAPTER 16

A s he'd planned, Harry reports in person to the Booth residence once he sees David's Hudson is in the driveway. He assumes he'll be invited inside, given a pat on the head, and his choice out of the Whitman's Sampler box, and if Dorothy is there, who knows what then.

David Booth answers the door, tells Harry to stand fast, and steps outside as he throws on a coat. "Let's take a walk around the block."

"Dave, I've been walking around blocks all day long. I'm an icicle."

"This is important," he says leading the way. "We lost another one."

"A B-17?"

"Yes. Over the Atlantic. In the last transmission within radio range on this side, the pilot complained of a vibration."

"Damn," Harry says.

"It's not in the news yet, so mum's the word. This makes our work even more imperative."

Harry proudly relates the Dewey news to him.

"The Dorrinsen Arms? Excellent work, Harry. If we can get something on that character, it may be a start."

"That hotel is big, you know. He'll be a needle in a haystack."

91

"Regardless, if there is a needle, we will find it."

"Yeah, well," Harry says. "Not if *we* freeze to death first."

As they approach Rainier Avenue, David stops and says, "We shall see about that needle posthaste. While I hustle home to make a phone call, Harry, continue strolling around the block. I'll meet you—"

"You'll meet me there," Harry says, pointing at a tavern he has occasionally frequented. "The only thing cold in that joint is the beer."

David shakes his head, but doesn't argue.

Harry walks inside and feels right at home. Although the tavern has changed hands since he went off to Europe, the decor is unchanged: *no* decor, just how it should be. The tavern's layout is a stretched rectangle. After four or seven beers, he recalls that the corners weren't square. There's no point in posting a menu, for the offerings are on the back bar: jarred pickled eggs and beef jerky.

Harry orders a glass of whatever they have on tap.

"Hey, Antonelli."

Harry looks to a rear corner, adjusting his eyes.

A guy at a table says, "Hey, it's Harry Antonelli, the Jap lover. What're you gonna do now that your boyfriend's gone?"

Harry recognizes him by his greasy duck-tail: Rolan Snails, a know-nothing do-nothing. Harry remembers that he dropped out of Jefferson in the 10th or 11th grade.

HISTORICAL NOTE: The duck-tail haircut didn't come along until after the War, but if it was in vogue in late-1941 among marginal types, Rolan Snails would certainly have had one.

Harry turns back to his beer.

The bartender says to Harry. "They walked in five seconds after you. I don't want no trouble in here."

Harry says, "Did I say a word?"

Snails persists. "Big, strong, tough football star, how come you ain't in the Army yet?"

Snails has two companions, who laugh.

Harry grips his beer glass tightly, looking at nothing. Snails' pals are scrawny and greasy, too. If Harry does what he's dying to do, David will have a cow, and the bartender will call the cops.

"I don't gotta tell you that the Jap has a little sister. How is that stuff?"

Harry grips his beer with both hands. The bartender starts a conversation with him, Harry believes, to distract him. The bartender's name is Bob and, like half the town, he knows who Harry is and all about his football exploits. They talk football and the war and the weather, until Snails yells and yells for more rounds of beer.

Bob is doing most of the talking, speaking in particular of a USC game, recalling it in greater detail than Harry does. In the second quarter, he was carried off the field and given smelling salts. Two plays later, he was back in, unsure of many things, such as who they were playing and where. Next play, though, he assisted on a tackle for a loss.

Harry smiles at Bob and nods politely, trying not to listen to Snails' yelling. Bob is trying hard to stop something before it starts. Harry understands. The tavern is Bob's bread and butter.

Bartender Bob finally points at Snails and says, "You're not gonna be served. Get the hell out of here."

"The hell I will," Snails yells. "This is a free country even if Antonelli wants to hand it over to the Japs."

Harry has had enough. He's on his feet just as David walks in.

"What's the matter, Harry? You're as red as a beet."

"Not a thing. Too much cold, fresh air today. That was fast, even for a secret agent. Buy you a beer?"

David sits on the stool beside him. "Yes, thank you. The Dorrinsen Arms Hotel is two-thirds full. Nobody with a name remotely similar to the person in question is registered."

"No surprise there. Physical similarities?"

"He's recognized by front desk employees and has been there for approximately two months. Visiting, so the word is. The elevator operators on duty now remember him riding to the top-floor suites."

"He's a top-floor kind of guy," Harry says, growing even angrier. "That's for sure."

"There are three suites that occupy the entire floor. They rent for sixty dollars per day."

"Wow."

"Wow, indeed," David says, nodding thanks to Bob for his beer. "One is vacant. One has been occupied long-term by an eighty-two-year-old *grande dame*, an heiress to a logging fortune. She stays to herself and has her meals delivered."

"Like Greta Garbo, huh? Is she in the market for a younger boyfriend?"

Snails yells, "Hey, Antonelli, you still fucking that schoolmarm too, her *and* the little Jap girl?"

David says, "Does he mean who I think he means?"

Harry is on his feet. "This is too much. I'm gonna mop the floor with those assholes."

Bob says, "No. Don't. I'm gonna kick 'em out. I mean it."

"Harry," David says.

Harry stops. "Okay, okay. It's his bar. Bob, if you need help..."

"I'm fine. I was in the Marines in the Great War, and I got a baseball bat I know how to use if I gotta."

Harry sits back down and says, "That other top-floor suite?"

"It's a corporation named HH and Company. We're exploring it."

"Exploring. That means you don't know?"

"Correct. Not presently."

Bob is marching Snails and his pals toward the door.

"Who's the beanpole with you, Antonelli? He looks like a fairy. You turned queer?"

"Dave. He's gotta make his acquaintance with the floor."

David has reddened, Harry notices. The "fairy" remark has

definitely struck a nerve.

David says, "Permit me."

He swivels on his barstool as Rolan Snails passes and squeezes his shoulder, rotating his thumb at the base of Snails' neck.

Snails screams, then drops to his knees whimpering.

Harry stares at his pals, who waste no time detouring around Snails and running outside.

"You are rude beyond societal rules," David says, looking down at a writhing Snails. "Will you promise to behave, or do I have to wash your mouth out with soap?"

"No. No. I promise. I give."

I give. Harry remembers that from grade school while on top of bullies. *Lemme up. I give.*

Snails bangs his head against the door as he stumbles outside.

"That's secret-agent jujitsu if I ever saw it. Where'd you learn that?"

Avoiding the question, David sips his beer and says, "Those ruffians are beneath contempt."

They finish their beer without conversation and order another.

Harry says, "Snails sure knew about me, and about me being here. I don't think I said three words to him throughout high school. He hung out with others like him between periods, smoking behind the metal shop."

"Perhaps he was playing the odds, presuming that you would turn up here eventually."

"I used to be an occasional regular, but not since I got back from Europe and Havana."

David smiles. "Occasional regular. An oxymoron if I ever heard one."

Those jerks have Harry thinking, all their jabber about Chuck and his family.

He says, "Have your boys seen anything suspicious at the Shimizus' place?"

David, who usually answers right off the bat, doesn't.

"Nothing so far, Harry."

Dammit, Harry thinks. He's forgotten his promise to keep an eye on it.

CHAPTER 17

Seattle.
Saturday, December 20, 1941.

Dinner at the Antonellis' tonight is macaroni and cheese, iceberg lettuce wedges with French dressing, and dago red. Nothing that requires ration coupons, Joanne proudly proclaims.

Tonight's main topic is football. How they've moved the Rose Bowl from Pasadena, California, to Durham, North Carolina.

Is it worth ruining tradition on the remote chance Japan might make the 100,000 seat stadium the second Pearl Harbor?

Nobody at the table is sure. Harry mostly stays out of it; he hasn't gotten over his disappointment that his Washington Huskies never won the Pacific Coast Conference, denying them the chance to play at Pasadena on New Year's Day. His senior year, they went 7-2-2 and played twice in Hawaii, though, on January the first and January the sixth. He vaguely recalls celebrating: a bar, hula dancing on the bar itself with a local beauty, teammates clapping hands to the rhythm of the band, but the aftermath is fuzzy.

He does grudgingly agree with the Rose Bowl move, even though Stanford has a two- or three-day train ride because the game is on the campus of their opponent, Duke. Harry is relieved that no Jap airplanes will make history by dropping bombs on a crowd of 100,000.

After they finish dinner and clean up, Harry asks Lou if he wants to go for a spin.

Lou says, "Sure." Louis Antonelli idolizes his older brother and will go anywhere he wants.

Joanne says to go easy on the gas pedal of the Booths' Chrysler. There'll be gasoline ration coupons soon, and every extra drop of gasoline is needed for Army tanks and planes.

Rocco says nothing. The boys are acting funny. He's hoping Harry's influence on Lou doesn't take too strong a hold.

After Harry and Lou are out the door, Rocco looks at the goddamn cat. Tabby is glaring at him, angry that there are no palatable leftovers. Macaroni and cheese is not among his favorites.

Rocco picks up on that and smiles at the goddamn thing as he turns on the Philco. Fibber McGee and Molly will be on shortly.

In the Chrysler Airflow, Lou pats the dashboard and says, "How's it running?"

"Sounds okay," Harry says, who knows little about mechanical devices.

"These L-head, eight-cylinder mills are known for blowing head gaskets."

Harry knows that Lou is curious where they're going, but is waiting for big brother to tell him. Whatever it is Lou said about what's going on under the hood, Harry says, "I'll be careful not to run it too hard."

"I can replace one at the shop on a weekend."

Harry tells him about the encounter in the tavern. He's already confessed his three-day absence to him. Lou likes the Shimizu family, too.

"I thought we'd go by and see if their house is okay."

"Wow. I remember Snails. What a jerk. I smell a rat."

"Him and his pals. Three rats."

"We can walk over there, you know."

"Let's be sneaky. We know they are. They could have a lookout."

They cross Rainier and park three blocks from the Shimizus' on the opposite side, then walk to the alley behind the house.

Harry's hunch is right. The only light inside is small and moving, darting: a flashlight. Pulled in diagonally in the driveway two doors down is a beat-up '35 Plymouth sedan, a coil of rope on the roof.

"Snails," Harry says. "In the tavern, he just about dared me to come here and check if everything's okay."

"Let's go do it," Lou says.

On their tiptoes, they slip through the gate and see one of the guys from the tavern. He's carrying something out the back door.

"May I?" Lou whispers.

"Be my guest."

Before the guy has a chance to blink, let alone yell, Lou lunges and drives a shoulder into his gut. Just like he did at Jefferson High, blocking for Harry.

The guy falls to his knees, emitting a *whoosh.*

Harry grabs his loot—a box of silverware—before it drops, takes the guy by the hair, and whispers, "You say one word and I'll kick your teeth out. You'll be living on milkshakes."

The guy nods.

"Scram out of here and don't stop running."

When they stop hearing the guy's footfalls, the Antonelli brothers go inside and hear giggling and the tinkling of glass. It's coming from upstairs. Harry is so angry he can hardly see.

Lou holds on to him before he can race upstairs.

"I hear 'em, They're moving. Gotta come down sometime, you know. Let's wait, okay?"

Harry catches his breath and mouths "okay."

The brothers duck behind a sofa as two guys carry a headboard down the steps. A lacquered antique with inlays from one dynasty or another, according to Chuck. Snails has recruited a fourth guy, which means he was planning on four against one. Harry mind starts going berserk.

They reach the bottom of the stairs and turn. The headboard is heavy, so the maneuver is awkward. The Antonellis rush out. Harry takes the trailing one by the shirt and drives a fist into his kidneys, the punch coming from his toes. Lou swings as if his arm is a baseball bat and gives his guy a bleeding earache.

Harry's guy is gasping, half paralyzed. He shoves him toward Lou, who takes the other by the hair and bangs their heads together, a la The Three Stooges. They rest the headboard against a wall.

"Now we're cooking with gas," Harry says as he charges upstairs. "They won't need that rope anymore."

All by himself, Snails comes out of a bedroom. "Hey, you guys, wait till you get a load of this brassiere they left behind. These Nip gals they got tiny tits, the size of—"

Which is the last thing he will be able to say for an indefinite period of time. Lou has to pull Harry off.

"Harry, don't kill him. You'll get the chair."

"Udagh," Rolan Snails says in agreement, flat on his back, his mouth and lips bloodied.

"Who put you up to this, Snails?"

"Nuh-un, nuh-un di."

"We'll talk later, Snails. Count on it."

In the car, after they've cleaned up and secured the home the best they can, Harry says, "Lou, can I buy you a beer?"

"Hell ya. We worked up a thirst."

They drive to the tavern where this all started earlier in the day.

They don't know the night bartender, who's busy and not talkative. On their third beer, Lou departs from football, Rolan Snails, and other small talk. "You know anything about this fertility deal with gals?"

"Some. Not much," Harry says. "Fertility is like fertility with plants. You know, things grow if the soil is fertile."

Actually, he knows more about fertility than he wishes he did. Women have brought it up with him before and after intimacy in one context or another. Any way you look at it, a frightening topic.

"Well, Julia says she'll be at her peak fertility next week. She said so just today."

"Ah," Harry says.

"Her folks, Mr. and Mrs. Wilson, and this couple they're friends with, they're going to the ocean for New Year's Eve and New Year's Day. They've rented cabins right on the coast, where they'll watch storms and get drunk and stuff."

"You'll have their house to yourselves is what you're saying?"

"Yeah. What do you think I oughta do, Harry?"

"Lou, I'm the worst person in the world to ask about gals."

"I know. That's what everyone says."

"Let me think about this. It's a tough question. Fertility. I don't even like the sound of that word. The way it's said, it can be, you know, a threat. Even if it's said with a smile and a kiss."

"What would you do?"

"Gals get headaches when we're all hot and bothered. I know that for a fact. Why can't guys, too?"

"I'll think about it," Lou says, nodding at his beer glass.

"That's good. Don't be hasty," replies a relieved Harry.

*****

Rolan Snails has gotten out of the Shimizu house, into the back yard. He drops to a knee, waiting for the double vision to go away. He spits out a second tooth, thinking that no amount of money is worth this.

The guy paid him to follow Antonelli, run in the back door of the tavern when Antonelli went in the front. His buddies were there, like they often were, so that part of it, needling Antonelli about the Japs, it went like clockwork. Knowing Antonelli would check out the Jap house. They'd be paid and get to keep whatever they found.

If they hurt Antonelli real bad, the guy said, just short of sending him to the funeral parlor, he'd give him a fat bonus.

The guy with Antonelli who did the shoulder thing to him, and his buddies running away, he should have known to quit then. He didn't. The money was too good. Four guys against Antonelli.

Should've been easy. He didn't count on Lou Antonelli being along.

Rolan Snails is seeing kind of okay and makes it to his feet.

He can't breathe hard or it feels like his chest is being knifed.

The guy, he dressed and talked like a rich swell. Should've asked for more money, Snails thinks. Like *double*. He'd lied to his buddies about how much he'd been paid so to short them on their cut, but what he's got in his pocket right now? If he misses work or has to go the hospital, he's losing dough.

A third tooth is loose, but maybe he won't lose it.

CHAPTER 18

Seattle.
Sunday, December 21, 1941.

Benjamin (Bugsy) Siegel steps off the DC-3 airliner at the Seattle airport, down the steps of the portable ramp, him and twenty-four others, every seat taken. Head hunched, braced against the damp chill, he gets into a black Ford sedan waiting for him on the taxiway.

"All day long on the fucking thing," Siegel complains to the driver. "Stops in Frisco and Portland to let people on and off. Off and on, on and off. My ass is sore and my ears are ringing from the motors. The food was okay, though, and the stews got curves. One gave me her phone number."

"That's swell, Mr. Siegel," the driver says as he pulls away toward Highway 99.

The driver is awestruck, and scared too, knowing Siegel's reputation. The Mob has no real presence in Seattle, but the driver and a few others in town do odd jobs for LA, collecting debts and looking up people, like he's doing now.

"I could've taken the train, but down in Havana, the boys are in a big hurry."

"You done the right thing by putting up with the plane," the driver says.

"How far do we have to go?"

"A half hour, sir, if the traffic's okay, and it damn well oughta be at eight o'clock Sunday night."

"What've you found out for me on this Antonelli bird?"

"He played football at the local college here. A big star. He went away to Europe or somewheres for a coupla years but now he's back, living with his folks. Hanging around, not doing much of nothing."

"College boy, huh?"

"Yes sir. They say he's a tough guy. Likes to put up his dukes."

"We'll see how fucking tough he is. I gotta get this done tonight and back to LA. I'm freezing my nuts off."

"You don't got to if you don't want to, sir. I got a hotel room reserved for you and a return ticket on the airline tomorrow in case you wanna take a load off."

"The hotel?"

"Ritzy. It got hot and cold running water, and a hot chick if you like."

Bugsy rubs his hands together. "Hot and hot. This is good. Let's get the job done. Thing is, it ain't clear whether Meyer and the boys want him ventilated or just roughed up, taught some manners. I guess they're leaving it up to me to decide on the spot."

They drive deeper into the city, quietly, Bugsy thinking about plugging a guy, and later on, a hot chick in a hotel room, plugging him and her in different ways. This while the driver is thinking of how many different ways the night can turn out bad for him, getting him in a jam. Siegel can blow his stack, like a volcano.

He finally says, "You want a gat, sir?"

Bugsy pats his pocket, feeling his .38 Special. "Don't worry about it none. I'm all set. How're we gonna get me and him alone?"

"What I can do is this, I seen him yesterday in this tavern on this main street close to his house. I'll call him from a phone booth, say I got somebody at the tavern who wants to see him real bad and hang up."

Bugsy smiles. "Yeah, it'll be real bad. For him."

The driver laughs and says, "His house, it's around the next corner off this here Rainier Avenue highway, coupla blocks on our right. Hey, wow, that's him there with that girl, walking our direction. We don't have to call nobody."

"Stop and lemme out. Keep the motor running."

Bugsy Siegel steps out of the Ford, walks up to Harry and says, "You Antonelli?"

"Who wants to—"

Bugsy gives him a right cross to the jaw. Harry lands flat on his ass.

Dorothy opens her mouth to scream, but Bugsy gets in her face and says, "I done you a favor. You look like a classy dame. This gigolo punk motherfucker, you're way too good for him. Pardon my language."

"I know I'm too good for him, but that gives you no right to—"

Bugsy pulls out his .38 and says, "You saved his bacon, lady. If it wasn't for you being here, I woulda plugged the bum."

With his other hand, Bugsy takes a 50-cent piece out of his pants pocket, flips it in Harry's lap, and says, "Use that to hire yourself a cab to take yourself to the hospital. And think it over next time you wanna treat a classy dame like a whore."

As the coin lands on his trousers, Harry believes that this is the hardest he's ever been hit. Harry is seeing spots as the guy gets back in the car and roars off. Whoever he is, he's dressed like a million bucks. Topcoat, suit, tie and hat—an outfit worth more than every item of clothing Harry's ever owned, combined.

He thinks of the Lone Ranger, riding out of town with Tonto.

Who was that masked man?

Then: *Gigolo.*

Oh shit.

Havana, Gabrielle, Meyer Lansky, the general.

The long arm of the Mob.

Dorothy has Harry by a bicep and helps him to his feet. The half dollar rolls into the gutter.

"Who was that, Harry, and why did he call you a gigolo? Not that you don't have those tendencies."

"Ancient history."

"Well, that's preferable to you lying and saying it was a case of mistaken identity."

Harry doesn't comment.

In an uproar about the lack of security David had promised at the Shimizus, Harry had gone to the Booths under the pretext of seeing David, even though his Hudson was nowhere to be seen. He asked Dorothy over to a malt shop on Rainier, and she surprised him by accepting. They discovered that it was closed, as most everything is on Sunday nights. It was cold and dry, a nice evening for a walk, though.

They were on their way back when the guy came out of nowhere and clobbered him.

It isn't all bad. As he runs his tongue over his teeth to check for any loose or broken, Dorothy clings to him. So tightly he can smell her perfume and the toothpaste she used.

"Why don't you come inside and warm up, Harry? I'll make us some hot chocolate."

His jaw feels like Ted Williams clobbered it while swinging for the fences. He's in trouble with the law, gangsters want an ounce (or much more) of his flesh, *and*, under orders by her brother, he has to dupe a woman he probably loves. Or *else*.

A woman who's assisting him home like a wounded bird.

All in all, not completely a rotten evening.

EDITORIAL NOTE: There is no evidence that Bugsy Siegel ever visited Seattle for any reason. For the sake of this story he had to. Harry would be disinclined to go to Los Angeles for a beating.

CHAPTER 19

Seattle.
Monday, December 22, 1941.

U p in the morning, head throbbing, Harry is thinking of Dorothy last night. He wanted to woo her the way *he* wanted to woo her, but she was having none of it. She was Florence Nightingale with washcloths and aspirin and a thermometer in case of a fever. That was sweet of her, but not his preferred idea of being nursed.

As he gingerly cleans up and dresses, he thinks about the sabotaged B-17s. His aching skull reminds him of hangovers and Herbie Barnwell. Something pops into his mind, something that's between a brilliant inspiration and a wild stab in the dark.

Guys I knew from the Brigade, they hear things they pass along. The more dangerous breed of roaches are out there, looking for a chance to help out Hitler.

Dorothy's phony Dewey may be a dead end now, but there's more than one way to skin a cat, he thinks, dressing as Tabby carefully watches him.

"In case you're tuned in to my thoughts, that's an expression," Harry tells his cat, who is in loaf-of-bread configuration on the lower bunk. "All I've ever skinned is a knee."

Relieved, the animal yawns and closes his eyes.

Out of the house before Mom can have a good look at the fresh bruise on his chin, Harry heads to the heart of Skid Row. There are guys standing around, bundled up, with nothing to do and even less hope. The third one Harry asks points him to Reverend Snell's.

The combination flophouse and mission is located between a dormant warehouse and a tavern with steel bars fronting every piece of filthy glass. Windswept garbage and newspapers are piled against a long-abandoned building across the street, a putrid berm of flotsam.

A simple wooden cross nailed above the mission door serves as identification. Butcher paper taped to the inside of a window advertises: BEDS 19¢ PER NITE.

The price of a meal to go with the room, he assumes, is a sermon, because one is just wrapping up. Reverend Snell's flock, seated on folding chairs, their heads bowed, say their amens.

While the guys chow down on macaroni and cheese—surely inferior to Mom's—Harry asks Reverend Snell about Herbie Barnwell.

A thin, graying man in his fifties or sixties, Snell pages through a ledger and says, "It's been a few weeks since I've seen him. I heard through the grapevine... Is it true about Herbert Barnwell? He's locked up again?"

"Yes sir. Just wondering if he's out yet."

"You could check at the jail yourself."

"I'd, uh, rather keep my distance."

Reverend Snell looks at Harry hard, then cocks a thumb toward the hungry faithful. "Herbie Barnwell is very much like the majority of men I see here. Not a bad person, but forlorn and enveloped in the snares of Demon Drink. How was he doing when you last saw him?"

Partly because of who Reverend Snell is, and partly because he'll get nowhere unless he confesses, Harry does, telling his tale. "Locked up, he had no choice but to sober up. Herbie's a good guy."

"The action you took at your friend's home was brave, Mr. Antonelli, but, I must say, foolhardy."

Harry smiles. "This isn't the first time I've been called foolhardy."

"What they're doing to Japanese-Americans is reprehensible, sinful. But it is, unfortunately, the law. Someday, in the distant future, the shamefulness of it will be confessed and apologies made to their descendants."

Harry is skeptical, but hopes so.

He says, "Herbie told me he was planning to give you a call because you knew a volunteer lawyer who could get him out."

"There are several," Reverend Snell says. "I get a call or two a week, but none of late from Herbie."

"So he may be out on his own recognizance?"

"Yes."

"Well, good for him."

"What is your interest in Herbie, Mr. Antonelli?"

"I took a liking to him and vice versa. I'd like to see how he's doing," Harry says.

Reverend Snell studies Harry for a moment, consults his notebook, makes a call, identifies himself, asks about Herbie, listens, and hangs up.

"He was released on Saturday."

"Released to someone or just cut loose?"

"Released to a friend without bail. They are sick and tired of Mr. Barnwell, thoroughly sick and tired of feeding him. Both the friend and Herbie have worked as laborers infrequently during their adult lives, although his friend has intellectual potential he has squandered. A jack-of-all-trades sort."

"Anybody you know by name?"

Reverend Snell nods. "Paul Miller. Like Herbie, Paul is an occasional visitor to our mission who also drinks too much."

"Was he in Spain with Herbie?"

"You know about that horrifying experience? Yes he was." The reverend scribbles an address on note paper and gives it to Harry. "Be warned, this is a shantytown."

"I'll be careful," says Harry, who seldom is.

"Mr. Miller goes by Pegleg Paul. It will be obvious why."

Pegleg Paul Miller lives directly south of what remains of Hooverville, a ramshackle collection of makeshift shacks thrown up during the Depression. Named in dubious homage to President Herbert Hoover, who was in office when the stock market took its nosedive on Black Tuesday, October 29, 1929.

The population of Hooverville once numbered over 1,000, primarily occupied by single men who could not find work. Hooverville is ninety-percent bulldozed now. What remains is an odor and a feeling of gloom. Mocking the residents every single day, history-major Harry thinks, is downtown Seattle, not far to the north, prosperous and well-fed.

Downtown's crown jewel is the sky-scraping Smith Tower: thirty-eight stories, 484-feet high, the tallest building west of the Mississippi when built in 1914, and the fourth largest building in the nation. It had to be as hard to reach from Hooverville as a wingtip of Wonder Woman's invisible airplane.

Paul Miller's address is on Railroad Avenue. It's a cockeyed cabin constructed of scavenged lumber and sections of boxes, typical of its neighbors.

Herbie Barnwell comes out to the front porch holding a bottle of Jack Daniel's by the neck. A death grip, Harry thinks.

"Harry, my boy. A lovely surprise. Right on time for cocktail hour."

"Don't open that bottle yet, Herbie. We have to talk."

"Paul is frying hamburgers for lunch. You're invited. You can stretch your food coupons like a rubber band if you stick to hamburger, you know. Stretching out the hamburger itself with added ingredients."

"If you use food coupons and creative recipes," comes a voice from inside, followed by a cackle.

Harry doesn't like the sound of "creative recipes." He follows Herbie inside. It's dim, not an improvement over the exterior, with packing-crate furnishings and the smell of a tramp steamer's hold.

"I've just eaten, a late breakfast, but thanks anyhow," he says.

"Pegleg Paul was a cook in the Brigade. Lost his leg there, too."

Paul Miller is cooking his hamburgers on a camp stove, powered by an electrical cord that goes through a rear window to an unknown outlet.

Miller, a pudgy man with uncombed broom-straw hair, raps on his peg leg with his spatula. "Knock on wood. Herbie here saved my life at Jarama. Me and this leg, we got too chummy with a fascist machine gun nest. Herbie did magic with a tourniquet made out of his shirt. Kept me from bleeding to death till I got back to the aid tent."

Harry looks at Herbie, who shrugs.

"Gotta plug my ears when I hear a saw sawin' too. Mix that with screaming, not so good."

Anxious to change the subject, Harry says, "In town here, see any of the guys you were with over there?"

"A few in Seattle I know by sight, but except for Herbie, no."

"Know anything about them now?"

Pegleg Paul flips the burgers over and says, "You hear of this 'America First' deal?"

"Some," Harry says. "Charles Lindbergh was one of the leaders. Their aim was to keep us out of the war. For them, what was happening in Europe was none of our business."

Pegleg Paul says, "That's it in a nutshell. Like the Bund, after Pearl Harbor they're rats on a sinking ship is what they are. Lucky Lindy even went to Germany and thought the Nazis were the cat's pajamas. In thirty-eight, Göring pinned a medal on him. That's how friendly they were."

Harry says, "How do you guys fit in?"

"The Brigade? Well, you know, after Franco won in Spain, and then a week later, Ribbentrop and Molotov signed their non-aggression pact—which cleared the way for Hitler to invade Poland—that had a whole bunch of the Brigade guys confused, like we'd been stabbed in the back."

"Us, too," Herbie says, after taking a long belt and wiping his mouth on a sleeve. "Like I told you in the hoosegow, we was fighting for the Republicans against Franco's Nationalists, who were fascists. Until Hitler invaded Russia last summer, it was topsy-turvy to some of the guys' way of thinking."

"Some of the guys?"

"But not to most," Paul says. "We stayed in full support of the Republicans fighting that dirty bastard Franco."

"The guys who switched allegiance to the Axis, do they still want to lick their jackboots?"

"Hard to say, but I'd guess yes," Paul says. "The ones I talked to, this was a few months ago, they said they wanted to stay on the winning side. They firmly believe Hitler can't lose."

Herbie taps his head with his non-Jack Daniel's hand. "They may've been shell-shocked. Your head goes goofy then, and the goofiness, it don't always go away in due course."

"Those you talked to, are they from around here?"

"They are. Bill Randall and Ray Helms. Met them in this tavern, me and Herbie did."

"What tavern?"

"Why?"

"Just making conversation."

"The Owl Tavern. Up off Broadway."

"They're rough trade, Randall and Helms. The Owl, it's their hangout. A rowdy joint, even without that pair. A normal person enters at their own risk, day or night."

"How're those two guys so rough?"

"You can tell by looking at them. They got tattoos and they ain't even sailors."

"What do they do for a living?"

"According to them, they're working at Boeing on the B-17 line."

"Yeah?"

"They got some friends that're Owl regulars, too."

"From the Brigade?"

"Some are, some not."

"Where do they work?"

"They're at Boeing, too, building bomber planes. With the war, if you can fog a mirror and spell your own name, you're hired. There's a spot for you, even if it's pushing a broom."

"Lunch is served," Paul Miller says.

Harry says, "Hey, thanks fellas, but like I said, I had a late breakfast."

CHAPTER 20

Seattle.
Monday, December 22, 1941.

Harry stops at the first phone booth he comes to outside a dry goods store next to a FLYING A gas station. As he calls David, he sees on a pump that gas is twelve cents a gallon. With the war, it's gonna skyrocket, if you can even find it.

"Booth."

"Secret-est of all secret agents Booth?"

A sigh. Typewriters clattering in the background.

"Harry. What is it?"

"We gotta meet."

"Why?"

"Nazis."

An identical sigh.

David says, "Forty-five minutes. The five-and-dime on Rainier just north of us."

*****

Forty-four minutes later, after being jostled by holiday shoppers going in and out of stores, snatching up what they can before shortages and rationing set in, Harry climbs into David's Hudson.

"You're late," he says.

David frowns at his wristwatch. "No, I am not late."

"Yeah, you are. You're only one minute early."

Booth ignores the dig, drives around the corner, and parks. "Your Nazis, Harry?"

"Speaking of. I'm fresh out of nickels and running extra low on the folding stuff. I can't chase fifth columnists if I'm damn near broke."

"I will put in a requisition for an additional payment. Harry, what happened to your face? Your jawline?"

"Just frostbite settling in. First order of business: Dave, Lou, and I had to knock some heads at Chuck's last weekend. Some punks broke in. With that kind of security from your G-men, Adolf Hitler could be downtown playing a department store Santa."

"Broke into the Shimizu home?"

"Yeah. We showed them the door."

"That repulsive Snails among them?"

"Yep. He'll be on a porridge diet until 1943. Which reminds me, will you teach me that shoulder thing you did to him?"

"Harry. I am so sorry regarding the Shimizu vandalism. We've been stretched thin since Pearl Harbor and the B-17 sabotage. I honestly will try to do better. We have so many irons in the fire."

"How are you doing on this HH and Company investigation at the Dorrinsen Arms?"

"I told you on Saturday that we are exploring it and today is only Monday."

"So you've drawn a blank that's even blanker, even after I trailed phony Dewey there?"

"Please, Harry, can we get back to your Nazis?"

Harry relates his meeting with Herbie Barnwell and Pegleg Paul Miller.

David thinks for a moment and says, "I don't mean to make light of your story, but can you trust their veracity?"

"You and your veracity, Dave, just bird-dog Bill Randall and Ray Helms. Can't be that tough."

"I will give it the utmost priority, and I want to pass something along to you in confidence. I don't know if it is related to anything that concerns you or us, but a colleague got in late yesterday evening after a flight from Washington and saw a notorious crime figure as he was boarding another plane. We made inquiries and learned that he had arrived from Los Angeles earlier in the day."

"What's that have to do with Abraham Lincoln Brigade veterans turned Nazi traitors?"

"Probably not a thing," David says, shaking his head. "Even if not, it may be a concern, perhaps to you, dealing as you do with less than upstanding citizens."

"Who is this bird?"

"He is the criminal in charge of the Los Angeles mob, which has close connections with New York gangsters. He and his subordinates are associated with every type of crime. Murder, extortion, prostitution, illegal gambling."

"Al Capone?"

"No. Capone ruled Chicago's underworld. These scoundrels are beholden to New York. "

"You're thinking they're in on the B-17 sabotage?"

"If there's a dirty dollar to be made, who knows?"

"This bird who flew in and out, who is he and what's he like?"

"He is handsome and charming and dresses like a million dollars, but the man is a mad-dog killer with a violent temper. His name is Bugsy Siegel. He reports directly to Meyer Lansky and the imprisoned Lucky Luciano."

Harry takes a deep breath. "Lansky? The name's kind of familiar."

"Meyer Lansky is their money man, said to be a financial genius. If he sent that gunsel here only for a day, there has to be a nefarious reason."

Who was that masked man?

Suspicion confirmed, Harry thinks, as he rubs his tongue against a loose tooth.

"You worry too much, Dave," he says, knowing that if there's secret-agenting to be done at the Owl Tavern, it'll have to be done by him. "I'm sure it's a coincidence or mistaken identity."

"I do hope so. We have ample problems without having to deal with organized crime."

Stepping out of the car, Harry says, "Don't worry yourself into an ulcer. Life's too short."

CHAPTER 21

Seattle.
Tuesday, December 23, 1941.

It's 9 AM and the other two men in the family are off to the body shop for a day of honest labor. Harry feeds Tabby, and thanks to Mom's cooking, he then feeds himself.

After a breakfast of eggs and toast, Horatio Alger (Harry) Antonelli decides to live up to his namesake: bravery, perseverance, hard work. But not necessarily honesty.

He can smell the Christmas tree, the Douglas fir Dad and Lou brought home yesterday in the Antonelli Body and Paint truck while Harry was out being a secret agent. The tree is decorated, presents already underneath, his and Lou's childhood stockings hanging beside the fireplace.

Presents, Harry thinks. He's gotta get busy.

Joanne Antonelli studies her older boy, curious why he's dressed in tan slacks, blue blazer, white shirt and tie, the outfit issued by the University of Washington football team when they travelled to road games. She specifically remembers the Washington State College game in his senior year, the big cross-state rivalry in Pullman known as the Apple Cup.

The family listened on the radio in horror when Harry was carried off in a stretcher after a collision between him and a WSC Cougar. To their relief, Harry returned two plays later and intercepted a pass.

HISTORICAL NOTE: The game ended in a 7-7 tie, one of two ties in a 7-2-2 record. Harry Antonelli had no impact on the outcome, nor on any other game that season, in which the Huskies outscored the opposition by a combined total of 187 to 52.

As Harry dutifully takes his plates to the sink and washes them, she wonders too about his unexplained absence last week, as she wonders about so many things where he's concerned.

While Harry rinses his dishes, he feels Mom's eyes on the back of his head. She's serene and relaxed, though. He knows Lou hasn't dropped the Marine Corps enlistment and/or Julia Wilson's fertility bombshells yet.

His valise is already in the Airflow. He did that on the sly earlier. Too many questions to answer if he hadn't.

Harry drives downtown to the Dorrinsen Arms Hotel, then eastbound, alternating streets, until he finds a parking place without a meter, catty-corner from a DeSoto-Plymouth dealer. It's six blocks away and freezing out, but no rain or snow in sight. He walks to the hotel, a half-baked plan in mind. He'll let David in on it later. Maybe.

Into the hotel lobby Harry walks like he belongs there, long strides and unswerving gaze. His scheme—such as it is—is to ride to the top floor of ritzy suites and find out where the phony Dewey Concannon IV hides out. According to David, one suite is vacant, one occupied by a rich old lady, the third by the mysterious HH and Company.

Into the elevator he goes, crowded in with others. The uniformed operator asks which floor and Harry says the top. He's the last passenger when the elevator stops.

"This is it, sir."

"This isn't the top. I counted."

"This is the ninth floor."

"The ninth isn't the top."

"You have to have authorization, sir."

"How do you get that?"

"The hotel manager has to sign a chit."

Harry pats his pockets and says, "I know. Where did I put it?"

The elevator operator smiles "Hey, you're Harry Antonelli, ain't you? You played for Jefferson High."

A question? "Yeah, I did."

"I played on the Garfield team, on the lines. You scored three touchdowns and broke my nose when you plowed into me from the one-yard line."

The guy's uniform is similar to the bellhop in the Philip Morris cigarette ads: black pants, red jacket with silver buttons, and a cap that's like a fez without the tassel. He's tall and chubby. The silver buttons are about to burst, and his nose isn't on exactly straight. His brass nameplate is stamped STEVE.

"Uh, oh, sorry Steve."

"That's okay. It was football. Your brother ruined a teammate's knee with a block. Do you want off here or right back on down?"

Harry points upward. "What's this HH and Company?"

"I hear it's perfume. Real expensive perfume."

"They sell it up there?"

"Nah, hotel rules won't let you sell to the public. What I hear is people take up samples they got from Paris, France, and they pick out the kind they sell in New York and places like that."

"Yeah, I know how that works," says Harry.

"Do wanna get out? I can't stay here all day."

"You have many passengers headed up there?"

"Hardly any. You want out?"

Harry gets out and walks the hallway. The rooms are numbered 901, 902, 903... Two floors from the top. There are unlocked stairs at one end, a fire escape. He goes up the steps to the next landing, and walks in: 1000, 1001, 1002... Just rooms, not suites.

Then on up to the top floor and a locked door. Through a small window, he sees three doors and no one in the hallway.

Anticipating locked doors, he has brought bobby pins along.

He learned how to use them from a girlfriend in Amsterdam who supplemented her income as a clerk in a millinery shop with burglary.

Harry's thinking, as he searches for tumblers, what a disappointment he can be to his parents. He'd been named Horatio Alger at his mother's insistence, known from an early age as Harry by everyone else. He'd been the only member of his family to attend college, let alone graduate.

Harry had spent four long years at the University of Washington and couldn't have done so during the Depression without washing dishes at the dorm, getting free tuition for playing football, and working in the summer at a beverage distributor, lugging cases of sodas, a job arranged by the football coaches to keep players fit.

The lock is sturdy and he's out of practice. It takes five minutes until he has it.

The hallway is quiet. There is one door on his left, two on his right: 1100, 1101, 1103. He tiptoes along, having not a clue what to do next. Getting inside the vacant unit, he thinks, is probably a good first step.

As he reaches the elevator on the other end, he hears music playing softly inside the nearest door: 1101. He presses an ear against the door and listens. A minuet? Played on a harpsichord. Something like that from the olden days.

The doorknob clicks from the inside. Harry jumps back as if electrified.

A petite old woman steps into the doorway. She's wearing a brocaded robe and a frown.

"Where's my food?"

"Uh..." Harry says.

"You're not from the kitchen?"

"No ma'am. I'm here to see the vacant suite."

"By yourself? That's hogwash. Are you an outlaw?"

Her eyes are steady and blue. They bore through him. Like Wonder Woman and her magic lasso, she has rendered him unable to lie.

"Not all the time, ma'am. Not in this country."

She cackles, thinking that he's joking. "Get inside before someone sees you."

Harry does, into a spacious drawing room filled with Victorian furniture. The music is coming from a gramophone on an armoire shelf.

"What's your name?"

"Harry Antonelli."

"Harry is your formal name?"

"No ma'am. Horatio Alger is."

"Are you like him, full of merit and pluck?"

"No."

"That was such a lovely tale. It isn't too late for such a young man to aspire to its wonderful ending."

Harry smiles. "It is for me."

She extends a bony hand, three fingers of which are bejeweled. "I'm Alice Haymarket. Do you recognize the name?"

"No, ma'am."

She sweeps an arm toward the windows. "Half the framing lumber in those buildings came from trees my late husband's company chopped down. He passed away ten years ago."

"Gee, I'm sorry."

"No, you're not."

Harry says nothing.

"Neither am I. The skirt-chasing bastard drank himself to death on the finest European wines and spirits. If he'd guzzled rotgut, he would've died six months earlier and spared us both considerable money and grief."

They hear the elevator. Alice says, "That's room service. Hurry. Into the bathroom."

Harry waits in the ritziest bathroom he's ever seen, wondering if the gold on the fixtures is real. Or if it can be scraped off.

He hears, "Thank you, Hughie. You're such a dear."

Alice raps on the door, tells Harry to come out, and asks if he'd like to share her oatmeal and toast.

He sits down at a table across from her. There's a candelabra in the center and room for eight more diners.

"I had a big breakfast."

"I don't blame you. This gruel is on doctor's orders. Now, Harry, tell me *truthfully,* what the hell you are about, and why have you sneaked up to this floor?"

Harry begins by laying the bobby pins on the table. He rambles on for fifteen uninterrupted minutes.

"My goodness, Harry Antonelli, you have led quite a life for so young a man."

Harry agrees with a nod.

Alice Haymarket smiles. "If I were forty years younger, I'd be out of my bloomers and have my way with you. I'd wear you down to a frazzle. You'd limp out of here with a grin plastered on your face."

Harry stares at her, peeling away those forty years; for certain, Alice was a looker. Blonde, hourglass figure, and still-gorgeous eyes.

"I'd be ready, willing, and able, Alice."

"All right. Now that we have the dirty talk out of the way, what're we going to do?"

"We?"

"Yes, *we,* you poor frustrated thing. This phony Dewey character is treating your former flame like shit, and who knows what else. These Boeing bombers that are crashing and killing our innocent boys. Those poor old drunks and their Nazis. You are tangled up in a *mess.* You need my help, and I need an important mission. I am so fucking sick of twiddling my thumbs here, waiting to die."

"What I told you, Alice, it's a secret."

"Good Lord, look around you, Harry. Who the hell am I going to blab to, the waiters? I'm a recluse, for God's sake."

Stalling the *we* business, Harry says, "Why are you?"

"Why am I what?"

123

"A recluse."

"I hate people, and I want to be alone."

"Like that actress, Garbo?" Harry says.

"Those Hollywood dames are all sluts. Don't be comparing them to me, buster," Alice says, reaching across the table and jabbing him so hard in the chest that it hurts.

"Yeah, well…"

"*We* is what I said, and what I *mean*. Let's get cracking."

"Okay. David Booth and I are ninety-percent sure that phony Dewey is hiding out on this floor."

"He's not in here with me. That leaves two choices. The suite next to me has been vacant for a year."

"Sixty bucks a night is a small fortune."

"I get a monthly discount," Alice Haymarket says. "But, yes, I agree. The other suite…"

"HH and Company."

"Twice the size of mine. And, no, that's the first I heard that name."

"Do you see who comes and goes from there?"

"I hear the door open and close often."

"How often?"

"Twice a day. I am an old snoop and peek out as soon as I can. By then, they're gone."

"That fast, they'd have to take the stairs," Harry says.

"You are a bright boy, aren't you?" Alice says. "If they waited for the elevator, I'd see them."

"They walk up and down two or three flights, then hop the elevator. Nobody's the wiser."

Alice smiles.

"What?"

She opens an armoire drawer, brings out a key, and swings it on its chain.

CHAPTER 22

Seattle.
Tuesday, December 23, 1941.

Alice takes a stethoscope from a drawer and says, "An absent-minded doctor left it behind once when he was examining my late husband. He said Max's lungs sounded like they had cancer. He claimed it was from all the cigarettes Max smoked. I have my doubts, but who knows or cares. I sure as hell didn't."

Harry looks at her as she presses the stethoscope against the common wall and listens.

"Not a peep."

"You *are* an old snoop."

"Don't be snippy with me, young man."

"Do you ever hear noises when you do that?"

"At times, a faint rustling sound is all."

"Right now?"

"Nary a rustle or a peep."

"Let's go pay a neighborly call on nobody," Harry says.

Alice swings the key chain and says, "I'll lead the way. Stay on your tiptoes. You boys with big muscles, you sound like a herd of elephants."

"Bossy," Harry mutters, as he obediently raises to his toes.

She opens the door an inch and squints. "We're clear. Scoot."

Up on his toes like a ballerina, Harry scoots.

Her hand steady, Alice has the door unlocked in a jiffy as her other hand reaches back for Harry. "For God's sake, hurry up. We haven't got all day."

Harry hurries up and in they go.

"Quietly close the door."

Harry quietly closes the door.

They don't turn on lights, taking a moment to let their eyes adjust to daylight coming through the curtains. The suite is sparsely furnished: table, chairs and sofa, better quality than the Antonellis have, but a far cry from Alice's.

Alice sniffs dismissively. "Odds and ends they store in the basement with the spiders. You aren't afraid of spiders, are you?"

Harry, who fears nothing but guns and clowns, says, "Nope."

Alice says, "People have lived in this suite. Coming and going, I think, not staying long."

"How do you know?"

"I can sense it. It has a lived-in feel I can't explain."

"Good enough for me," Harry says. "Let's start looking."

They search the obvious places, including the empty refrigerator.

"Alice, where would you hide something? Something extremely valuable you wouldn't want a soul to know about or find?"

"Well, my Max was a cheater. He had brazen hussies on the side."

"That's hard to believe," Harry says, meaning it.

"Stop the sweet talk. I'm not taking my knickers off for you, young man."

Harry replies by blushing, then says, "If you were hiding something valuable from Max, where would you hide it?"

She smiles. "Next, you're going to ask me why I stayed with Max?"

"Do I want to ask?"

"Yes you do, Harry."

"Okay, why did you stay with Max?"

"For the money, silly, some of which I converted into jewels and hid."

She goes into the bathroom and wiggles the built-in medicine cabinet. "It's loose, Harry. It wiggles just a hair. A faulty installation by the suite builders?"

"You hid your jewels behind your medicine cabinet?"

"None of your business. Can you yank it loose? My old muscles aren't even as strong as rubber bands."

"Let's find out."

Harry yanks, pulling the heavy wooden cabinet straight out. Behind it is a steel-lined box inserted into cut-out framing. It's the size of a shoe box. Instead of tiaras and bracelets, cards fall out onto the floor.

Harry lays the cabinet down and picks up the cards. They aren't playing cards, though the haul is as thick as a deck of them. It's an assortment of identification cards: driver's licenses, union membership, and Social Security Board.

HISTORICAL NOTE: The Social Security Board (SSB) began on August 14, 1935, and was renamed the Social Security Administration (SSA) on July, 16, 1946. The first SSB beneficiary was Ida Mae Fuller, who was issued a $22.54 check on January 31, 1940.

The SSB cards Harry and Alice are examining belong to William Randall, Raymond Helms, Jack Stormson, Philip Jones, and Leroy Hoopsma. There is a lapel pin, too, with an enameled flag on it.

"Know any of these birds, Alice?"

She blanches. "Thank goodness I don't."

CHAPTER 23

An aide has stacked another log on the fire and quietly left the room. The Führer's study remains toasty. Blondi, his Alsatian bitch, is at his feet. The dog was a gift from Martin Bormann, who many whisper is *also* an obedient bitch.

Eva Braun, the other female in the Führer's life, is in the next room, reading.

Adolf Hitler scratches Blondi's head, thinking that at least *she* makes no demands on him.

Eva has been cajoling him for conventional intercourse "as our God in Heaven meant." As opposed to acts she finds disgusting and repulsive, incorporating pain and screaming (his) and excrement (hers). She does not dare criticize him to his face, though. Her Dolphie's temper is not something to encourage.

Hitler turns his attention to the dispatches on his desk. News from the Russian Front is growing worse and worse. Earlier in the month, because of the severe winter weather, he had been compelled to halt all offensive operations and go on the defensive.

Tanks and artillery and trucks are buried in snow, and with forty-below temperatures, it's the harshest Russian winter in memory. Vehicle fluids are frozen solid and moving parts are bonded by ice. Wehrmacht troops are suffering and dying in summer uniforms.

Virtually within sight of Moscow. An unmitigated tragedy.

He recalls World War I, Corporal Adolf Hitler wallowing in the trenches clogged with filth, corpses, disease, and rats. Illuminated by artillery flashes. Raise your head too high and you would be decapitated by machine gun fire.

Soldiers on the Russian front have it no worse than he had, the Führer believes. In service to the Reich, they can endure until the spring thaw. He knows there are critics of the invasion, naysayers and defeatists. Those who compare his invasion to Napoleon's *will* eat their words.

He is the most powerful man on Earth, but can he be blamed for the weather? Is it his fault that the invasion began on June 22 instead of in early May as originally scheduled? There were circumstances, betrayals, and blatant stupidity that cost Operation Barbarossa six precious weeks. Most notably, Mussolini's ill-conceived invasion of Greece that required a German rescue of Il Duce's pathetic troops.

America's declaration of war against the Reich subsequent to Pearl Harbor is doubly vexing, an abomination. It is squarely on Roosevelt, the Führer believes. The wheelchair cripple is the lackey of the Jews who orchestrated his election, all under the control of the Wall Street bankers and Bolshevik Russia.

Heinrich Himmler's latest report is expected to be one bright glimmer. Heinrich is due in tomorrow to explain it in further detail. The Führer knows the purpose of the visit is a request for increased funding and permission for the second phase. His Seattle-in-America project has been successful thus far, damaging aluminum, a B-17 crash here and there, but America's entry into the war has changed everything. Roosevelt's belligerence has made Heinrich's second-phase request a formality.

Bombing of Germany has been tolerable thus far, on a par with the destruction he is bringing to England. The few B-17s, B-24s, and Lancasters have been a nuisance. The B-17 Flying Fortress, however, with America at war, will be manufactured at unprecedented speed and quantity, like automobiles off an assembly line. Quantities that may fill the skies above the Reich.

Unless stopped.

HISTORICAL NOTE: Hitler's fears will be realized. By the time production is ceased in 1945, 12,371 B-17s will have been manufactured in Seattle (6981), Long Beach (3000), and Burbank (2750).

Himmler has promised that he will eliminate B-17 production. Permanently.

Hitler smiles. If Heinrich is convincing, he can have all the money he wants.

Heinrich and his magical potion.

CHAPTER 24

Seattle.
Tuesday, December 23, 1941.

It's Harry's turn to be bossy.

He stuffs the ID and lapel pin into a pocket and orders Alice to peek outside. "If the coast is clear, we'll reverse direction."

It is, so they do, and once back in Alice's suite, they spread the identification and pin out on her table.

"Bill Randall and Ray Helms," Harry says. "We know about them. David and his super-secret agency is looking them up in their files."

"The other three," Alice says. "They are most certainly the same type of traitorous reprobate."

"Yeah. Birds of a feather. I'll have David get after them, too."

"Harry, I'm afraid it's become extra complicated."

He gets it. "If they're 'Helms' and 'Randall' hidden behind that medicine cabinet, they're out and about as somebody else."

She pats his hand. "You're becoming a mind reader. That occurs between lovers, you know."

"Yeah, well," Harry says, clearing his throat as he holds up the lapel pin. It's a red rectangle centered by a white ring, and a blue circle split by a white lightning bolt. "What do you make of this?"

"It is aggressive."

"Yeah, it is. A design a Nazi could love. David will know."

He stands and writes down his phone number and asks for hers. "Alice, you be careful. Make sure you only open your door for me or Hughie with your meals. Absolutely nobody else. Any hint of trouble, jam a chair against your doorknob and call me."

She smiles. "This is so exciting. I have a gun, you know."

A mountain range of goose bumps erupt on Harry's arms. "Oh?"

"It's a darling little thing. If firearms as jewelry existed, I have one. Want to see it?"

"Uh, nah, that's okay."

"Aren't you even curious? I've thought of having jewels inlayed in the baby handle. Would you care to give me an opinion?"

"Uh, nope. I don't know a thing about jewels. I'd just give you a bum steer. We have other things to do."

"Young man, you've turned white as a sheet. Did I say something wrong?"

Harry is already out the door. Halfway down the steps, it strikes him that Alice has no Christmas tree or decorations.

*****

"Well, Harry, you have taken initiative," David says.

Spoken flatly, no inflection whatsoever. Does he approve, disapprove? Is a lecture forthcoming, or a pat on the back?

"Aw shucks," he says.

They are in Harry's and Lou's bedroom, seated at a table. Mom is upstairs baking cookies and singing carols, singing along with Bing Crosby on the radio.

David is uncomfortable confined in the small room. Lou and Harry, in Cub Scout uniforms, plotted mischief here, impossible things from comic strips they never carried out, despite trying and creating havoc as they did so.

Rope swings that landed them in mud puddles rather than onto the next jungle vine. Darting into traffic as they chased phantom bad guys on their bikes, a la Dick Tracy. This while David read and studied in his room.

"I agree with your theory that these men have assumed new identities and are at Boeing attempting dastardly deeds."

"Here's what I don't get," Harry says. "They have new IDs. Why not destroy the old stuff?"

"The obvious reason is that if they're found out and manage to escape, they can assume their original personas and flee the immediate area."

Harry shakes his head. "That's assuming HH and Company or whoever stashed it behind the medicine cabinet wants the saboteurs returning when every policeman and federal agent in town is chasing them."

David nods. "Your assumption is perplexing. As is the perfume story? I must admit that you've gotten further with HH and Company than we have."

"The only 'HH' I can think of is Heinrich Himmler."

"That monster, unfortunately, is far away and otherwise occupied."

"Can't you raid the perfume parlor, bust the door down and arrest them all? Billy-club the ones that resist?"

"Arrest whom for what, Harry?"

"I don't know. It's wartime. For looking shifty?"

"We can't behave like the Nazis. This isn't a police state."

Harry firmly believes that there are exceptions to every rule. He thinks of the Phantom and Superman doing what they have to do. Flash Gordon and Buck Rogers in their rocket ships, throughout the universe, making their own rules, the end justifying the means.

"What if they're spies? In wartime, they can be hung or shot. If it's strictly perfume, you can apologize."

David evades, saying, "This elderly woman you befriended sounds like an interesting person."

"She is. I just hope Alice cools off and doesn't get herself in a jam, doesn't think she's Mata Hari. I'll keep checking in with her."

"It is disturbing how you gained access to that eleventh floor, Harry. Don't get yourself in a pickle."

Harry dodges by fishing the lapel pin out of his pocket, flicking it across the table, and saying, "I almost forgot. Know what this is? Doesn't look like anything I'd want to wear."

David holds it at eye level. "Indeed you do not. It's the badge and flag of the British Order of Fascists, led by a notorious character named Oswald Mosley. The BOF is the English equivalent of the German-American Bund. Fascist troublemakers and agitators with a substantial following in the mid-thirties. When Hitler invaded Poland and Britain declared war, it was banned and their membership scurried under rocks. The leaders have been interned."

"Okay, you have what you have to have to arrest them for treason."

"I wish it were that simple, Harry. You can keep a picture of Hitler under your pillow if your desires are so sickening. Again, this isn't a police —"

"If we find the bird who belongs to this, you can interview him, right? I'd be happy to help."

"Thank you anyway, Harry."

"Which brings to mind our phony Dewey."

"He visited Dorothy this morning."

"Huh? Christmas shopping?"

"He drove her to Boeing Plant Two, to work. They telephoned last night and called her in to start today."

CHAPTER 25

Seattle and Minidoka, Idaho.
Tuesday, December 23, 1941.

DOROTHY BOOTH is with Dewey Concannon IV in his Lincoln. Dewey is being embarrassingly chivalrous. After he stops at the Boeing 'WOMEN ONLY' gate, he runs out and opens her door. Lends her a hand that she politely refuses as she steps out with her lunchbox, sandwich, and vacuum canister full of hot coffee inside, wearing her Rosie the Riveter garb—khaki pants and shirt, hair up in a bun, wrapped with a scarf for protection from machinery.

"May I pick you up afterward?"

"Oh, no thanks, Dewey. That's so kind. I'll catch a bus. There's a stop three blocks from home."

Dorothy goes in to the guardhouse and receives a badge. They have been expecting her. As instructed, she walks toward the factory. A man in a suit meets her halfway. They shake hands and she goes with him in the direction of a large office building.

She feels Dewey's eyes on her. Whatever this is about, and his interest in her in general, Dorothy is increasingly aware that there is not a stitch of purity in his motives. She will take David and his doubts seriously from now on.

*****

Saburo (Chuck) Shimizu sits on the front steps of the Minidoka barracks to which he has been assigned. Mother, Father, and Kiku, his younger sister, are inside, settled in, as settled as a family can be with flimsy partitions, communal bathrooms, and dining halls.

Perhaps the worst, he thinks, is the barbed wire fencing and the guard towers. As if they are inmates, killers and robbers and spies. Where could he escape to in this frigid moonscape? There are nearby towns, Jerome and Twin Falls, populated by wary, hostile people, from what little of them he has seen.

Let's say he does tunnel out. Uses nightfall and his sprinter's speed to escape machine-gun fire. Makes it to a town—only to be lynched. Or tarred and feathered, *then* lynched.

The governor of Idaho was quoted as saying, "The Japs live like rats, breed like rats, and act like rats. We don't want them."

Since the governor and his state *do* have *them*, does this mean he would be tarred, feathered, and lynched simultaneously?

Until the internment, Chuck doubts if these locals have ever seen a person with Oriental roots. They may think a Japanese-American is from a foreign planet like a character in one Harry's beloved comic strips.

There are rumors that young Japanese-American men will be recruited to fight in Europe. He has mixed feelings. It will be a legal escape from this place, only to be killed by Nazis. Or if he survives, using his badly-needed medical training, functioning as a full-fledged doctor. There is no way of knowing unless he volunteers.

He has no mixed feelings about Harry Antonelli. How he took the police and MPs on, knowing that it was fruitless. Seeing him dragged off to jail. Chuck hopes, but does not pray—there cannot possibly be a God in 1941—that Harry can work his way out of this predicament, and the others he will surely get himself into.

*****

"Whatever he's up to, Harry's bitten off more than he can chew," Pegleg Paul Miller says, stirring a pot of mulligan stew that is in its fifth or sixth incarnation.

"That boy, he can take of himself," Herbie Barnwell says. "He's handy with his fists."

"Harry does look like he's gone a round or two. Randall and Helms, one at a time, sure. Easy money, even *with* the knives they carry night and day. But if they corner him and gang up? He ain't got a prayer."

Herbie sniffs the stew. Another belt of Mr. Daniel's and it'll smell better, he thinks. Like fancy restaurant cuisine. If he had his druthers, he'd be at the mission for chow, but that'd be impolite to Paul.

He says, "Let's hope that don't happen. I'd fear for the boy's life."

*****

The Killer Klown Gang is driving around Seattle. The way they're rubbernecking, you'd think they were tourists, hayseeds from the country taking in the big city. Of course, they're not. They're scouting for and choosing next Friday's bank. Leamy's at the wheel of a stolen Plymouth sedan. Rob is taking mental notes, figuring where the most dough might be and where the best getaway routes are.

*****

Alice Haymarket has the stethoscope pressed against the common wall. This is so much fun!

She hears shuffling, then slamming and yelling. *Oh my goodness*, they've found out the ID is gone, she thinks. Will they suspect her? She pushes a chair and tries to wedge it against the doorknob. It keeps falling over.

She'll be defenseless if they suspect her. They'll break down the door and do bestial things to her to make her confess!

She goes to the phone. Call the police? No, she's in too deep, whatever it is exactly that she's into.

Her fingers are trembling so badly that she misdials three times before correctly dialing Harry's number.

*****

Horatio Alger (Harry) Antonelli is angry and frustrated about the phony Dewey driving Dorothy to work. She has confided *nothing* to him except her egg white problem at school. The way he's treated her over the years, he deserves nothing from her, but that's no excuse, he thinks, as he throws on a jacket, kisses Mom on the cheek, and heads out the door, bound for the Owl Tavern.

*****

David Booth sits in his room at home, thinking. His head is spinning, pondering what to do next. Harry is running off somewhere, half-cocked as usual, although he has produced materials and information that may be important. Dorothy and her infatuation with an impostor he and his agency cannot identify. The B-17 sabotage continues unabated. Rolan Snails and the pseudo Dewey, he knows there is a connection, but he cannot bring it into focus.

*****

Joanne Antonelli is forming peanut-butter cookies to put in the oven. She is singing *Jingle Bells* with Bing Crosby. The telephone in the next room is ringing, but Bing's and her own voice drown it out.

*****

Diana Doe can be on the move in five minutes.

She realizes that they're closing in on her. Dewey, that *idiot*, and the Rolan Snails fiasco. Too many mistakes. It must be done as soon as possible. As soon as the remainder of deadly surprise arrives and is dispersed.

The money will be hers.

CHAPTER 26

Seattle.
Tuesday, December 23, 1941.

Harry drives to Broadway Avenue East, the main north-south thoroughfare on Capitol Hill, and parks across from the Broadway Theatre. MOON OVER MIAMI is on the marquis, starring Don Ameche and Betty Grable. There are posters in the windows, one of Grable in a swimsuit.

Nice chassis, Harry thinks, as he pauses for a closer look. Same as Wonder Woman's, maybe ever curvier. But no magic bracelets, no truth lasso for Betty.

He walks down the hill a couple of blocks, turns a corner, and comes to the Owl Tavern. It's got sooty brick walls and shares an alley with a pawn shop. Sticking out above the Owl's door is a baseball, outlined in neon. Should be an owl, shouldn't it?

Harry enters a fog bank of cigarette smoke and stale beer. Gabrielle had made him quit cigarettes, saying the smoke hurt her sinuses. It was a choice of her sleeping in his bed or him back on the rocky beach on the water side of the Malecón wall, so he endured the nicotine withdrawal. Something god-awful unpleasant that the ads showing doctors happily puffing away don't tell you.

Hanging on the wall to his immediate left is a large chalkboard, lined in baseball innings. On hooks are the Pacific Coast League teams, easily adjustable for a day's games: SEATTLE RAINIERS,

SACRAMENTO SOLONS, SAN DIEGO PADRES, HOLLYWOOD STARS, OAKLAND OAKS, SAN FRANCISCO SEALS, LOS ANGELES ANGELS, PORTLAND BEAVERS. On a shelf underneath it is a tiny Zenith radio, a machine no bigger than six toasters, half the front a station dial, the other half the speaker.

Harry had a baseball bat in his hands for as long as he could remember. He'd played on the Jefferson High team. Swinging for the outfield seats, he could hit it a mile, tying the school record for home runs in his senior year, but for the life of him, he couldn't hit a good curveball or field a hot grounder. He was all power, no refinement. The story of his life.

The Owl is a dump, long and narrow. The wall decor after the chalkboard is tobacco tar and cobwebs. Harry perches on a barstool, wondering what they bet on in the offseason. There are ten or fifteen other patrons. They are older, ratty-looking, unshaven. He feels their eyes on him, an intruder.

The bartender, a fat guy wearing a dirty apron, says, "What'll it be?"

Harry lays a dime on the bar. "A schooner of beer. And an answer to a question. Why is this place named the Owl? I'm not seeing any owls."

Drawing Harry's beer, he snorts and says, "Know how many times I been asked that?"

"Not once by me."

Foam runs over the sides of the glass and onto the bar. The barkeep doesn't bother to mop up the spillage.

"Long time ago, the owner had an owl in here in a cage. It died. The name stuck. Any other questions?"

"Yeah. I'm told a couple of guys named Ray Helms and Bill Randall do their drinking here."

"Who told you that?"

"Sorry. It's confidential."

"You a cop?"

"Secret agent."

The bartender snorts. "Sure you are, kid. Never heard of them boys. You're barkin' up the wrong tree."

Harry shows him Randall's and Helms' SSB cards. "They lost these. Might be, they want 'em back. I'm just trying to be a good citizen."

The bartender reaches for them. "If they show, I'll return them."

Harry pulls the cards back and sticks them in his pocket. "Nah. How're you gonna return them to those boys if you never heard of them? Not even Mandrake the Magician can pull *that* off."

Harry drains his beer. The bartender takes the glass.

Harry says, "You didn't ask if I want a refill."

"You can go wet your whistle somewheres else. I don't want your smart-mouth business."

Harry gets up and takes a long look around. All the eyes on him earlier are averted.

Loudly, he tells the bartender, "I'm going to take a leak in the alley next to this pigpen. I'm afraid I'll catch something if I use your bathroom."

The bartender is wiping the bar where Harry had sat. He freezes, his hand around the bar rag closing into a fist. He looks at a smiling Harry and knows not to try to do what he wants to do.

Harry walks out to the middle of the alley and waits.

Not for long; three minutes tops. Two guys enter the alley, one from each end. They're in their mid-thirties, with pencil necks and mean, dumb eyes. One has a bent nose, the other, the lowest hairline Harry has ever seen outside of a zoo.

"That was fast. Must be you were at the far end of the bar or close by when you got a phone call."

One says, "Hear tell you got property on you that belongs to us."

"Who tipped you off?"

"Our *property*."

"What property would that be, asshole?"

Horatio Alger (Harry) Antonelli is an experienced street fighter. He learned long ago that fighting fair is for inside the ring, on canvas, with three-minute rounds, and a referee. Elsewhere, obedience to the Marquess of Queensbury rules can render you unconscious or worse.

"Asshole," has agitated the guy. Might make him act before thinking.

"Hand it over."

"Which one of you fairies is Randall and which is Helms?"

Harry hears a click behind him, turns and sees a switchblade pointed at him.

He hears another click behind him, turns back, and sees a switchblade pointed at him again.

"You got any nuts, boy? You'll see who's the fairy when we carve yours off."

"Make you one of them high-voice sopranos," says the other.

Harry wrinkles his face, swivels his head back and forth, and pleads, "Oh, God, I'm so sorry, I didn't mean it. I say stuff I don't mean. Please don't. I'll give you the ID cards. Okay, okay? Don't hurt me. Please, please."

He reaches into his pocket as he moves toward one. Both are laughing at him, giving Harry a single second to surprise the one he's facing, a single second to lunge as if out of the blocks at the start of the 100-yard dash.

Harry is alongside the guy's switchblade arm, twisting it hard with his left hand, rotating and slamming his opposite elbow into the guy's temple. The switchblade falls and so does the guy, as Harry rotates him between himself and his partner.

Harry backpedals and kicks him in the jaw. *Hard.*

Harry Antonelli, backup placement kicker at the University of Washington, recalls his two misses against Oregon State, both wide to the right. Luckily for him and the team, they won, 26-7.

HISTORICAL NOTE: *Harry has it wrong. On October 9, 1937, his Huskies lost to Oregon State, 3-6. Harry Antonelli wasn't called on to kick.*

This boot is so strong and straight that it lifts the guy off his knees. It would've been a field goal straight through the uprights from fifty yards. Making a sound like a cupboard full of china breaking, bone and teeth crushed, the guy tumbles against the other one, who drops his knife and runs for it.

Harry catches him after two strides, takes him by the scruff of the neck, and slams him against a wall. The guy is groggy, but upright.

"You killed Ray."

"That narrows it down," Harry says. "You must be Bill Randall."

"Look at him. He ain't moving."

"No, you look at *me*," Harry says, squeezing his cheeks, jerking his face around. "Talk to me about you and him and Boeing."

"Ain't nothing to talk about. We're working stiffs, having us a few belts before we clock in on swing shift."

"A tipsy guy working on B-17 Flying Fortresses, that's not good. He'd screw up and cause metal fatigue to a part."

"We never did. We're good at our jobs."

"I'll bet you aren't good at anything. A part that falls off in midair and brings the airplane down. You boys do that accidentally on purpose?"

Randall tries to shake his head but only manages a grunt.

"Sabotage in wartime gets you the noose, Billy boy."

"I don't know what you're talkin' about. Why'd you have to go and kill him?"

"Let's see some ID," Harry says, digging into Randall's pocket and helping himself to his Boeing badge. It's round, has his name and photo inside it, and is attached with a safety pin on the back.

"Hey, if you take that, I can't—"

"Tough shit, traitor. You're headed for a necktie party,

compliments of the law."

"I ain't no traitor, and you're a killer! You're the one who's gonna get the noose."

Harry is wondering now if he *had* killed the guy. Discretion might be the better part of being arrested for murder. He releases Randall with a gut punch and runs to Helms. The guy's not breathing, the bleeding has stopped, and his head is cockeyed. Deader than a doornail.

He sees Randall stagger out of the alley, clutching his midsection. To call the cops?

Harry pats Helms down for a wallet, finds only wadded-up cash and a Boeing badge. He takes the money and the badge, and scrams.

CHAPTER 27

Seattle.
Tuesday, December 23, 1941.

"You killed the man, Harry?"
"Not exactly."

"Not exactly? Is he dead or not?"

"I'm no doctor, but he didn't look very spry. It was self defense, so I technically didn't kill him. He charged me like a rabid bull. Him and the guy with him had switchblades. They were coming at me from front and back. They were gonna carve me up, threatening to slice off my nuts first, Dave. They weren't nice guys. They were mean."

A rare event, David thinks: Harry may not be exaggerating. "So he is dead?"

"Again, I'm no doctor, but he wasn't breathing and his head wasn't connected to his neck in a natural way. His chest was abnormal, too."

"Why?"

"Why what?"

"Why were you in that confrontation with them?"

Harry relates the rudeness accorded him in the Owl Tavern. "I was trying to flush them outside for a chitchat and succeeded."

"Good Lord, that must have been a shock. You've never taken a human life before, have you?"

"I haven't. I swear."

David stares at him.

"Well, not in *this* country."

"Please spare me whatever you did in Europe. You should have notified me immediately."

"I couldn't. I was running and didn't have Dick's radio."

"What? Who?"

"Dick Tracy. His wrist radio."

They're in the Hudson coupe, around the corner from home, where Dorothy has safely arrived, having taken the bus after work. Harry should be feeling remorse about the killing, but he doesn't. Preachers and priests would surely chastise him, pointing out passages in the Bible on the taking of a human life. Harry would then have to point out to them that he had two switchblades *pointed at him.*

Shaking his head, David says, "I wish you had questioned them thoroughly before the violence."

"*They* started the violence, and weren't in a talkative mood," Harry says. "The dead one wasn't talking at all, and the live one was lying like a rug. Not a truthful word. Five minutes later I heard sirens. I figure the bums in the Owl came out, saw the stiff, and called the law. The sirens, they were singing their tunes at me."

The Boeing badges are laid out between them on the seat. Harry has kept the cash, a grand total of $28.

They are round, leather-enclosed ID cards inside plastic, with leather thongs to hold around the neck. They were issued to Dick Jenson and Lan Williams.

"Familiar names?" David asks.

"Not to me," Harry says, sorting the ID cards as if a poker hand. "Here they are. Their SSB cards."

"No driver's licenses or union cards or anything that could narrow them down," David says, going through the pile.

"Nope," Harry says. "My hobo friends know them as Randall and

147

Hayes because those are the names they gave Reverend Snell at his mission. They could be anybody. One of them still can be."

David goes through the cards again. "No Dewey Concannon the Fourth."

"Nope. Phony Dewey's was the first name I hunted for. You need to put your secret agency to work on this, giving it the highest priority, Dave. Have them work overtime."

They are startled by a rapping on David's window.

Joanne is standing there, draped in an overcoat, shivering.

"Harry, an elderly lady called for you. She's upset and won't say why."

*****

Dorothy's brain is spinning like a top. An hour after clocking out, she's still in a tizzy. She's home, boiling water for a cup of tea. Thinking of her day, she barely notices David and Harry in David's car, Joanne going to them, then running back into her house. Or David and Harry tearing out in David's car, obviously up to something.

The man who met her inside the Boeing gate, such a nice man in an expensive suit and stylish hat, escorted her to a large room occupied primarily by women like herself, dressed as Rosie the Riveters. The room was soundproofed, her ears ringing for a few seconds from the rivet guns outside. Her escort and another man welcomed them, explaining the importance of their work, but not explaining why. It was easy enough to read between the lines, though.

Other welcomes were given from men and women who said that one or the other spoke Japanese, German, and Russian fluently. Write down your answers, they said, never mind the context.

Exercises like *56812 44825 90536 41514 96296 44994 21569 85294 77336 31753 MARY HAS A LITTLE LAMB* were child's play compared to today's assignment. Dorothy believes she had contributed, but is unsure how.

After their shift ended, there were whispers amongst the ladies what they had deciphered: the latest message in its entirety, the word *aileron* being the key. She knows that an aileron is a control surface, mounted on the airplane's wings, turning in opposite directions so it can roll as part of a turn along with the rudder.

Dewey is as much a puzzle as her codes. Out of nowhere, he arrived in the morning to drive her to work. He promised to pick her up afterward, but didn't show. A relief.

She knows how David and Harry feel about him, but she's hesitant to mention what happened today to David. It might slip out to Harry, who would take matters into his own hands. After he doubled them into fists.

Dewey, him and his opaque feelings toward her.

So unlike Harry. Dear lustful, reckless Harry, impulsive as a child. You know what you have with Harry, even if he conceals things and prevaricates, such as why that gangster punched him in the face.

Her teapot whistles. Dorothy goes to it, thinking that she may have to reuse the bags. If it's rationed in Britain, perhaps it will be here too.

She remembers what Sadie, the girl at the desk next to her, had written down: *2LEFT4AILERON1HINGE8*. It was confidential because it hadn't been verified, from wherever the source of the transmission, by whomever. Sadie is an expert at Morse code, the raw source of the transmissions, and has a well-tuned ear for gossip.

The supervisors had been excited beyond excited.

She was certain she heard one say to another, "Go. We have them. This will bring an end to the sabotage."

If this is it, the end of the sabotage and the end of their code-breaking mission, she wonders, dipping the bag to steep every last bit, it was too easy.

Much too easy.

The message had been spoon-fed to them, she thinks.

CHAPTER 28

Seattle.
Tuesday, December 23, 1941.

Harry tries Alice Haymarket's number from the nearest phone booth: EL-2681. He lets it ring twenty times, slams down the receiver, and yells as he dives back into the Hudson, "Shit! Goddammit. David, let's move out!"

Davis grinds the gears as he shifts from neutral to first and moves out.

But not fast enough to suit Harry, who says, "Can't you goose this thing, make it go faster?"

They are northbound on Empire Way. David recklessly (for him) passes under yellow lights and rolls through stop signs.

"This may be nothing, Harry. The woman is a recluse. Thanks to you, she's become excitable and foolhardy."

"Dave, Alice is no birdbrain. Next-door to her, they came for the ID and threw a fit. Then putting two-plus-two together: they're trying to bust in and snatch her. That's why she was calling me."

"A big guess on your part. We shall see."

"When we get there, can you call in the rest of your agents so we can raid the eleventh floor?"

David Booth sighs. "Harry, this isn't Prohibition, where we can barge in and take an axe to beer barrels."

"A-ha. That was your agency that ruined everybody's fun, huh?"

David doesn't answer until they park across the street from the Dorrinsen Arms Hotel. "How do you propose to get to her?"

Harry begins running. "Same way as before. C'mon."

Luckily, it's a different elevator operator, one who hadn't been maimed playing high-school football against Harry. He's in a front-desk uniform like an ocean liner valet, so Harry figures Steve's on a break. They step out two floors from the top, the maximum allowed.

Harry leads David to the stairs and up to the top floor. He has the access door open in under a minute, manipulating the bobby pins like they were miniature chopsticks.

"Practice makes perfect," he tells David, who doesn't respond.

Harry knocks gently on Alice's door. No answer, not a sound inside.

"This is gonna be tough," he tells David. "It's a double lock. The upper one is a deadbolt."

"Allow me," David says, as he turns the doorknob and the unlocked door opens. They go in to find no Alice Haymarket and no sign of violence.

They look around and David says, "I have to believe that she went out voluntarily, Harry."

"No she didn't. Not after that phone call. I know her."

"You met her briefly. What proof do we have? This suite is undisturbed. It's the lap of luxury, and nothing appears to be out of place."

Harry prowls everywhere. "Something's missing, Dave."

"What?"

"I—I can't put my finger on it. C'mon next door."

The vacant suite is unlocked, too. Harry enters it and points, "Look at that."

The medicine cabinet is on the parlor floor, and just above it, the chunk it had taken out of the wall.

"Well," David says.

Harry doesn't answer. He's already across the hall, ear pressed to HH and Company's door.

151

"Not a peep," he says.

"They are gone, Harry. We should be, too. The entire floor is vacant."

"They have her."

"They?"

"*They.*"

"We cannot be certain of that, of your 'they'. We can file a missing person's report on Alice. That way, we will have police looking for her, too."

"We need faster action than that," Harry says, a whirling dervish now.

David just looks at him, knowing that it's pointless to argue with Harry when he's like this.

Harry, by now frantic, is checking one end of the hall and the other, looking at the fire alarms and axes, one set above the stairs, the other above the elevator.

"Alice's stethoscope," he says.

"What about it?"

"It's gone is 'what.' That's what's missing."

Harry runs to one end, pulls the fire alarm lever down, then runs and does the other.

"Let's get the hell outta here before we get scorched."

*****

Harry and David stand outside the Dorrinsen Arms as fire trucks respond to the alarm, men hooking up hoses to fire hydrants, others charging inside with axes. They're in the midst of a crowd scanning the art deco surface of the hotel for smoke and flames. Harry watches the entrance as people are marched out into a cold drizzle.

Some hotel guests are panicked, some are puzzled, all are shivering. Few are dressed for the weather. Most are angry when they look up and see no fire, a false alarm confirmed by angry firemen who come outside.

Harry sees one person he recognizes, Steve, the elevator operator whose nose he broke when playing high school football. Steve isn't angry. He lights a cigarette, appearing happy for this unscheduled extension of his work break.

David says, "Harry, we have to go before you cause any more trouble."

"Okay. One more minute. We have to know if Alice is hiding in there."

A woman emerges, tall and slender in pleated skirt, ruffled blouse, and golden bracelets. Her dark hair is long, her eyes as hard and deep as blue topaz. She is not dressed for the weather but seems oblivious to the cold.

Harry cannot move, cannot take his eyes off her.

Diana Doe is scanning the crowd, and locks on them with hatred and contempt. Not just him, but David too, Harry sees.

Harry's knees weaken and his pulse races.

Whoever she is, Harry thinks, she's a dead ringer for Diana Prince, Wonder Woman's alter ego. Or her evil twin.

Her eyes harden further. Harry can't believe his own. Her eyes are going from blue to blue-black to black as obsidian. Like the Dragon Lady in 'Terry and the Pirates,' one of his favorite comic strips. She's every bit as hot as Wonder Woman, but wicked as all get-out.

She scares the bejesus out of him while giving him a monster of a boner.

"Harry, what is the matter? You are trembling and it is not the cold."

"Dave, what are we waiting for? No reason to hang around."

CHAPTER 29

The Seattle Daily News
Wednesday, December 24, 1941. Price: Five Cents.

MURDER VICTIM DISCOVERED
IN SEEDY ALLEYWAY.

*Man's inhumanity to man isn't confined to the purview
of Hitler, Tojo and Mussolini. Yesterday, in an alley in
a disreputable neighborhood, an unidentified man in
his thirties was found savagely beaten to death.*

*He had no personal identification, so the presumed
motive was robbery. The only identifying features were
tattoos, so he is thought to perhaps be a sailor or an
out-of-town criminal, with whom his murderer had
an insidious dispute. Police questioned patrons of a
seedy tavern adjoining the alley. No one could provide
information that could aid the invest—*

Joanne Antonelli puts the newspaper aside for Harry and shakes
her head.

"A grisly murder on the eve of our Lord's birthday. A false alarm,
too, at a big ritzy downtown hotel. Sending our fire department there
when they need to be on alert for damage that could be done by

154

Japanese bombers. This on top of the war. If you ask me, we have spies and fifth columnists running loose. They ought to be rounded up and shot. Every last one of them."

"Erg," Harry says.

Joanne reaches across the table to feel her boy's forehead. "Hmm, you're very pale, but I don't feel a fever."

All four Antonellis are having an oatmeal and toast breakfast. Rocco and Lou are discussing a 1937 LaSalle coupe they have in the shop, how badly the passenger door is caved in, how GM stopped making the model in 1940. Now, thanks to the Japs and Nazis and the war, General Motors and the rest of Detroit don't make parts for any of their models, the precious metal going instead into the manufacture of tanks and cannons.

"Parts for LaSalles were scarce as hen's teeth before the war," Lou says.

"We'll have to skin the door, beat out the panel and fill every bump and dimple with lead. Not perfect, not the kind of work I want to send out of the shop, but it's the best we can do," Rocco says. "We're working till noon today. We promised the Johnsons we'd have their Plymouth done. Let's worry about the LaSalle the day after tomorrow."

Harry barely hears them, turning pages and skimming.

Wondering why there's no mention of the switchblades—probably swiped by whoever found the stiff—Harry turns to the piece on the false alarm at the Dorrinsen Arms Hotel, which was blamed on juvenile delinquents, not Axis spies.

Christmas shopping today. A good trick without much money and no way to buy on time, Harry thinks, putting on his jacket.

HISTORICAL NOTE: Harry had no credit rating, so "buying on time" was out of the question. Credit cards did exist in 1941, but they were merchant-specific and run against charger plates when used. The Diner's Club Card debuted in 1950, much too late for Harry. As are *the ubiquitous Visa and MasterCards that Harry would blithely max out even if he qualified for them.*

He can't stop thinking about Alice. He *has* to find her. Dave's missing person report isn't worth a hill of beans.

At the door, Joanne says, "It's not too late to invite a guest. Other guests too, if you like. We have plenty of food I am so thankful for."

A guest. Meaning a lady friend, Mom hoping it'll be Dorothy. Harry says he'll think about it and let her know as soon as he can. On the sidewalk, without the foggiest notion what to do next, he sees his very own Santa Claus unlocking the Hudson.

Harry waves his arms like a semaphore as he runs to him.

"Merry Christmas, Dave."

"Whatever it is, Harry, the answer is no."

"Since you mention it, I have to have a couple of things in order to continue my mission."

David digs cash out of his pocket.

"Here. That's the first of your 'couple,' I know without being told. Please don't ruin my day by telling me the second."

"I can't give you the details except that it's urgent. Does your secret agency have a yard for cars you've impounded from bad guys?"

David stares at him.

"No, no. I'm not prying into any deep, dark secrets of yours."

"Well, certain agencies do share impound facilities."

"Can you inquire if there's a thirty-seven LaSalle with an undamaged passenger door?"

"I can if it's important."

"Grab the door for me if there is one. You won't regret it, Dave," Harry says, running to the Airflow.

"Harry, it's Christmas Eve. Don't be imperious. I am confident Mrs. Haymarket took refuge with friends."

"I'm her only friend."

"The only friend that you know of. Please stay out of trouble."

"Scout's honor. I will."

David laughs.

"C'mon Dave. What am I gonna do, rob a bank?"

"Since you mentioned it, while you were still in Cuba, a bank-robbery streak began. There is a bank robber who wears a clown's mask and carries a large pistol, a .45 Colt. He strikes on Fridays, typical paydays, and the day before holidays when banks carry substantial amounts of cash. He's hit seventeen banks thus far. His getaway driver always has a souped-up stolen car. They're known as the Killer Klown Gang. They are vicious killers, too, having taken two lives. Human life has no meaning to them."

"Umph. I've heard about them. Why are you bringing it up? What the hell's that got to do with anything?"

"Don't yell at me. I am bringing it up to emphasize that all official agencies have their hands full. Because of the war, we have to wear many hats. Please behave."

Harry drives into town, suspicious that Dorothy has spilled the beans to Dave about his only two fears in the whole wide world: guns and clowns. But she's never dangled it over his head like her brother has the trumped-up charges filed against him after the incident at the Shimizus, or the self-defense death at the nearby Owl Tavern that the press and everybody else is calling murder. Blackmail and yellow journalism, as if he doesn't have enough problems.

As he drives, he mentally prepares a Christmas shopping list. On this, his traditional shopping day, scant hours remain until Santa flies out of the North Pole. Harry's Christmas wish for himself is that the law leaves him alone. A Public Enemy Number One poster will not please his family. Any way you look at it, it's been tough for him to catch a break lately.

Downtown, thanks to a heavy fog, is lit up everywhere, every store window and street lamp on. Shoppers are out in force, so

Harry has to park ten blocks from the Dorrinsen Arms.

Pummeled by fellow pedestrians, nose running from the cold, humid air, Harry believes he's overdue for some luck. His plan is vague, but one element in it is standing outside, smoking a cigarette again: Steve, the elevator operator. Steve, who might be his lucky charm.

"Hey, Steve, fancy seeing you here."

Steve blows a smoke ring. "I work here, Antonelli."

"Yeah, hey, you do, don't you? I read that somebody set off a fire alarm yesterday."

"Yeah. Punk kids, they think."

"The little bastards," Harry says, slapping a fist into a palm. "They belong in reform school, getting slapped silly by the guards."

"You said it, but you know, I was really enjoying my break till you came along, Antonelli."

"Everybody was evacuated anyway, huh?"

"What do you care?"

"How about the rich old lady on the top floor nobody ever sees?"

"None of your beeswax," Steve says, flicking the butt into the street.

"How much do you make an hour, riding up and down all day?"

"Go to hell, Antonelli."

"Nice talk," Harry says. "The minimum wage for anything is thirty cents an hour. You're in that general range?"

Steve's jaw tightens, so Harry knows he is.

He takes a ten-dollar bill from the money David Booth gave him. Ten bucks, he calculates, is four days work for an elevator jockey.

"Answer that simple question and one or two more, and the sawbuck is yours."

"I think it was her, dressed up like she was going to the opera or somewheres."

"She went outside when the alarm sounded?"

Steve smiles.

Harry gives him another five. "This fin is the end of the rainbow, Steve."

"Before that. To the basement. If she came back up, she didn't during my shift."

"What's in the basement?"

"Storage. Empty rooms. How the hell should I know? Hardly anyone goes there. I think you have to have a key to use the stairs."

Harry says, "Let's go for a ride, Steve."

CHAPTER 30

Seattle.
Wednesday, December 24, 1941.

Harry steps out of the elevator into dim light and dust. Steve shuts the door so quickly that it scrapes Harry's back heel. The basement seems to be first and foremost for storage; half the doors are open, with surplus furniture piled willy-nilly. All the doors on one side of the hallway are closed. Only one isn't covered with dust.

Harry knocks on it. "Alice?"

No response. He knocks harder. "Alice?"

"Go away. I'm not here."

"Alice, it's Harry. Open up. Let me in."

The door opens a crack.

"It's all right. It's me and I'm alone. Are you okay?"

"Oh, if you only knew! How did you find me?"

"C'mon, let me in before we draw a crowd."

"There's no crowd down here except for the spiders and rats."

"Alice."

She admits Harry to a single room, substantially smaller than her suite. He's blinded by the reds and pinks on everything: walls, bedding, furniture. Everything except the ceiling over the bed, which is mirrored.

"Do you like it, Harry?"

Eyes blinking, adjusting to the decor, he says, "I'd go for different colors, Alice, if I was doing the painting."

"This is Max's den of iniquity, where he fucked his harlots and who knows what else. He thought I didn't know. In a pig's eye I didn't!"

She thinks, *Well, my Max was a cheater. He had brazen hussies on the side.*

"Ah."

She sits in a chair that's striped like a candy cane. "How did you find me?"

"I have my ways. When did you get down here? During the fire alarm yesterday?"

"Is that what the commotion was about? The bells ringing. The people up above. It sounded like a herd of elephants. Was there a fire?"

"No. It was a false alarm."

"People who do that are dreadful. Hateful."

"I agree wholeheartedly. The punk kids, they ought to be in reform school. You scared the hell out of me, Alice, when you called my house and spoke to my mother, and then didn't answer my call later."

Alice gets up and touches her bedside phone, which is gold and red. "Would you care for a meal or a toddy, Harry? Hughie delivers to me down here on the q.t. I know he wants to get into my knickers, but I just string him along."

"No thanks. I had a big breakfast. You called for me. Mom said you were upset, but wouldn't say why."

"I did. It was the suite next door. I heard someone over there, and whoever it was, they were throwing a tantrum, making a terrifying racket. It had to be concerning the identification cards. Do you have anything to report on Randall and Helms?"

"Nope."

"Harry, are you sure? I know when you lie to me. Randall and Helms?"

"I would never lie to you, Alice. I wish I could, but, dammit, I can't. Those two bums jumped me in an alley outside of a tavern. One of them came out on the short end of it."

"Oh? How short?"

"As short as can be. You really don't want the fine details."

"Very well. Have it your way."

"What did you do next, after the racket next door to you?"

"I waited until it calmed down. Then I packed a few essentials and took the elevator down here. Including this."

She opens a dresser drawer by the bed, and pulls out her stethoscope and a Derringer. "Anybody tries to break in on me here gets his head blown off. Harry, what's wrong?"

Harry is looking away. "Careful with that thing. It could go off."

"It can go off. It's made to go off. Goodness, you're as white as a ghost."

"Your stethoscope was gone when I checked out your suite. I was worried sick. Put that goddamn gun away, Alice."

"There is no cause to curse, Harry, to take the Lord's name in vain," Alice says as she drops the Derringer into the drawer.

Harry is able to look at her again.

"You poor dear. I'm at my wit's end. You're the only person I can trust and you're so rattled."

Harry looks around at the confectionery colors and upward at himself. "Alice, you can't stay here."

"Oh, I know. The very sight of this. The bed where he… It makes me want to kill Max all over again."

To kill Max all over again?

A killer in his own right, inhabitant of a glass house, Harry lets it slide.

"Seriously, Alice."

"Oh, where would I go? I've lived at the Dorrinsen Arms forever and ever."

"I think I've asked you this before, Alice, but have you ever seen anybody from HH and Company?"

"No, not that I recall."

"A lady?"

"I'd remember a lady."

"Do you read the Sunday funnies? 'Terry and the Pirates' or any other strips?"

"Goodness, no. The comic pages, they're for children. Why?"

"Yeah, they are."

"Once again, why?"

"Well, I remember when I was younger and read the comics, 'Terry and the Pirates' had a Dragon Lady character."

"You do ask strange questions and make odd remarks, Harry. They trail off to nowhere."

Harry jumps up, takes her hand, and gently coaxes her to her feet.

"Throw a coat on, girl. We're going Christmas shopping."

*****

Outside for the first time in who knows how long, Alice inhales the chilled air and perks up. Her kitchen sink of a purse slung over her shoulder, she takes Harry's hand. "Come with me. Since we're doing this, I know best."

She tugs him along to Frederick & Nelson on Fifth and Pine, Seattle's leading department store.

"They're expensive, aren't they?" Harry says, taking longer strides in order to keep up.

"Don't you worry, young man."

She steers him through mobs of crazed last-minute shoppers, knowing right where to go. She makes him buy a heart-shaped locket for Dorothy (by then, Alice had pried loose Harry's confused and conflicted feelings for her), and a fruitcake for Mom, her favorite dessert. The only person on her list is Hughie. In the kitchenware department she finds a top-of-the-line set of knives, and spends a pretty penny for it with a wad of cash in her purse.

"Hughie's told me his kitchen knives are low quality and won't hold an edge no matter how many times he sharpens them," she says. "He's been dropping hints since October."

Back in the late Max Haymarket's basement den of iniquity, Harry lays the heavy knife set on the dresser and is absently jingling the change in his pocket—all he has left from the shopping expedition—preparing to invite her to Christmas dinner, when he feels the little flag.

He removes it and says, "I damn near forgot. David identified this. It's the flag of the British Union of Fascists."

"Nazis?"

"The closest thing England had to them. They raised hell in the thirties, but when Hitler invaded Poland, that was the end. The big shots were arrested and interned."

"Someone belonging to that stack of IDs was an English Nazi?"

"I think so. Know any Limeys around the hotel?"

"Only one." She pauses, "No, it couldn't be him."

"Who?"

"My friend in the kitchen, Hughie."

Harry smiles and says, "I have an idea."

CHAPTER 31

Seattle.
Wednesday, December 24, 1941.

It's Harry's brainstorm to gift-wrap Hughie's knives and invite him down to wish him a Merry Christmas. That, as Alice orders a meal.

"The yuletide spirit," he says.

"You are such a naughty, naughty boy," Alice says, blowing him a kiss.

"Make it a big portion," Harry says. "We're having lunch, not tea and crumpets, whatever the hell a crumpet is."

It had taken some convincing to persuade her that Hughie may be a rotten apple. She admits that—come to think of it—he abruptly replaced Lillian, his predecessor who had been here for ages, without any explanation, and only a headshake and a shrug whenever she pressed him.

"How long ago?"

"Earlier this year. I don't remember the precise date. Lillian didn't even stop by to tell me in person. That was unlike her. I was suspicious."

"What's Hughie's background according to Hughie?"

"I thought nothing of it until now, seeing him in a completely different light. Hughie is evasive, Harry. Some people naturally like to keep their own business to themselves. He values his privacy so much that I gave up and stopped prying. He may as well have dropped

165

out of the sky in a Martian spaceship. Like in Orson Welles' *The War of the Worlds*. He will only say that he fled the Nazis."

"Hmm," Harry says, rubbing his hands. "If he's English like he claims, the last I read, Hitler hasn't landed in Britain yet and isn't likely to."

"I know what you're thinking, young man. Resist your natural urges. Fisticuffs doesn't solve anything."

An odd thing to say. Attempting to look innocent, Harry nods and suggests another tactic.

Alice agrees and telephones her order. Within five minutes, there is a tap on the door. She lets in a pear-shaped man in his mid-thirties. His reddish hair is combed from where it grows to where it doesn't. He's startled by the sight of Harry as he sets down the tray of club sandwiches, French fries, and bottles of Olympia beer, which vibrate and wobble, but don't topple.

Harry picks up a beer and, eyes unnaturally wide, sneers at Hughie.

"Hughie, this is my son, Horatio. He's visiting for the Holidays."

Harry chug-a-lugs the beer, belches, twitches and says, "Out on parole, to tell you the honest truth."

Hughie freezes.

Harry presents a lopsided smile. "Relax. Those electric shock treatments they gave me made me into a new man."

"He's fairly harmless, dear," Alice assures Hughie. "The shock treatments? They shocked loose some of the violent behavior that got him sent up the river."

"*Some of*, mum?"

"Please have a seat so we can have a little chat."

Hughie backs to the door. "I'd love to, mum, but the kitchen is overwhelmed."

Harry smiles again, trying for twisted. He pats Hughie on the back hard enough to move him, and pushes him down into a chair.

"Really, ma'am," he says, sitting. "I can't."

The look Harry gives him stills him in the chair.

Alice sets the gift-wrapped knives on his lap. "Merry Christmas, dear."

"Blimey. You shouldn't have, Mrs. Haymarket."

Harry drops the lapel pin on the knives and says, "Lose something, mate?"

Mouth open, Hughie shakes his head.

Alice squeezes Hughie's thigh, digging her nails in, and says, "Confession so relieves the soul, and sheds oodles of light on the day."

"Are you delivering meals to HH and Company, too?" Harry asks. "Way up on the top floor?"

Hughie looks up at Harry. His first instinct is to spring for the door, but his survival instinct is to evade, hoping to get out of this nutty old biddy's room in one piece, and away from her and her crazy, criminal boy. He has read about his kind in the *Police Gazette*, has seen front-page sketches of blood dripping from their hands.

"You might say so. They send somebody down, or we send somebody up. It varies."

"How many people are in that suite to be fed?"

"That varies, too. Some, I think, are quartered across the hallway."

Harry flexes his fists, demonstrating his impatience. He begins to drool.

"Numbers."

"Two to seven, if I have to guess."

"Ever smell perfume?"

"From the main suite?"

Harry's twitch is becoming palsied. "Yeah. That suite. What suite do you think I'm talkin' about?"

"No. No perfume."

"We hear tell they get perfume samples delivered to them."

"Once or twice when I was there, I saw parcels left by the door. Round canister-size things inside the paper wrappings is what they looked like."

"Canister size?"

"Yes sir, like the kind that go into lunch boxes, to keep coffee hot."

"Faces?"

"Faces?"

Harry pats both sides of Hughie's. "Faces. Belonging to bodies who picked up those parcels."

"Honest true, I never saw a soul. They'd call their order downstairs. We'd leave it at the door and come back later for the trays. I'd come for the trays, and the parcels would be gone."

"Names of who called the food orders?"

Hughie purses his lips.

"Does the name Dewey Concannon the Fourth ring a bell?"

Hughie shakes his head too vigorously. As if he's been wrapped up in Wonder Woman's magic lasso.

Harry looks at Alice. "Mother, may I?"

"Oh dear, Horatio, I do so hate savagery. It's the cause of you doing so many years in that dreadful prison with those awful beasts who assaulted you in the shower room."

Harry stamps a foot. "Mommy!"

Alice stands up. "Oh, very well. You always did get your way as a child. I'm going for a walk. All this tension is detrimental to an old lady's heart. Hughie, please, for your own sake, don't agitate this boy of mine any further. I couldn't control his temper from the day he was a toddler. Lord knows what the prison experience, with all the perverts and slashers and armed robbers and killers, has done to him."

Alice chokes up, her acting technique even superior to Harry's psychotic twitching and drooling and lopsided smirking.

Harry grins. "Enjoy your walk, Mommy, and take your time."

As Alice turns the doorknob, Hughie begs her not to go and starts talking. Blathering, in fact. Even if they want to, Alice and Harry doubt if they can shut him up without slapping him.

Lillian was sacked, no reason stated. She was given five minutes to pack her stuff and clear out, he says, so Hughie could be installed in the kitchen. Hughie, who was a *former* member of the British Union of Fascists. He served under Oswald Mosley, who was slated by the Führer to become Reichskommisar of Britain after the invasion and conquest. Before any of that occurred, Mosley and the other leading Union members were interned.

The rank and file, such as himself, scattered to the four winds. With his cooking background, he landed here. Persons unknown arranged for him to have this job, giving him no other choices, including the option to say no. This was before he left England.

Hughie stops talking and looks at his hosts, looking for approval. End of story?

Hughie draws back as Alice pats his knee. "And you were doing so well."

Harry cracks his knuckles and says, "Dewey Concannon the Fourth."

"Son, will you please stop behaving like a ruffian," Alice scolds. "Your vile temper is what put you behind bars for half your life."

"I know, Mommy. I try, but I can't help myself."

"Hughie, you *must* do your part. My boy is a powder keg and I am too old and frail to intervene. Please answer his question."

"Dewey who? The name is unfamiliar."

"This is the last time I'm asking polite-like," Harry tells Hughie as he bounces up and down, slapping his hands.

"All right, all right. A bloody charlatan, Dewey Concannon is. A BUF member, too, but higher up. Not at Mosley's level, but not far under. I saw them together at rallies. They chatted like they were close mates. With the Mitford sisters, too. Those ladies, they were Nazi-loving beauties. Oswald was married to Diana for a spell. That other, Unity, took a fancy to Hitler. His preferences in that regard are a mystery, so there's no telling how far she got with him, hot-blooded lady that she was."

169

"Stay on the topic of Dewey Concannon. He's a Brit, right?"

"Sounds like a Yankee Doodle, don't he?" Hughie says. "He can talk out of both sides of his mouth and you don't know who he is. Mosley sent him into the different districts to recruit. He spoke all the dialects and slang like he was born there. He's a German, but that's only my opinion. He's changeable like those lizards."

"Chameleons."

"Yes, ma'am. That's it. A chameleon."

"Did he have a different name then?"

"Don't remember. Just remember seeing him."

"Tell us more."

"I ran into him in the lobby some weeks back. One of your small-world encounters. In a country this size, amazing. He was none too chummy, said to keep him and his identity under my hat."

"What does he do?"

"All I know is that he isn't employed by the hotel. He's possibly a long-term guest."

"Keep talking."

"There was another time, he encountered me on the top floor after I left a tray. Laying in wait, I suspect. Asked if I had anything on me connecting me to fascists. This pin. He took it from me, called me stupid and other names. Pledged me to secrecy. I took the pledge, of course. Hard not to when you're pinned up against a wall. Bloke's stronger than he looks."

"I'll keep that in mind," Harry says. "Did Dewey ever speak of what he's doing here in Seattle?"

"Not in any specific terms."

"What's that mean? Did he speak of B-17s?"

"The bombers?"

"Know of any other B-17s, asshole?"

Alice says, "Horatio, your language. I apologize, Hughie. He's had a filthy mouth since the fourth grade. The prison time with those creatures has made it even worse."

"Third grade."

Hughie is perspiring heavily, wondering if he'll escape this madhouse alive.

"All I can gather is that he's in Seattle to win the confidence of a person."

"Did he mention her name?"

"He offered no name. I do recall this. He said *his*, not *her* confidence. And *confidence* is my word, not his. This is all innuendo on my part. He gave away little if anything. Our shared background went only so far."

"Hmm," Harry says.

"Last question, Hughie, before you go. Who or what is this HH?"

"I heard tales. They're only tales and I heard them years ago. Who knows what the truth is?"

"Tales are better than nothing."

"HH is or was Hubert Hennshaw, a chap who originally leased the suite around 1930. I recall his name because it's so alike mine. The suite fell into the hands of others when he went away in 1934."

"Went away where?"

"Back where he came from is what I hear. A bloody secret is what it is. Even the rumors are hogwash. You've drained me dry of information. I swear."

Alice sends a relieved Hughie on his way. She and Harry hug, congratulating each other for their acting jobs. As they separate, Alice slaps Harry on the ass and asks, "What next?"

"Two things. I hereby invite you to Christmas dinner. I'll let you know after talking to Mom what time I will pick you up."

"Harry, I can't impose."

"I accept your acceptance of my invitation. Mom will love you. Second, I'll use your phone now to have David research this Hubert guy."

CHAPTER 32

Seattle.
Thursday, December 25, 1941.

To Joanne Antonelli, Christmas dinner, a day devoted to the baby Jesus, is a day where it's the more, the merrier. Filling her home with tidings of comfort and joy, and thanks to the war, for the last time until who knows when. She shunts that thought aside before the waterworks start.

Last-minute invitations ok, Harry asked? Yes, please bring them. Again, son, the more the merrier on this, the most special of days. She revels in "taking the bull by the horns." On this particular day, there is no such thing as a party crasher.

Two smoked picnic hams are in the oven. The poor cousin of the more expensive regular ham, the "picnic" is, in Joanne's opinion, every bit as flavorful if cooked properly. Sweet potatoes adorned with marshmallows will follow. A garden's worth of white potatoes are awaiting peeling, boiling, and mashing.

Harry and Rocco have the card table set up in the living room, the table used exclusively for canasta parties and Christmas dinner overflow. These days, the table is more often covered with dust and fond memories. Long ago, it had been for the kids and their friends, the Kiddies' Table: Harry, Lou, and the Booth children. Doctor and Mrs. Booth at the adult table with her and Rocco.

Lou's Julia is celebrating Christmas with her family, he has told

Joanne, though she sees in his eyes a hint of friction between them. He'll confide in her if he feels like it, grown-up adult that he is, although compared to his brother, Lou is as transparent as glass.

Harry went to pick up a special lady friend, mysterious about her as he is about so many things. Him and his femme fatales. The lady and his two other mystery guests.

Now he's back with a delightful old lady in expensive clothes and two gentlemen in rags. The men are scruffy, but their hair is parted as if they used a ruler, and they've drenched themselves with cologne to conceal the odor of the whiskey she knows they had for breakfast.

Harry's hobos—Lord knows where he meets and makes friends— are very sweet. One man has a peg leg. Herbie Barnwell and Paul Miller, by name. They're at the end of the second table, regaling all with stories of the Spanish Civil War. Harry is between them and the table's jug of dago red. He fills their wine glasses with water. Herbie and Paul have the daintiest table manners of anyone there.

Dorothy, bless her, is lending a hand; it's all Joanne can do not to tell her and Harry to stop playing hard to get with each other. Dorothy's guest, Mr. Dewey Concannon the Fourth, is attempting to make small talk with Rocco and David, who fidgets as he holds his tongue. There is an air to Dewey she finds distasteful, him and his flashy $100 suit. It's her own fault for inviting Dorothy to bring a guest, thinking that she would being a lady friend from work or decline altogether.

Harry has an extreme dislike of Dewey Concannon, too. It is *so* obvious. When Mr. Concannon speaks of his parents' giant iron-casting plant in Pittsburgh, and how he could reunite with them and receive a draft deferment because it is a critical industry, how he has instead chosen to do his patriotic duty.

When Mr. Concannon wraps himself in the flag, she sees in Harry's eyes the urge to plunge across the table and take him by the neck. There is also the green-eyed monster in her boy to consider, too, when passing judgment on his mood and their arrogant guest. She is relieved when conversation drifts to the vapid, confined to the weather and the wonderful food.

Of the presents piled under the tree, one is the oddest ever, a secondhand car door that Harry leaned precariously against the adjacent wall. Its window is rolled partially down so a ribbon can be wrapped around it, a tag saying it's from Santa. The recipients, her husband and younger son, are gaga over the door.

If the war isn't enough, this promises to be the strangest Antonelli Christmas *ever*. Her own present from Harry, a fruitcake stuffed with cherries and walnuts, is delightful.

Tabby has been carefully removed from his chair by Rocco. Harry's kitty is in a far corner of the kitchen. Having gorged himself on table scraps, he is sound asleep in a happy coma. After dinner, Dorothy comes into the kitchen to assist Joanne with the plum pudding. Mrs. Haymarket comes in to help, too, but not before ordering Harry into the hallway with a small and clumsily wrapped gift he holds, and then sidling Dorothy in that direction. Joanne is impressed at how the lady can be overbearing without being overbearing. Cupid with a crossbow.

As Alice assists her hostess in apportioning the plum pudding onto plates, she positions herself so she can catch a glimpse of the hallway doings. In an unspoken alliance, Joanne and Alice cannot separate sweet Dorothy from sinister Dewey soon enough.

Farther down the hallway, out of sight, Dorothy is holding the locket chain, grinning from ear to ear. Harry starts to put it around her neck, but she shakes her head. No, later. But she gives him a thank-you hug, which metamorphoses into the hug Alice hopes it will be. Harry, the naughty boy, roams with his hands under her dress and her garter belt, and Dorothy's whispered protests of "Stop it, Harry" are not protests at all.

"Ditch that guy," Harry whispers back.

"For you?" she counters.

His hands are almost inside her panties when he says, "You can do a whole lot better than either one of us."

Dorothy places both fists on his chest and pushes him out of reach.

"I'd love to know why you're doing this, Harry, you and your flowers and candy and roaming hands."

She is out of the hallway before he can answer, a relief to him since he doesn't have one.

The meal is over, presents opened, conversation exhausted, the men speaking of brandy and cigars. Joanne lays down the law: no cigar smoke in her house.

Only 365 days until Christmas, Joanne thinks, as she stacks dishes in the sink. Will there ever be another as good as this one? She doesn't kid herself. She lost her brother Fred in the Great War. It seems like small potatoes compared to this one, Hitler on one side, Tojo on the other.

*****

Harry is giddy about Dorothy, what they had in the hallway. If that's not courting her, he doesn't know what is.

He has taken David aside, saying it's urgent they speak after he runs his guests home. Herbie and Peg Leg Paul first, rudely denied wine with dinner, offer no objections. Mr. Jack awaits at home.

Alice, on the other hand, informs him, "You're not dumping me off, Harry. Not on your life. I'm in on this, too. If you're playing Junior G-Man, we are solving crimes as a pair, a *team*."

HISTORICAL NOTE: Junior G-Men was a popular phenomenon of that era. It began as a radio program starring a real-life G-Man named Melvin Purvis, an FBI agent and national hero who led the manhunt for John Dillinger. The Junior G-Men spun off into radio programs, slogans, and other "war on crime" incentives. Focused on boys, there was no known restriction banning older men, or even women *from honorary membership.*

Harry ignores the Junior G-man crack, but yields, and the twosome return to the Booths, hoping to catch David alone.

"Mrs. Haymarket," David says at the door, surprised.

She brushes by him, saying, "Go back inside, young man. It takes two to tell *this* tale."

David obeys, taking the easy chair.

Alice and Harry sit on the sofa.

"Where's Dorothy, Dave?"

"Concannon dropped her off at work."

"On Christmas?"

"Only a half day. Don't ask for details. She was suddenly called in. She won't give me a hint at what she does there, but I noticed she was surprised by the call."

"By the way," Harry says. "Thanks for that thirty-seven LaSalle door. To Dad and Lou, you're a magician."

"My pleasure. Now, what is this all about? When you telephoned yesterday, you asked me to check out this Hennshaw individual, keeping other things to yourself."

Alice says, "Harry told me you were all business. I'll start."

She starts and ends, so thoroughly that Harry has nothing to add about Hughie, but says, "The phony Dewey, it's high time we sit him down and question him."

"The Nazis pull out fingernails with pliers," Alice says, bony fists clenched. "They get answers."

David says, "We are aware that the man is a scoundrel, but I didn't realize the depth of his venality. Are you certain this kitchen worker, this Hughie, gave you the true story?"

Alice smiles and pats Harry's knee. "Oh yes. It's all true. Harry scared the shit out of him."

Harry smiles. "Not a drop of blood was shed."

"I am their target, not Dorothy? This makes no sense."

Harry says, "The phony false alarm some sick-in-the-head vandal set off at the Dorrinsen?"

Alice covers her mouth to suppress a giggle.

David can't prevent himself from smiling. "What of it?"

"We waited outside when the fire department went in. I said nothing at the time, but a woman who came out of the Dorrinsen Arms stared daggers at me. It gave me the willies."

David says, "More young women should stare daggers at you. It would save them grief later on."

"She was a dead ringer for the Dragon Lady in Terry and the Pirates or Diana Prince in Wonder Woman. Take your choice."

David closes his eyes. "How much of Rocco's wine did you have, Harry?"

"It wasn't just me getting her evil eye. You were, too. I wasn't the object of her attention, Dave. You were. You more than me."

David has no answer.

"You and your spies, you do be careful, Mr. Booth. Super agents are only human," Alice tells him.

"So, Hubert Hennshaw?" Harry says.

David takes a piece of paper from his shirt pocket. "This information dates to 1930. It seems that he is out of the picture. He was a Bremerton attorney who lost his practice during the Depression. He went to work for a large law firm in Seattle in a junior position. It was a take-it-or-leave-it time. Hennshaw stayed there less than a year, then resigned. Where he went from there is a mystery."

Harry says, "Where is he now?"

"That we do know. He was killed by his wife at their Bremerton home in 1934."

Harry nods. "Which explains why you're drawing a blank on his work record."

"Killed how?" Alice asks.

"Elizabeth Hennshaw, his wife, was acquitted of the murder charge, successfully citing self-defense. She alleged that he was a belligerent drunk who was two-timing her with a Seattle woman. She lived with the treachery and shame until she could endure it no longer and demanded a divorce. He had abused her physically in the past, and came at her again with his fists, more brutally than ever. She had no choice but to fend him off with whatever was within reach. In this case, a large kitchen knife."

"Ouch," Harry says.

"Ooh-la-la. Lollapalooza," Alice says, clapping her hands. "What a lady."

David and Harry look at Alice, as Harry inches away from her.

"What happened to the widow?"

"The prosecuting attorney decided not to file charges. Apparently Elizabeth Hennshaw still lives in the family home, all alone. She has no friends or family."

"The poor lonely dear," Alice says.

"Hennshaw's Seattle gal?"

"I gather that the investigation into her came up empty."

"Hmm," Harry says.

"They didn't pursue the incident vigorously because the mystery woman wasn't as germane to the trial as was the question of self-defense or cold-blooded murder. Mrs. Hennshaw was able to prove the former rather easily. She had defensive bruises and the neighbors testified to past troubles between the two. Harry, you have that look on your face."

"Yeah, I do have an idea, but it has nothing to do with those lovebirds. I know how to work off some of that Christmas dinner."

*****

Diana Doe spends Christmas alone. This is her preference. In her childhood, Christmas was merely another day of horror.

She sits in her suite and waits. The money is safely stashed. After one last pickup, it will be time.

Dewey comes in and even before his coat is all the way off, says, "It was a bizarre day."

"I don't care if the potatoes were lumpy. What do you think?"

"I know they're suspicious. He was looking at me strangely."

"The hothead?"

"He has from the day I met him. The girl's brother, the agent, was unfriendly, too. After dinner, the girl was called in to work."

"Today? Christmas day?"

"Yes."

"Do you know why?"

"No. She doesn't confide in anyone. Should we worry?"

"No. It's a fool's errand, her and her team. They're taking the bait."

"What do we do?"

"Pack."

"I can be ready to move out in ten minutes."

"We have what we need. We're set to begin the final phase."

CHAPTER 33

Harry has talked David Booth into playing along with him. Furthermore, he has persuaded the secret agent to provide the transportation, him and his government-issued 1939 Hudson coupe.

"Might as well let Uncle Sam pay for the gas, huh?"

"It has to be HH and Company, this phony perfume outfit, which we've infiltrated and penetrated and neutralized. I'd bet my bottom dollar," says Alice, euphoric in her role as an assistant secret agent. A Junior G-Lady.

David downshifts from third to second gear as they approach a red light. There is a Christmas tree inside the window of a hardware store on the corner. Its lights are blinking. By tomorrow, needles will be falling, the limbs drooping, and there will be post-Christmas gloominess.

Only 365 days until the next one, Harry thinks. Where will he be then? Shooting Jap Zeros out of the air, he hopes. Them or Nazi Messerschmitts. The fact that fighter planes have guns doesn't disturb him. They're way out on the wings, and they're not aimed at him.

Dorothy will be safe and well, he hopes, not riveting Boeing bombers, but in a job that utilizes her brainpower. He continues to tingle from their hallway clinch and grope. Him and her after we win the war, he cannot imagine. One day they're hotsy-totsy, the next

180

they're just friends, by and large his fault. This going back to grade school, him already a butterfly.

"Your super-duper secret agency hasn't got the drop on them yet, has it?"

Alice says, "Harry, you're being pushy and rude again."

David stops at a red light.

David sighs and says, "You have not revealed the fine details of your wonderful plan, but I am sure it breaks no fewer than five laws."

"I haven't exactly formed it fully in my head yet, other than keeping with the Christmas spirit and having a toddy with Dewey. Even British fascists celebrate Christmas, don't they? At dinner, he was a windbag, not celebrating anything but himself and his lies."

Alice snaps her bony fingers. "The light inside my head just came on. It's low wattage at my age, but it's still burning. Your plan has formed fully in *my* head, Harry. You youngsters are headed to the right place, but for the wrong reason."

"I'm listening," Harry says.

"I'm sorry. I should have said, for the wrong *reasons.*"

Harry reaches back and squeezes Alice's knee. "I'm really and truly listening even if David isn't."

She slaps his hand. "Don't get fresh unless you're willing to do the dirty deed."

"Jeez, Alice."

David says, "I am listening, Alice."

"The Dorrinsen Arms has eleven floors, plus basement rooms where my late husband rendezvoused with his whores, doing unspeakable things with them. Two at a time, I suspect. He had the money…"

It makes me want to kill Max all over again, she thinks.

She pats David's shoulder. "I'm sorry, Mr. Booth. Your neck is reddening. I'll be careful with my language. As I was saying, the hotel has eleven floors. The first is the lobby. Two through eleven are guest rooms and suites. The elevator cannot go higher than the ninth without special authorization, but Harry was able to enter the tenth floor from the fire stairs simply by opening the door. However, he had to employ his skills as a second-story man to gain entry to the eleventh. There is much to be said for a common burglar in certain circumstances."

"C'mon, Alice. You're hurting my feelings."

She laughs and says, "The tenth floor."

"What of it? The tenth has no suites," Harry says. "Just rooms like the other floors, right?"

"Yes, so why will the elevator not transport a person to the tenth floor without permission?"

"Uh-huh," Harry says.

"Interesting," David says.

"My second reason: Our Dewey Concannon the Fourth is not an Englishman."

"Why do you say that?" David says.

"Because, Mr. Booth, if Concannon was English, he would have been scooped up with other high-ranking British Fascists and interned. He'd be behind barbed wire and kicked in the balls by guards to practice their soccer skills. That poor excuse for a human being claims he was cozy with Oswald Mosley and those Mitford Nazi sluts. Unity Mitford was fucking Hitler. If the horrid little man is actually capable of doing so. Did you know about that?"

David clears his throat.

"*If* we believe everything Hughie told us, Alice."

"Harry dear, he would have sworn the earth was flat if you ordered him to."

"I'll take that as a compliment."

"It was meant as one, as proof that Hughie was truthful with us."

"I anticipate your answer, Alice. You have the floor," David says.

She leans back in the seat and says, "Hughie told us what he thought we wanted to hear. If Dewey's not German, I'm Barbara Stanwyck."

*****

Outside, the Dorrinsen Arms, carolers dressed like elves are singing. Inside, the lobby consists of a front desk, concierge kiosk, bar, and dining room. Finely-dressed civilians and military officers are having a meal.

The threesome rides the elevator to the ninth, gets off, and walks the stairs to the tenth. Harry tries knobs at random. All locked.

"Doesn't mean nobody's home," he says.

"It *could* mean nobody's home," David says.

Harry takes bobby pins from his shirt pocket.

"If somebody *is* home, that's a surefire way to get your face blown off, dear," Alice says.

"Yeah, well," Harry says.

"My plan has an additional component," Alice says.

They look at her.

"Silent night, holy night," she sings in a quaking falsetto. "All is calm, all is bright."

David laughs out loud.

Harry says, "I can't sing and I don't know the words."

Alice says, "What a couple of babies you are. Choose a door, knock on it, and I'll start singing. You can hum along. We're carolers. What is more innocent than that on this most holy of days?"

"Best plan I've heard all holy day," Harry says.

"No argument here," David says.

Harry leads the way to 1019, raps hard, waits, and Alice begins.

"Christ the Savior is born," she ends.

Harry presses an ear against 1019's door and shakes his head.

Alice trills, "'O Come All Ye Faithful' next?"

David says, "There is no need to continue, Alice. There has not been a whisper anywhere on this floor. Harry?"

Harry goes to work on 1019's keyhole, turns the knob, and shoves the door wide open.

David enters first. If he has a pistol on him and pulls it, Harry will be looking elsewhere.

But no gun needed, as there are no visible guests.

They look around and see two single beds, made up. Fresh towels in the bathroom. No personal belongings anywhere.

They randomly pick two other rooms: 1003 and 1026.

They are identical in layout and unoccupied.

"Stand by," David says. "I'm going to the front desk."

Alice and Harry sit on a bed.

"I have to ask, Alice. Did you really kill your husband?"

She smiles. "Wouldn't you like to know?"

"Well, yeah..." he says, then pauses. "Actually, when you come right down to it, maybe not."

"That's a good boy," she says. "You and that Dorothy, you are such a darling couple. I watched you in the hallway. If you and her had some privacy, what would you have done? "

He smiles. "Wouldn't *you* like to know."

"Once we get our mitts on her Nazi lover boy, it'll be just you and her."

Harry smiles again, but makes no comment.

Alice says, "Do you like mushrooms?"

"Sure. Why?"

"Max did, too."

Harry looks at her.

Alice smiles.

Harry says, "Maybe I don't like them so much anymore."

David doesn't take long. "I had a word with the manager. He confirms what we have already deduced. The entire tenth and eleventh floors are on a long-term lease to HH and Company. As they aren't regarded as single rooms, there is no record kept of individuals' comings and goings."

"Their dormitory," Alice says. "Like a college."

Harry is on his feet. "Or their barracks. Like an army."

CHAPTER 34

Seattle.
Thursday, December 25, 1941.

Harry is out the door and into the hallway before his companions can react.

"Harry," David says, in the hallway.

Harry has already picked the lock and is on the eleventh floor, axe mounted by the fire alarm taken down and in his hands like a baseball bat.

"Harry, whatever you are going to do, *don't*," David says.

Alice has arrived, out of breath. "Harry, you're bound and determined to tucker me out and give me a heart attack."

David is standing between Harry and HH and Company. "Think."

"What is there to think about? I bust in. We get answers."

David says, "Who is in there, Harry? Do they have guns? We are unarmed."

Guns.

Harry lowers the axe. He can almost smell Diana Prince's evil twin's perfume. "We gotta do something. If the phony Dewey is in there…"

David says, "If he is, he drove here, yes?"

"What're you saying?"

David cocks his head toward the door.

"Shall we see what is parked in the hotel garage?"

185

Alice says, "Brilliant, dear boy, brilliant."

"It is," Harry says.

"If his Lincoln is here, he is probably here. If not, then he is probably elsewhere," David says. "If it *is* here, perhaps we may find a clue in it."

Harry hates it when David's right, but he drops the axe. "Okay, okay. Lead the way."

Behind him, Alice says, "Will you youngsters please slow down. Kids these days are so impatient. This isn't the Olympic Games."

In the landing, David initiates a meeting. "Harry, in the event we encounter Dewey in the garage, I know you would love to use that axe on him and I don't blame you."

"You're a mind-reader, Dave. I didn't bring the axe, but my fists will do. We're killing time out here."

"Listen to me. Then you will be guilty of another murder."

"Like I explained over and over, the first murder wasn't a murder. It was self defense."

"We don't know precisely who he is, and if he is not alive, he cannot tell us."

"One or two or however many dead men," Alice says. "It's the same in the eyes of the police."

They look at her.

She says, "Your plan is to ask for the garage keys at the front desk, is it not?"

"Our next stop," David says.

"Those people are as gossipy as Hughie."

"A risk we shall have to take," David says.

"He drives a fancy car, doesn't he?" Alice asks.

"A forty-one Lincoln Zephyr," Harry says.

She reaches into her kitchen-sink purse and pulls out a key ring.

"Max parked his Duesenberg in there. I never turned in the garage keys after I sold it. We can forgo a stop at the desk."

Harry says, "That's swell, Alice. Dave, we gotta get to a phone before Lou leaves the house. I can break into every building this side of Fort Knox, but not into a car without it looking like it's been in a serious accident."

*****

Harry calls from Alice's suite and catches Lou. They arrange to meet at the garage, which is a block south and a block east of the hotel entrance.

In thirty minutes, Lou Antonelli arrives in a 1936 Chevy pickup with ANTONELLI BODY AND PAINT on the sides. They've repainted the truck sky blue with black lettering. Hard to miss, Harry thinks, damn good advertising.

Sheepishly, Lou steps out with a key ring the diameter of a saucer. Harry counts twenty-five to thirty keys.

Lou asks Harry, "Are you getting me mixed up in something illegal?"

His older brother smiles. "Probably."

"Nifty," Lou says, ready for some excitement in his life before "the ball and chain" as Harry had put it, or the Marine Corps in the Pacific, where he may be treated to way too much excitement, courtesy of the Japs.

They enter the garage through the people door and turn on lights. It smells like oil and rubber, and is half full.

Harry whistles. "Two snazzy Caddies, a Mercedes-Benz, a Packard, and there's our Lincoln, in the front corner. Lou, you sure you can open it up?"

Lou tinkles the key ring. "I can open any car ever built."

He feels the hood. "Warm, not hot. He didn't just get here."

Lou tries several keys before finding the one that opens the driver-side door.

Harry paws around, then David does.

"Anything we can string him up with, Dave? Car registration with the hotel address and road maps is all I see."

"Unfortunately, no. Lou, can we try the trunk?" David says.

When Lou opens it, Harry says, "A spare tire and a rubber mat."

Lou says, "Let me."

He removes the spare tire and peels back the mat.

"Aha, pay dirt," Harry says, reaching all the way in.

He comes out with passports and fans them in his hand. "A royal flush plus one."

David takes them one by one, saying, "United States, England, Mexico, Portugal, Argentina, Germany. All issued to Dewey Concannon IV on the same date, April 1, 1940."

"Not long before the Sitzkrieg ended," Alice says.

David says, "The Nazis are proficient at counterfeiting documents. We have reports that they use inmates in their camps to do the work."

Harry says, "Dewey can scram anywhere on a moment's notice. Unless…"

"Unless indeed," David says, pocketing the passports. "It's time to lock up his car and go."

"Nah," Harry says. "It's time to go. That's all."

"Excuse me?"

"Lou, can you make the trunk stick wide open? If Dewey boy doesn't see it quickly, someone else may and report it to the hotel. We'll be flushing him out."

"We won't know how long that will take," David says.

"We will if I make the call to the front desk from a phone booth," Harry says. "An anonymous call from a good citizen."

"After I phone in and request men to do surveillance," David says.

Alice hugs Harry, then David, then Lou.

"You naughty, naughty boys. If I'd ever had children, I'd want them to be exactly like you."

CHAPTER 35

Seattle.
Friday, December 26, 1941.

"Everything costs too goldurn much, you know. I been going out for sixteen-ounce T-bones with all the trimmings and Baked Alaska for dessert, before they go and ration them cows. Sets me back five bucks and some change," Leamy complains.

"Yup. Highway robbery is what that is," Joe Bobby (Rob) Banks says.

Behind the wheel of a freshly-stolen black 1939 Ford coupe with white sidewall tires, Leamy says, "This gas rationing, too, Rob. Gonna be harder for me to find a car with a tank that ain't three-quarters empty."

"We gotta dump it quicker and git in the next car is all, Leamy."

Leamy downshifts and shakes his head. "Easier said than done."

The two-man gang lives in cheap hotels, one step up from flophouses, keeping the loot they don't pocket in bus station lockers. They move weekly, figuring to keep one step ahead of the law in case the law is only one step behind them. This is a smart thing to do, Leamy believes, but decent getaway cars are hard to find in crummy neighborhoods. He has to take the bus to scout out a good set of wheels, and feels that riding buses is beneath him, a man of his skills.

They've come to an agreement that this is their next-to-last heist. They'll have enough dough stashed, around $12,000 each, to retire from doing banks to doing things they'd rather do. For Rob Banks, that's going home to poach alligators. Sell the meat and the hides and drink moonshine.

For Leamy, it's poaching cars and selling them to shops for parts. With the war on, he'll get top dollar and won't have to worry about being chased by bank guards and cops, or getting shot. Two more banks and they'll be in the gravy.

They pass by one in the heart of downtown, on Third and Madison. It's made of concrete with art-deco doodads and brass doors, this in keeping with Rob Banks' notion that the loftier the building, the richer the take. He is often correct in this evaluation.

"This one here, it looks ripe for the takin'. Go on around the block, Leamy."

"I dunno, Rob. The day after Christmas? All this traffic, too. Is that a snowflake on the windshield?"

"It's Friday. There's still big paydays on any ol' Friday."

"Worth a try, I reckon. I don't see no guard by the door," Leamy says. "This girl I been going out with, I done gave her a ring yesterday so she'll be more friendly in some ways, if you know what I'm sayin'. She tells me she needs a magnifying glass to see the rock."

"There's other fish in the sea. Stop here," Rob Banks says after they've rounded the block. "We'll do it."

"This is closer to downtown than we usually do. All these cars, the traffic…"

"You're a worrywart, you know. People returning presents, buying other stuff with the money they get back. The bank, it'll have a lotta dough on hand."

The clown mask disguise is a choice made by fate, Rob thinks. He found one on the ground two Halloweens ago. It's been his lucky charm ever since, and their luck's held so far.

Rob Banks bought another mask, and selects the one with the smile. He likes to alternate it and the sourpuss one with the droopy lips, a bone to throw at the newspapers, who love him and his style. He steps out of the car and slips it on.

Colt .45 pressed against his side, he walks into the bank. Walking in like he owns the place.

*****

At the very minute the clown-masked robber enters the bank to commit his eighteenth robbery, David Booth pounds on the Antonelli door. Harry, who has been reading the paper, jumps up and answers.

"Get a jacket on. Let's go."

Harry doesn't argue. The paper's all bad news anyway. The Japs are all over the Philippines, running wild in Malaya and the Dutch East Indies. They're knocking on Singapore's door, too.

David's super secret agency Hudson is outside, engine running, passenger door open.

Harry yells goodbye to his mom and runs to the car. Snow is falling lightly, a white day-after-Christmas.

David lurches away, throwing Harry back into his seat. He's driving like a crazy man with a telephone receiver to his ear. They had waited ninety minutes outside the Dorrinsen garage after Harry made the call before David ran Harry home. They assumed Dewey wasn't at the hotel or had doped out the trap.

David says, "He did spend the night at the hotel. Fortunately, our people spotted him a short while ago."

"Why do you think he waited until today?"

"To formulate a strategy, I believe. The man does not panic."

"Where'd he go when he came out of the garage?" Harry asks.

Harry's looking at the telephone, thinking of Dick Tracy and his wrist radio, which is a ten thousand times smaller. Too bad there's no such thing and never will be, not until the real Buck Rogers and his rocket ship comes along. Harry is half-expecting David to be dragging a telephone cable along.

"Is that one of your G-men you're talking to?" Harry asks.

Ignoring him, David yells into the phone, "On foot? Which direction?"

Harry looks in the back seat, sees two large metal boxes the telephone cord is connected to, and says, "Dave, what the hell is this thing?"

"A two-way radio. A walkie-talkie."

"Talkie-walkie?"

"No. Walkie-talkie. It's designed to be portable, carried on one's back. It works just fine in a car, too."

HISTORICAL NOTE: In 1940, the Galvin Manufacturing Company (now Motorola) was given a War Department contract to develop a portable, battery-powered, two-way radio that could be worn by infantry troops. Their SCR-300 weighed thirty-eight pounds and contained eighteen vacuum tubes. It first went into service in the Pacific in 1943. How David obtained a unit in late-1941 remains classified, as does his agency.

David is driving with one hand, slipping and sliding under a red light, talking and listening.

"He's what?"

"On foot?"

"Not? What?"

"He jumped on a bus? Which bus?"

"Well, that helps us."

"Do I hear sirens?"

"Roger. Standing by."

When he puts the receiver on his lap, Harry says, "Fill me in."

David says. "Concannon went into the garage approximately"—he checks his watch—"forty-nine and a half minutes ago."

"That's approximate?"

"And ran back to the Dorrinsen Arms. Running as if he had caught on fire. Brushing people aside. To an unknown room for unknown reasons, then back out and to the bus. The bus is westbound, progressing slowly. Traffic is a mess, made worse by a number of police cars with their lights and sirens going. Apparently, there has just been another bank robbery, thought to be by the Killer Klown robber. A witness claims to have heard gunfire."

"Ooh," Harry says.

"We are short on manpower," David says. "Wait. Just a minute."

Phone to his ear, glancing at Harry, he says, "Third and Seneca Streets. He is staying on? Good. I have somebody with me."

"Why me? I'm not a secret agent."

"And you never will be, given your criminal propensities."

"I'm flattered, but you didn't answer my question, Dave,"

"Speaking of. The man you killed?"

"In self-defense."

"Preceding the autopsy, they found a tattoo on an upper arm. The Nazi eagle with the swastika. He had an identical one on his back."

"Hey, I self-defensed a Nazi spy."

"You did. I will use my influence. You will be in the clear, Harry."

"So, I've been acquitted?"

"You cannot be acquitted if you have not stood trial, but for all intents and purposes, yes. Law enforcement cares little about solving the murder of a Nazi. The case will soon be forgotten. In the event it is not, I will do as I did with that brouhaha at the Shimizus that landed you in jail."

"Okay, Dave. I get the message, loud and clear."

Another wild turn and Harry is slammed against his door. "As you were saying, me and your manpower shortage?"

"I want someone available on foot. You're faster than anyone we have."

"Carrying a football, yeah. But—"

Telephone to his ear, David says, "Off where? Yes. I'll send him. Waving a gun?"

"Gun. Gun? Who has a gun?"

"The bank robber. Outside the bank, he had been waving it out the window of their car, attempting to clear an escape route."

"Not Dewey? Dewey isn't waving a gun?"

"No. Not Dewey. He got off the bus at Second and Madison. Harry, we're south of there and only ten or eleven blocks southeast of him. Get out now. Go!"

David slams on the brakes. Harry opens the door and says, "And do what?"

"Stay on his trail, for God's sake."

"And keep in touch with you how? You got an extra talkie-walkie?"

"You will think of something. You usually do. Go!"

Harry goes. He piles out of the car, around the front of it, jay-running into horn-honking traffic.

CHAPTER 36

Seattle.
Friday, December 26, 1941.

Legs pumping, avoiding obstacles both stationary and moving, as if returning a kickoff, Harry Antonelli charges into traffic, evading cars like they're tacklers, horns bleating at him from every direction. Referee penalty flags that weigh two tons are flying.

Some lunatic driver jumps onto the sidewalk in a black 1939 Ford coupe with white sidewall tires and clobbers a parking meter, barely missing Harry, tires spinning in the new snow as it races through an intersection. Harry shakes a fist at the crazy bastard.

Westbound toward Elliott Bay, on a steep downhill street like a skier, Harry turns sideways to skid on the steeper parts, the snowfall thankfully now half rain. Two green lights, three reds, and Harry is two streets from the water.

There Dewey is, frenzied as described, stepping onto a southbound bus. Harry plunges onto it through the rear door just as it closes. He'll worry about the fare later.

He sees Dewey in a front seat, directly behind the driver. Where the hell's he headed?

They're on First Avenue now, merging onto Highway 99. Harry knows US 99 to be the main route from the Canadian border to the Mexican, from Blaine, Washington, to National City, California.

Phony Dewey Concannon the Fourth is unlikely to be traveling that far. They're past downtown, making fewer stops. Whichever one Dewey takes, Harry will take. If Dewey spots him, he'll grin, make a stupid "small world" comment, and obey his first instinct by knocking the son of a bitch's teeth out. Secret Agent Booth didn't say *not* to.

Let Booth and his G-man secret agents give what's left of Concannon the third degree.

The bus is staying on 99, doglegging to the left. Boeing Field is not far. Harry sees the tarmac jam-packed with newly-completed B-17s lined up, shiny and silvery. Harry refocuses on the phony Dewey Concannon IV and where he'll get off.

He doesn't have to wait long. Dewey pulls the stop cord at the Boeing main gate.

Dorothy.

This is where she checks in and out of work.

Dewey gets off with two-thirds of the other passengers.

Harry waits until the next stop, drops a quarter into the box, and runs back toward the main gate. The temperature has fallen, snow is falling harder, and the ground is crunchy under his feet.

A hundred yards from the gate, he can't see Dewey, who must've gone inside. He presses against the fence and waits.

Ten minutes later, Dewey emerges, an arm around Dorothy, who holds a hankie to her eyes. Moist red eyes.

What the fuck has he told her to make her cry?

Snow continues to fall. Harry is looking at them as if he's gazing into a snow globe invented by the goddamn Devil himself.

No time to behave like a counterspy. Time to play defensive back and put the phony Dewey on the ground.

In the street now, hoping for better traction, Harry breaks into a sprint, screaming, "Dorothy, no!"

They look at him.

He sees a southbound car pulling up to the curb. It's a gray sedan, maybe an Oldsmobile. Not that it matters.

"Dorothy, no!" Harry screams again, waving his arms away from the car.

She looks at him, looks at Dewey.

Dewey looks at her as the car stops.

He opens the car's back door and takes Dorothy by the sleeve.

Harry is yelling incoherently now.

Dorothy jerks free of Dewey, who grabs for her, catching her coat. She yanks loose and he dives into the car.

It accelerates, headed for Harry. He hops on to the sidewalk, but so does the car. There's a grassy, rocky strip between the sidewalk and the metal fence. He reaches down and grabs a pool-ball-sized rock.

Him and baseball. Not a great player, but he did have a rifle arm.

Still does. He flings the rock, smashing the driver-side windshield, a direct hit. It doesn't break through, but shatters the outer laminate into a spider pattern.

Good as the final strike that wins the World Series, as it probably just saved his life. Flying blind now, the driver swerves back into the street and out of sight.

Off balance, clinging to the fence, Harry sees little of the driver but long hair.

The evil Diana twin? The Dragon Lady from Hades?

He looks back at Dorothy, who is wiping away tears.

He runs to her and takes her into her arms.

*****

"I had her until—"

"Shut up, you idiot, and help guide us. I can barely see," Diana says.

Dewey does as ordered. Going south and westward, managing to keep the car on the road, they eventually arrive in White Center, an unincorporated area at the edge of Seattle's city limits. Diana has rented a small house on a quiet street there for such a contingency.

It's three blocks from a two-street business district.

There is a bedroom for each of them, with appropriate clothing in the closets. The half basement where they were going to interrogate Dorothy Booth is windowless and virtually soundproof.

Behind the house sits a large detached garage. Dewey runs out and opens one of its doors. Diana drives in so fast that she almost hits him, and parks next to a 1936 Pontiac sedan she had purchased from a retiring cab driver. It's an oxidized dark green, with TAXI stenciled on the front doors.

"We will be driver and passenger when we next go out," she says. "We'll be invisible."

"Ingenious," he says after they're in the house and she has ordered him to start a fire.

"You are full of surprises," he says as he stuffs old newspapers into a freestanding stove. "Why?"

"Why what? Hurry. Get it started and pile kindling on top of the paper."

"I know how to start a fire. Why do you conceal so many things from me? I knew nothing about this place."

Diana says, "I inform you when you have to know."

"Interrogation techniques, for instance. You didn't elaborate."

"Now a couple of larger logs. Until Antonelli got in the way, you were getting set to learn what they've discovered with their decoding." She smiles. "You could have some fun with Dorothy Booth, too."

Dewey doesn't reply, blowing into the stove.

She says, "Move aside and let me do it before we freeze to death. Have you had fun with her? You haven't said."

"She didn't seem interested. I didn't want to push it."

"A shame."

"I don't even know your last name. I know 'Doe' isn't it."

"See what I'm doing? Kindling, then the smallest, driest logs."

CHAPTER 37

Seattle.
Friday, December 26, 1941.

Fast becoming a snowman and snowwoman, Harry and Dorothy attempt to calm each other.

Dorothy had been frantic because Dewey called her out of work, claiming an emergency, then telling her that her brother David had been in a head-on car accident and was taken to the hospital in critical condition.

Harry responds that David is hunky-dory, and it's Dewey who's gonna be in critical condition the next time Harry can get within punching range of him.

Dorothy says her head is gyrating. It's hard to stand on her own two feet, let alone think.

Harry asks if she can get the guard shack to let her use the phone, to call the Dorrinsen Arms desk, to send someone to locate David.

Though out of breath, in two minutes, she has David on the phone.

"Safe and sound," he tells his relieved sister, how he's been waiting to hear from Harry or whoever has Harry in custody.

"David, Harry is in *my* custody. He just saved me from I don't know what. Please get here as fast as you can."

Her brother arrives in the Hudson faster than Harry thinks possible. In it they go, headed for home.

David tells what they've learned about the pseudonymous Dewey

Concannon and the rest.

Harry is in the back, keeping his yap shut, not even complaining about what a tight squeeze it is, competing for space with the talkie-walkie.

"Dorothy, you have to be candid with me about your Boeing assignment. After we drop Harry off."

"Bullshit on dumping me, Dave. I'm smack-dab in the middle of this thing."

"You have no security clearance."

"Look, we wouldn't be here, the three of us, if I hadn't chased Dewey and his gal friend away."

Dorothy says, "David, he's right."

"Yeah, c'mon. I'll be going into the Army Air Corps soon," Harry says. "We're all on the same team, fighting Japs and Nazis and their cockroaches in this country."

David sighs. "Very well. When we get home."

"Ever wonder if there have been listening gadgets installed in your house?"

David sighs louder. "Harry."

Dorothy pats his shoulder. "David, I know how you hate it when I take Harry's side. When Harry's right, you hate, hate, hate it."

"You don't know the half of it."

Harry laughs and says, "I recommend we go someplace noisy so nobody can aim a secret microphone in our direction."

*****

"The principle of somewhere noisy is good, Harry, but this venue is less than ideal."

They share a booth at the tavern where the confrontation with Rolan Snails occurred. Half the booths and barstools are taken, and it's loud but not *too* loud. Harry has plugged nickels into the jukebox to spin Artie Shaw's "Stardust" and the Andrews Sisters'

"Boogie Woogie Bugle Boy. "

Harry hoists his beer in toast. "Perfect, huh?"

Dorothy, seated across from him with her brother, smiles and clinks his glass. David Booth does neither.

David says, "Dorothy, please reveal what you actually do at Boeing."

She doesn't speak.

Harry does. "It's okay. He's a G-man."

"Shut up, Harry," she says.

Harry shuts up.

"Very well. David, you were like this as a child, unrelenting until you got your way."

David thrusts his jaw. "In light of the front-gate incident, please, Dorothy."

She looks around and sees serious drinkers, nary a spy amongst them. "It has to come out sometime, but what I say cannot leave this table. I took an oath. I'm part of a team that decodes messages. We believe they're sent from Germany through intermediaries to fifth columnists who are workers on the B-17 production line, assembly mechanics and riveters. These awful men have applied a chemical that accelerates metal fatigue to vital parts of the planes. That's what is to blame for the parts' failures that have caused the bombers being ferried to England to crash."

Dorothy pauses to sip her beer. David stares at her. Harry gulps his beer.

"On this last Tuesday, three days ago, our department broke the code," Dorothy continues. "The raw transmissions are in Morse code, which I don't know, but they're broken down into five-digit groups for us. The message was 'two-left-four-aileron-one-hinge-eight'. Our supervisors ran out of our station. They came back smiling like Cheshire Cats. They didn't say what happened, but gossip travels fast. We think that the saboteurs were nabbed in the act."

"The 'two-left-four-aileron-one-hinge-eight' on what plane?" Harry asks. "There are three shifts and a long assembly line in there. I saw them parked on the field when I was on the bus with our phony Dewey. It was a line of B-17s a mile long."

"Airplanes are assigned sequential numbers when nearing completion. The left aileron hinge or hinges on the plane with the two-four-one-eight serial number. If the hinges fail in midair and the left aileron flies off or locks up, I'm told, the pilots would lose control of the airplane. I'm presuming that two-four-one-eight hadn't left the factory floor."

When she stops talking, David says. "Are you worried about that—*individual*? If so, fear not. He is on the run, and their Dorrinsen Arms spy nest is being shut down."

"Yeah. And what did that son of a bitch have that I don't?" Harry says.

Dorothy smooches the air and pats his hand. "We'll talk about that another time, Horatio Alger."

David says, "So what is troubling you?"

"'Two-left-four-aileron-one-hinge-eight.' We decoded it so quickly and easily. *Too* easily," Dorothy says. "The girls and I are new code-breakers in a new department. This was our first and only success, and it broke the sabotage ring wide open."

"What do the bosses have you doing now that was so important to have you called in to work yesterday?" Harry asks.

Dorothy makes a face. "Practice exercises. We've heard that we'll be shut down after the first of the year. I'm going to be a Rosie the Riveter. This is okay with me. *If*."

"If?" Harry says.

"If this is the end of the cloak-and-dagger bit."

"Shouldn't it be?"

"It should," Dorothy says. "Us doing busy work."

"Unless there is another project on the horizon," David says.

"Unless," Harry says, "they're hanging on to you just in case."

"Just in case of what?" David says.

"Just in case of anything. This isn't gonna be over with any time soon."

They sit with their beer and their thoughts until Harry says, "I'm doing some sightseeing tomorrow."

David says, "If you go to Palm Springs, say hello to our parents."

"I'm going a whole lot closer than that. Bremerton."

CHAPTER 38

Seattle and Bremerton.
Saturday, December 27, 1941.

All RED and BLUE stamps in War Ration Book 4 are WORTH 10 POINTS EACH. RED and BLUE TOKENS are WORTH 1 POINT EACH. RED and BLUE TOKENS are used to make CHANGE for RED and BLUE stamps only when a purchase is made. POINT VALUES of BROWN and GREEN STAMPS are NOT changed.

Harry is reading this in the paper on the one-hour ferry ride from Seattle to Bremerton. Poor Mom, he's thinking, having to deal with that day in and day out.

The weather has perked up. It's a good five degrees warmer and the snow at the Seattle ferry landing has turned into slop. Alice Haymarket is sitting across from him, not knitting like the passersby think little old ladies should be doing. She's working the paper's crossword puzzle, doing it in ink.

She is tagging along with Harry because he knows he'd never have a minute's peace if he left her behind. They're going to Bremerton with the hope of seeing Lizzie Hennshaw, who committed the town's crime of the century and got away with it. Alice talks about Lizzie like she's a gun moll, for Christ's sake. Like she's Bonnie Parker. Harry hopes to hell she isn't.

HISTORICAL NOTE: Bremerton, Washington, did have a "crime of the century," a mass murder in March 1934. In the Erlands Point neighborhood, somewhat isolated and distant from the city proper, six people were shot or bludgeoned to death, their throats slashed for good measure. The motive was robbery. A huge dragnet was put out, to no avail. Months went by without a clue. One day in a Seattle beer parlor, two men were overheard talking, mentioning the crime and dropping a man's name. At long last, the killer was apprehended. He was tried, convicted, and sent to the gallows on September 11, 1936.

They drive to 112 Olympic Avenue, a mile from the ferry dock and a bustling business district, a miniature of Seattle's. For a town of around 15,000, the weekend traffic is heavy, much of it forming in lines at gas stations, everybody knowing that rationing is soon to come. What few know or guess is that, because of the Puget Sound Naval Shipyard, Bremerton's population will reach 75,000 by war's end, a figure it will probably never approach again.

Olympic Avenue is a tidy strip of average-sized homes built during the last war to house PSNS workers. Lizzie Hennshaw's is easy to pick out: peeling paint, bumper crop of dandelions, and oozing roof moss.

Alice is out of the car first.

"Cold feet?" she asks Harry.

"No," he lies.

"Well, move along then."

"I'm not keen on getting shot."

"Don't be silly. She knifed her man to death like she was carving a ham. She might not even own a gun."

"That'd be swell with me."

Up the steps to the enclosed porch they go, Alice leading the way. The front door is open a crack. Through the screen door, the odor of tobacco tar, stale booze, and bacon grease is strong.

"Hello, hello," Alice calls out.

A woman comes to the door. She's in a soiled housedress and curlers. She is formless, with the bloat of too many cocktails. Some years ago, she may have been a looker, Harry thinks, but the lines around her eyes speak of too many unresolved grievances.

"What the hell do you want?"

"We're stopping by for a friendly visit," Harry says.

"That's a new one," Lizzie Hennshaw says. "Neighbors see me outside, they grab their kiddies and run indoors."

"But you were acquitted," Alice says.

"Oh sure. Not to them and half the people in town I wasn't."

"I killed my husband, too," Alice says merrily. "The cheating, skirt-chasing bastard."

"You're a little old lady."

"That's what he thought, too."

"When did you get out of jail?"

Alice's smile puts her dentures on display. "The coppers never pinned it on me."

Lizzie swings the screen door open. "Well, come on inside, sister, before you catch your death of cold."

They go into a darkened living room, where they're invited to take seats on a couch with cushions that sink almost to the floor.

Lizzie offers drinks. Alice accepts. Harry declines.

Lizzie shuffles into the kitchen with her own empty glass and returns with two filled with a cloudy red liquid.

"I don't get to the store much, so I make my own red in a big ceramic jug in the bathtub like they did back in the Prohibition days. I get by on a small inheritance from a maiden aunt who hated all men, but it's not enough to buy booze off the top shelf."

Alice sips and says, "Tasty."

Lizzie looks at Harry and asks Alice, "Who's this cutie-pie? You knocked off your old man so you could land him?"

"His name is Harry. He's done marvelous things for me, but not what you're thinking, dear," she says as Harry attempts to shrink.

"Ah," Lizzie says. "I could throw a Glenn Miller on the Victrola. We could cut a rug, then have some fun with the boy. Teach him a few tricks."

Alice strokes Harry's thigh and says, "That *is* a thought, but we'd like to talk to you about a few things."

"You're my first visitors in a coon's age who aren't wearing uniforms. Dearie, you say you took your hubby's life. A rat, too, eh?"

"The dirtiest of rats."

"How'd you finish him off?"

"I fixed him mushrooms in a frying pan, the way he liked them. How was I to know they were poisonous? I never spent a day of my life in the woods looking for them."

Lizzie cackles. "My Hubie liked my cooking. Why didn't I think of that?"

Alice cackles, "The bastard always did complain about my cooking."

"Serves him right. The end of his complaining."

Horatio Alger (Harry) Antonelli, a history major, had been thinking about her mushrooms. He recalls classes in two quarters studying ancient Rome. Agrippina the Younger, the Emperor Claudius' last wife, widowed herself the same way, with a toadstool omelet or some such, so her son Nero could replace him. She was also Claudius' niece and sister of Caligula. Nero was a teenager when he took over, so Agrippina pulled his strings, effectively becoming the only female ruler in Roman history. This, until Nero, in his madness, tired of her bossiness and had her killed.

Harry has seen photos of busts of Agrippina the Younger. Not a raving beauty, not Miss Rome of 35 AD, but somehow *hot*. He'd been ashamed of the fantasies he had about Agrippina the Younger as he starred her in a term paper, which earned him an A.

Alice says, "They thought it was the cancer that had taken him. He was sick anyhow."

Lizzie says, "You did the right thing. You put him out of your misery."

They share a laugh.

Harry badly needs to be out of here.

When Alice starts on her second glass of Lizzie's bathtub concoction, Harry breaks into what's becoming a drunken hen party.

"What it boils down to," he says after a sketchy summary, "is that we'd sure like to know who, uh, your Hubie's Seattle lady friend was."

"She wasn't a *lady*, she was a dirty, filthy slut."

"That's what I meant to say," Harry says.

"Nobody ever found out, not even me or the coppers. But me and others, we had our suspicions."

Alice and Harry wait until she makes a trip for a refill.

"Hubie liked them young, you know. Me and him, we'd go downtown shopping on Pacific Avenue, at Bremer's and J.C. Penney's. This was when his law practice was doing good and we had some money to spend. The shop girls, the young ones, he'd give them the eye. One time he was staring so long and hard at this little blonde, I had to elbow him in the ribs.

"This is kind of a stab in the dark, but around ten or eleven years ago, out in the sticks west of here, in this little dump of a shack, there was a murder. Nobody talked about it much then on account of how it was done. This guy was living with a gal, him and her, they were a couple of mean drunks, and there was a daughter of the gal who the guy took liberties with, if you know what I'm saying. Beat her up, too. Beat her up bad.

"One day the mother woke up to find him dead, his throat slashed from ear to ear, and the little girl gone. The coppers, they didn't have to be Sam Spade to figure out who did him in, but nothing much was pursued as nobody missed the worthless drunk. It had to be the daughter, and she was nowhere to be found. She was seen getting on the Seattle ferry, a big city easy to disappear in. The girl, they said that she'd sawed his throat open from side to side with a kitchen knife."

"Why do you believe your husband was involved in this?"

"Not the murder, but not long after. It was the same time, late-1930, when he had to close down his law office here and he took a crummy job as a clerk in a Seattle law office. He was spending more and more time there, sometimes saying he had to work so late he slept at the office. I knew he was making better money, too. Leastways, he had more to spend, mostly on himself. I heard tell later on that Hubie was suspected of embezzling from the law firm, and they were closing in on him.

"Me and Hubie, it finally came to a head. He was crazy drunk one night, and I had to defend myself when the bastard came at me with his fists swinging. I still got that kitchen knife. They took it as evidence and gave it back after I got off the hook. Wanna see it?"

"No, not necessary," Harry blurts. "The girl, she was never located?"

"Never. For all I know, he might've killed her like he'd have done to me if I hadn't defended myself."

"Do you remember the girl's name?"

"Diana. Diana something."

"What happened to her mother?"

Lizzie says, "She went crazy when she woke up in the morning and saw the bloody corpse beside her. She was hauled off to an insane asylum where she died two or three years later."

Harry asks, "Does Diana have any relatives?"

"Not that anybody can find. Her father was long gone, and a brother went off and joined the military." Lizzie drains her glass. "She's an orphan and probably happy she is. I know I would be."

209

CHAPTER 39

On the ferry back to Seattle, Alice is bleary-eyed and cranky from the homemade hootch. Harry tells her to stretch out and take a nap.

"How the hell can I?" she says, "There are so many questions to be answered. They're flying around in my head like hornets."

"Take a nap, Alice."

"I can't," she says, slowly slipping to the horizontal.

As the boat slows to dock, after a nudge from Harry, she slowly resumes the vertical and says, "Harry, that post office box."

"Number one-thirty-seven."

"You saw that weaselly doo-doo Concannon, whoever he really is, take an envelope out of it."

"I did."

"Your brother-in-law, David Booth—"

"*Not* my brother-in-law."

"We shall see."

"You're talking like Mom."

Alice flutters a hand. "Regardless, David Booth is a secret agent, and he doesn't seem to care about you discovering Dewey going into the post office and going out with an envelope, does he?"

"Nope, he doesn't."

"He should have given you a badge and a raise. For that, and all else you've done."

"No badge and no raise since I'm not even on the payroll. But yeah, you're right, he should've."

"Dorothy's on the job at Boeing, marking time, although she believes it's not over, whatever *it* is."

"True."

"If Dewey and that Diana dame with the knife she used back in 1930 are on the run, doesn't it make sense that they would check that mail box? There's something in there they might need, don't you think? Fake passports or money or something."

"Yeah."

"Dear boy, are your bobby pins in your pocket?"

*****

Harry doesn't like her plan, but concedes that it's preferable to no plan at all. Naturally, he does have his bobby pins on him. You never know when they'll come in handy, so advised his Amsterdam girlfriend, the millinery worker and burglar.

He parks the Airflow three blocks from the main post office and, leaving the engine running, orders Alice to stay in it to stay warm. Since it's the deluxe model with a heater, she should stay toasty while he scouts.

He walks the same figure-eight path he did while on the lookout for Concannon, but this time for the good guys. He detects no agents in cars, fedoras pulled down low, no clean-cut boys with haircuts and fresh shaves huddled in doorways, dressed as bums. Nothing.

He goes for Alice, who complains that she's sweltering. He gives up the argument before it begins.

They start out, her arm tucked around his. "Being old doesn't mean I have poor circulation, young man."

"Alice, if anybody's curious while I work on the lock, distract

211

them. Talk to me about football. Like we're just standing there having a conversation."

"Football is why your nose looks like a truck ran over it. I don't approve of football, and I don't know anything about it."

"Make it up. Bend ears about this year's Army-Navy game. It's patriotic."

"Who won?"

"I don't remember. Army, I guess."

"Can they tie?"

"Yeah, but that's like kissing your sister."

"Oh, that's sick and dreadful."

HISTORICAL NOTE: On November 29, 1941, Navy defeated Army 14-6. The game was played as always in Philadelphia. There were 99,000 spectators in the stands.

It's Saturday, so the post office's counter is closed. The lobby will lock up in half an hour, so Harry knows he'll have to work fast. The lobby's busy, but not so busy that they're crushed.

As Harry fiddles with his bobby pins, Alice screens him from nosy-nellies the best she can.

"Army thrashed Navy, didn't they?" she says.

"No, I think you have it backwards."

As Alice explains to him loudly that his football knowledge isn't worth a hill of beans, Harry unlocks the box. It's so full of manila envelopes, it pops opens as if spring-loaded.

Simultaneously, Alice is shoved against Harry by men in topcoats, wearing fedoras, and others in hobo rags, all with haircuts and fresh shaves.

The envelopes fall on the floor as two guys are behind Harry, snapping on handcuffs.

"You're under arrest, Antonelli," one says.

"The old bat, too?" asks another.

"Hang on to her."

"Rape!" Alice screams, as she drops one of the envelopes into her kitchen-sink purse.

CHAPTER 40

Seattle.
Saturday, December 27, 1941.

"Where's Alice?"

"We took her home to sleep it off."

"You should be ashamed of yourselves, treating a harmless little old lady like that."

David says, "That harmless little old lady yelling 'rape' was on the verge of causing a riot. Then screaming that she was 'being pawed by animals'."

Harry doesn't comment. He had been rudely dragged out of the post office and shoved into the back seat of a waiting sedan, his head pushed down against the rear of the driver's seat. Destination meant to be unknown.

Five or ten minutes or twenty or thirty minutes later, they bounded into a basement garage. Harry knew that (or thought he knew) because of the darkness. Blindfolded before being yanked out of the car, there was an elevator ride, a beehive full of voices and cigarette smoke, and then into a room.

The blindfold is off and the room is windowless. Wherever he is, it's preferable to a stinking jail cell full of killers and perverts. He hopes it is.

Harry is seated in the middle of it on a wooden chair. He's triangulated by beefy, unfriendly guys in shirtsleeves, arms folded.

214

Their ties are loosened and they're wearing shoulder holsters. With large guns in them.

Harry makes firm eye contact in order to avoid seeing the cannons. "What the hell is this all about? You birds can get the noose for kidnapping, you know."

The guy in front of him, the largest one, a beefy redhead, says, "No more questions, wise guy. All we want out of you is answers."

"To what?"

"To picking the lock on a post-office box that doesn't belong to you. That's a federal offense, you know."

"That's crazy. I did no such thing. There were recruiting posters on the far wall. I was checking out my choices."

"The only uniform you'll be wearing will have stripes on it."

Harry spreads his hands. "What? What did I do? This mailbox you're talking about? What?"

"Box one-three-seven."

"Is that a question, Red? If it is, you'll have to spell it out in plain English instead of your riddles."

"You are one smart-mouthed asshole, Antonelli. Envelopes spilled out of that box a second before we slapped the cuffs on you."

"Okay, okay. I know the problem. It's all a big misunderstanding. My jacket snagged on something as I was going closer to those posters. That box must've been stuck partway open. Yeah, my jacket caught on the edge of it. I wasn't paying any attention at all to the boxes. I'll swear that under oath if you want."

The agent shakes his head slowly. "You're saying you didn't pick the lock?"

"With what? Find any burglary tools on me?"

"There were bobby pins on the floor. Where you dropped them when we apprehended you."

"Bobby pins? Some gal, they must've fallen out of her hair. Use your eyes. My hair's too short for bobby pins. I'm no burglar. I'm a law-abiding citizen who's gonna join up to fly fighter planes."

The three guys go to the door. The one who had been doing the talking says, "We'll be back in a while with rubber hoses to assist your memory, Antonelli. Take the time to decide if you want to keep lying."

They slam the door. The room echoes, then goes completely silent.

Harry waits. For how long, he doesn't know. He's in a big hurry to be out of here. Conversely, he's in no hurry for rubber hoses.

In five minutes or five hours, David Booth walks in.

"Wow, Dave, am I ever glad to see you. Those G-men were rude."

"Harry, shut up. Do you realize how many local and federal offenses you have committed in the month of December?"

Three, four, five, seven? Harry doesn't hazard a guess. He waits for David, who finally says, "We have had the post office under surveillance since you spotted Dewey-whoever-he-is removing an envelope from it. Thanks to your antics today, it will be pointless."

"Why the hell didn't you tell me? You wouldn't've known a damn thing about it if not for me."

"Harry, whoever you *think* you are, you aren't a member of our department."

"You and your department or agency you won't reveal to me. You could be the Black Hand for all I know."

"I will concede you that," David says, sighing. "But, believe me, I would not be sticking my neck out a mile for you again if Dorothy did not care for you. I have no idea why she does, but she does."

"Yeah. Why? What'd she say?"

"She said nothing."

"Nothing?"

David throws up his hands. "For God's sake, this is not junior high school!"

"Remember me saying I was going to Bremerton?"

"So?"

"After Bremerton, that post office box was just the continuation

216

of our investigation, Alice's and mine. The next step any smart and logical detective would take."

David closes his eyes.

Harry relates the visit with Lizzie Hennshaw.

David stares at him for a moment, then leaves the room. He returns with a blindfold and tosses it to Harry.

"Say one word until we are in the car and I will lead you off the side of the road and push you over a cliff."

CHAPTER 41

David pulls over and stops. "You can remove the mask and sit up now."

Harry's been bamboozled by time, distance, and Dave's jerky, gear-grinding driving. Could be ten minutes or an hour, fifty miles or twice around the block. He sits up and blinks.

They are on Highway 99, parked at Boeing's Plant Two. The tarmac is still jam-packed with newly-completed B-17s, lined up, gleaming in the low, winter sun like the family silver.

David says, "Dorothy is inside the plant working in her coding department, probably doing busywork. She packed her lunch box and coffee canister, as if it were a routine day on the job. I and others share her concern that the sabotage threat may not be over, that it may be, in fact, worse, *much* worse, with the perpetrators taking a different tack."

He pauses, giving Harry the floor. "Okay, Diana and the phony Dewey, the way I see it, they knew you were waiting for them, ready to pounce at the post office, but now you have to go to them, which is the best way, in my opinion, and *for* which Alice and I should be patted on the back, not blamed for spoiling your surveillance, though I *did* like playing defense better than offense, being that I liked hitting over being hit."

David impatiently drums the steering wheel. "Your football metaphor is entertaining, albeit obfuscatory and unhelpful."

"Okay, if you insist, you can blame me for today, the stew we're in, and I'll admit it, but when I first nailed down that post office and Dewey, I'm thinking that he might have seen me then. The weather was crummy, but he really scooted along to the Dorrinsen after he came out of the post office."

"Yes? So?"

"Could he have been picking up something else there, but nixed it because of me?"

David looks out the windshield at nothing.

"Then it's your blunder, Dave, for not hanging around."

"What you say is highly unlikely."

"Ha. So, it isn't anything else. Did you check what was in the envelopes?"

"We did. Of course we did."

"And?"

"Sorry."

"Yeah, yeah, I know. Classified. Top secret. C'mon. What was in the envelopes?"

"Harry."

"Will you tell me if I guess? That way, you're not telling me even though you're telling me, you're just answering yes or no to a guess. You can even just nod or shake your head."

David looks at him.

"Money?"

"Yes."

"A whole bunch of moola?"

"Yes."

"Enough dough to rent that Dorrinsen Arms suite and then some?"

"Yes."

"Renting it to the year two-thousand?"

"Perhaps."

"It's the 'then some' we gotta lose sleep over."

"Yes. Yes, I agree."

"You should have every cop and secret agent in town hunting for Dewey and Diana."

"We are searching thoroughly, with every available man."

"Why haven't you nabbed them yet?"

David stares at the B-17s and sighs. "They could be three states away by now."

"Yeah? That's believing they're all through here."

"That is one of a number of difficulties, Harry. Their motivation."

Harry says, "I saw Dewey take an envelope out of that box, right? And there were a lot more envelopes today. They haven't cleaned it out in a few days, knowing you'd be on them."

"Yes."

"Tell me what you can buy with all that dough."

"I cannot imagine."

"I can. People. Crumb-bums who'd do whatever you want if you pay them enough."

"I fear so," David says.

"Herbie and Pegleg Paul. You met them at Christmas dinner."

"I did."

"What did you think of them?"

"Well, they certainly have seen better days. Nice and thoughtful men, though."

"Think they'd take a big payoff to hurt their country?"

"Wherever you came upon these individuals, they certainly appear to have a shortage of money."

"Bullshit. You circled around the question, Dave, and answered yes. Wrong. The answer is *no*. These boys are the salt of the earth. Going to Spain and fighting Franco's fascists proves that. Paul donated a leg there."

"I stand corrected," David says, unconvincingly. "You chide me for lecturing you, Harry, but I believe I have just been the recipient of a lecture."

"Wrong. I was merely making a point. Those boys are on the skids, but they're true-blue, but *being* on the skids, they know the bird I accidentally killed in self-defense and other rotten apples I have in mind."

CHAPTER 42

Seattle.
Saturday, December 27, 1941.

Harry directs David to Pegleg Paul Miller's residence on Railroad Avenue.

David Booth looks at the cockeyed cabin and the bulldozed Hooverville directly to the north. He wrinkles his nose, but says nothing.

"There's no place like home, huh?" Harry goads.

"I see no signs of activity."

"These boys aren't early risers."

The front door is ajar.

David says, "Should we knock?"

"Nope. That's as far shut as the door goes. Their abode is open to visitors any old time."

Harry pushes the door open with a foot. He's carrying two bottles of Jack Daniel's in paper bags. At the liquor store, David had lectured him about how he's poisoning alcoholic derelicts as surely as bringing them arsenic. Harry had responded by saying that the whiskey was like a "hostess gift," arguing, "I don't think they'd appreciate a flower arrangement."

"Hey, boys, rise and shine," Harry calls out into the darkness.

Paul is already in the kitchen, stirring something in a pot. "Gentlemen. What a nice surprise."

"Where's Herbie?"

"In the outhouse."

"Where's that?"

"Out back. To what do we owe the honor?"

Harry gets right to it, saying, "The boys you were in Spain with, you talked with them a few months ago, and they said they wanted to stay on the winning side? We really want to get in touch with them. Immediately, if not sooner."

Herbie walks in then. "I gotta tell ya, there's really a lot to be said for indoor plumbing. Harry, always a pleasure."

Harry says, "Whatever you have out back, it beats the hell out of the jailhouse's."

"Mr. Booth," Herbie says. "An honor."

"No offense, but let's not shake hands," Harry says.

Pegleg Paul says, "Herbie, they're here asking about our treacherous comrades who favor the Nazis."

Herbie says, "One of them got hisself murdered last week, a little birdie told me. Helms, it was."

Harry says, "A little birdie told me that Helms attacked an innocent party and got himself killed by the innocent party's legal use of self-defense. That same birdie hears that Helms had Nazi tattoos, swastika and all."

"Ray Helms was that kind of guy," Paul says. "Not the pinnacle of American citizenship."

David says, "We have little time and it is extremely important that we know the whereabouts of the others, the Spain colleagues of yours who went to work at Boeing on the Flying Fortress production line."

"We know about Bill Randall. What you might not know is their Boeing badges were in the names of Dick Jensen and Lan Williams," Harry says. "Jack Stormson, Philip Jones, and Leroy Hoopsma are the birds we're after. There's no way of knowing who they're passing themselves off as at Boeing."

David taps his watch and says, "It is absolutely urgent that we locate them."

Paul says, "We can ask around. These bindle stiffs hereabouts know people who *know* people."

"Lowlifes knowing lowlifes," Harry says.

"That's a hurtful way of putting it," Paul says, smiling. "On the button, though."

Herbie says, "Whatcha got in them sacks you're holding, Harry?"

"Hostess gifts. Make them last."

He gives the whiskey to Herbie as David shakes his head and says, "When can you obtain this information for us?"

Paul says, "The wagon moves quicker if the axles are greased."

"Dave," Harry says, rubbing his fingers together.

David sighs and gives the men a wad of small bills. "Please do this before too much whiskey is consumed."

Herbie laughs and says, "Some of the contents of Mr. Daniel's here is the greasiest grease."

"When?" David asks. "We require results."

"It's Saturday night," Paul says. "We'll be painting the town red. Tomorrow. We'll be here."

*****

In the car, David says, "I do hope this scheme of yours bears fruit."

"Me too. There's another thing we can look at while we wait for that."

"What?"

"Rolan Snails."

"Why that cretin?"

"It's no coincidence that he was at that tavern when we were, don't you think? Then at Chuck's that same night."

"How many times must I apologize, Harry? I have agents going by the Shimizus' when they can."

"It was *meant* to be a trap for me. Four against one. If I was alone, it might've been curtains. They didn't count on Lou being along."

"If you are correct, then why?"

"Last I heard some time ago, Snails has a crummy job in a warehouse down on the waterfront. Somebody paid him off. Had to. Let's ask him who."

*****

Rolan Snails lives in a ratty duplex on a dead-end street, two blocks from Empire Way. Cars parked in yards outnumber those parked on the street.

"He's there with his mother, I think," Harry says as they go to the door. "Nobody else would have him."

"The father?"

"His old man went out for a pack of Chesterfields in 1936 and never came back," Harry says.

David looks at him.

"That's a guess."

David shakes his head.

"Hey, I've seen his mother."

A large unkempt woman who makes Lizzie Hennshaw look like a homecoming queen answers the door. "You! Antonelli, get your ass outta here."

"I came to apologize, ma'am," Harry says. "I really feel terrible if I hurt your son. Him and I were high school classmates."

"Get him outta here, Ma," Snails cries out.

"My Rollie says you jumped him from behind on a street corner for no good reason."

Harry lowers his head. "Yes, ma'am. I haven't been able to sleep at night. I gotta tell him I'm sorry, in order to soothe my conscience."

She steps aside and says, "Well, don't take too long. My boy, he's real sore and weak. Hasn't been able to get out of bed or go to work or nothing."

It's a two-bedroom dump that smells of last month's cooking and last week's garbage. Down a short hallway is a bathroom and two bedrooms. There are no wall hangings, no family photos. In a family like this, Harry thinks, no doubt descended from horse thieves and army deserters, it's just as well.

Snails' door is open and he's in bed, the covers pulled up to his chin.

Snails begins to yell for his mother, but Harry holds a finger to his lips. David shuts the door behind them.

Harry sits on the edge of the bed. Snails is black and blue, and could use some dental work. Should he be bedridden? Harry looked worse after the Idaho game in his senior year, when he was upended, somersaulted, and landed on by two or three linemen. Didn't fumble the ball, though. He was ready to go again the following Saturday against Oregon State.

He says, "We want an answer or two and we'll be gone."

Snails looks at David, who is standing over him, arms folded.

"Please don't let him touch me, sir," he says to David.

"That is entirely up to you, Snails. Who paid you?"

"Paid me to do what?"

Harry shakes his head and cracks his knuckles. "I don't care how much, just who."

David says, "Mr. Snails, we can continue this conversation downtown where the facilities are less homey."

"Okay, okay. This guy, I'd just got off work and was walking over to the bus, and he stepped in front of me. A real swell he was, dressed to the nines. He didn't introduce himself or nothing. He told me what he wanted, to trail you where I could do what I did, egging you on. It worked out good that you went into the tavern where a couple of guys I knew were. The swell, he gave me a chunk of dough that's like three weeks pay at the warehouse."

"No hesitation on your part," David says.

"Are you asking?"

David stares at him.

Snails looks at Harry and says, "Didn't take much thinking about it, Antonelli."

Harry shakes his head. "What did I ever do to you, Snails?"

"That don't make no never mind. I didn't think they'd take no for an answer."

"They?" Harry asks.

"This dame with him, he didn't scare me like she did. How she looked at me, I couldn't refuse."

"Describe the dame," Harry says.

"A real dish with eyes that stared icicles right through me."

"Come on, Harry," David says. "We are done with him."

"I'll send you a get-well card, Snails."

Out of the house, Harry says, "We make a good team, me suave, you the man with the hammer."

David laughs. "I am astounded. You did not have to lay a hand on him."

"He's no Einstein, but he remembers when I *did* lay a hand on him."

In the car, David turns the key, touches the starter button, then lays his head on the steering wheel.

"Harry, I know how this was initiated, how and why Snails was recruited."

Harry waits.

"Concannon was at the house one evening. He and Dorothy were paging through her high school annuals, enjoying the pictures, commenting on those most likely to succeed. Then he steered the topic to those least likely to succeed. Lo and behold, a brief comment was made concerning a dropout she had seen occasionally in the neighborhood. Guess who."

Harry pats his shoulder. "It's okay, Dave. Even secret agents slip up once in a blue moon. We'll get the phony Dewey. When we do, he'll be the least likely to ever eat solid food again."

CHAPTER 43

Seattle.
Sunday, December 28, 1941.

At the Antonelli's, on the surface, it's a typical Sunday.
Breakfast is over. Rocco and Joanne are listening to the radio while doing lackadaisical things—reading, knitting, dozing. They like the big bands, and Rocco has the schedules and stations down pat, so as to switch from Artie Shaw to Jimmy Dorsey to Gene Krupa to Benny Goodman without missing a beat.

Harry is lost in the funnies. He remains disappointed that Superman tested 4-F, but he's confident that the Man of Steel will be taking care of things on the home front, going after Nazi spies. Terry Lee in Terry and the Pirates has enlisted to be a pilot, which Harry will do the minute after he's done with his current entanglement.

The Phantom, the Ghost Who Walks. Harry relates to the guy. If somebody deserves to be punched in the face, the Phantom does it. Him and that big skull-and-crossbones ring. He puts the bad guy on the ground and that ring leaves a mark, like a notary stamp. Harry wonders if you can send away for one. If he can get his hands on the phony Dewey...

Lou comes upstairs, taking the steps two at a time, freshly shaven, in pressed slacks and clean sweater, smelling of Old Spice.

"Goodness, look at you," Joanne says. "Where are you off to?"

Rocco gives him the same suspicious narrow-eyed gaze he usually reserves for Harry.

"Julia and her folks asked me over for dinner."

That satisfies his parents' curiosity, but not his brother's.

Harry walks him outside.

"I thought it was gonna be New Year's Eve when her parents are gone."

"How'd you know it's now?"

"You're blushing like a ripe tomato is how."

"Her folks are gone most of the day at a church social. A potluck."

Harry thinks of advising him to have a window unlatched, to jump out of in the event the potluck is called off or ends early. In Europe, he'd had to amscray out of a few windows, some on upper floors, the risk of a broken ankle less unpleasant than the alternative. But he doesn't, and goes back inside, thinking *fertility*.

Joanne hands him the phone. "It's that sweet little old lady."

"Alice, how are you?"

"How are you, young man? Those horrid G-men. I thought they would have you on a chain gang by now."

"I was misunderstood. I'm innocent of all charges, past, present and future."

Rocco answers the doorbell. David Booth walks in, wags a finger at Harry, and says, "Time to pay a call on the hobos."

"I'm bored," Alice tells Harry. "Bored to tears."

"Want to go slumming?"

"That is so déclassé. I'd be delighted."

"The Dorrinsen Arms lobby in half an hour," Harry tells Alice.

*****

Harry is crushed sideways in the nonexistent back seat of David's Hudson. He has overruled David's objection to bringing Alice along. "She's tougher than you and me combined," he had argued. "Plus, remember, she got us into that parking garage."

On the way, David explains today's mission to her.

"Such nice young men."

"They can be when they choose to be," David has to admit.

At Pegleg Paul's, Alice watches where she steps, but seems otherwise unaffected by the squalor.

Harry shoves the door in and finds Paul in the kitchen, rummaging around, and Herbie Barnwell walking unsteadily in the back door, presumably from the outhouse.

Herbie gestures to the sofa and says, "Harry, ask and you shall receive."

Curled up is a tall, bony man of forty or so with tufts of hair like on a worn-out wire brush.

"Who?"

Pegleg Paul Miller says, "Mr. Leroy Hoopsma. We happened upon him during our social rounds."

Herbie says, "Brought him home with the promise of a party and female company."

"Where's the gals?" Harry asks.

Pegleg Paul says, "We were fibbing. Realistically, the only ladies who would, um, comply, are of the professional type who are at the end of their careers. If you catch my drift."

Alice tsk-tsks. "Such mischievous boys."

Harry is rummaging through Hoopsma's jacket and trousers, and comes up with a Boeing badge, round, with his picture and name on it, fastened by a safety pin on its back.

"The name's Larry Hill," Harry says, shaking him. "Larry. Leroy. Whoever you may be. Rise and shine."

"Sadly, he has a drinking problem," Paul says.

Harry has tugged him upright and shaken him semi-awake. "Guys, could you run out for a pail of water?"

Herbie says, "It really oughta be boiled if you're gonna douse him."

Harry says, "We'll take our chances with his health. Cholera is the least of his problems."

"Got one handy," Paul says, handing Harry a full pail.

Harry empties it in Larry/Leroy's face, point-blank.

They give him a minute to cough, sputter, and gag.

When he's fully awake and able to speak, David holds the Boeing badge in front of his face and says, "Whoever you are, are you aware that false entry into a war plant constitutes treason? A crime punishable by death."

"Fuck you."

Alice says, "There is a lady present, young man."

He laughs at her. "I got nothing to say about nothing, old lady."

Harry is in his face now, fist clenched an inch from his nose. "Talk, or you won't be *able* to anytime soon. They'll be digging your teeth out of your throat with a pair of pliers."

"Fuck you, too."

Alice says, "May I?"

Not waiting for an answer, she elbows Harry aside, takes the Derringer from her voluminous purse and holds it a foot from his face. "Whoever you are, you horrid creature, this is a Remington model Derringer 95. It holds two forty-one caliber rimfire cartridges. If I jam it against your ear like this…"

As Harry looks away, she jams the twin barrels against his left ear.

"And *bang*, you won't even have time to say your prayers. I am an old, old lady and you're a dirty, stinking, traitorous fucking rat. I won't even get a slap on the hand for ridding the nation of the likes of you. Why, President Roosevelt himself will pin a medal on me."

Harry says as he turns around, "G-man Booth and I will be out for our daily constitutional, so there'll be no witnesses."

Alice pulls the hammer back on her Derringer and says, "You gentlemen enjoy yourselves and take your time. It's a wonderful day for a walk."

"Let's go, Dave," Harry says. "We'll be back when we hear a bang, Alice."

"All right, get her the hell away from me! Stick around!"

"If we do?" David asks.

"Whadduya want to know?"

CHAPTER 44

Seattle.
Sunday, December 28, 1941.

A lice sits beside Larry/Leroy on the sofa, snuggling closely to him. It may appear romantic, but it isn't. Her Derringer is resting on his thigh, aimed at his crotch.

"Your family jewels are at stake, young man. A blind person couldn't miss from here. Do try to be forthright," Alice says with a benign smile.

HISTORICAL NOTE: "Family jewels," that wonderful neologism, didn't come into common use until 1946, but given the subject's anxiety, it seems appropriate.

Larry/Leroy's eyes blink as they dart from Alice to his family jewels. Harry's eyes dart from face to face, anywhere but at Alice's cannon.

She smiles sweetly at their prisoner. "Mr. Booth, any time you wish to proceed."

David's eyes aren't darting and he isn't smiling.

He says, "What is your real name?"

"LeRoy Hill," he says. "The 'R' is capitolated."

"You fought in the Spanish Civil War?"

"Yeah. Me and the other guys here and the dead one that got

murdered last week."

"Self defense killing of a Nazi," Harry says. "Nobody was murdered."

David continues, "You were in the infantry?"

"You could say that. I was keeping my head down is what I was doing. Jarama and other towns, it was like a shooting gallery."

"True. Thanks to German and Italian support of Franco's Nationalists. Which led most notably, among other things, to the destruction of the Basque town of Guernica, and the slaughter of its innocent inhabitants," David lectures.

LeRoy or Larry Hill shrugs. "Guernica and that other stuff, that's just the way the cookie crumbles. We should never have gone over there in the first place."

Herbie says, "He was a cowardly bastard. We couldn't depend on him."

David says, "You were quoted recently as saying that you planned to stay on the 'winning side,' meaning that your allegiance is foolishly with the Axis?"

"Who told you that?"

"Yes or no?"

"Lookit, I'm making common sense is all. The Japs are overrunning the Pacific. They're gonna be sailing into Elliott Bay before you know it. Hitler's so close to Moscow he can taste the vodka. Roosevelt, the commie, he picked the wrong side. We ain't got a chance."

Alice slides her Derringer even closer to his family jewels, saying, "You make me sick, whatever your real name is. If I had my way, we'd try, convict, and execute you right here, you revolting excuse for a man. We'd be saving the taxpayers some money."

Hill presses against the back of the sofa.

"You old bitch."

"You mind your manners and confine your filthy mouth to answering Mr. Booth's questions," she says. "If we want insults and propaganda, we'll ask for it."

"Thank you, Alice," David says. "Details, Mr. Hill. *Fast*."

"You're railroading me for treason is what you're fixin' to do."

"You have my word that you will not be arrested. That is, *if* you are cooperative. I promise that you will be granted immunity from prosecution."

"You swear?"

David raises his right hand. "I do."

Dave's lying through his teeth, Harry thinks. He loves it!

"Our coffee canisters."

"Excuse me?"

"What we carry in our lunchboxes to keep our coffee hot."

"What about them?"

"It ain't the real thing we carry into the plant inside our lunchboxes. You know, at the gate, you gotta open your lunch pail so the guards can look at your sandwich and that canister. We do that, then go in to work. Sometime during our shift, somebody switches out the phony canisters and sticks a real one in our lunch boxes. It ain't got coffee in it. It's got small bills stuffed inside, a whole bunch better pay than the thirty-five bucks a week Boeing's paying me."

"Your chums, too? Jones and Stormson and Randall?"

"I ain't seen them in a while."

"Could one or more of them be switching the canisters?"

"Your guess is as good as mine."

"A suspiciously ambiguous answer," David says. "Why the pseudonyms?"

"The what?"

"The phony names."

"Uh-huh. Yeah, well, if you got different names, it's easier to get lost if the shit hits the fan."

"Who recruited you and who gave you the phony names and the faux canisters?"

"Foe?"

David glares and waits.

235

"I don't know about nobody else doing it, but this rich-looking swell, I don't know how he picked me out, but we met in this bar one night and we got to talking and he made the offer. I said that it sounds too good to be true, and he said that all I gotta do is leave my empty lunchbox on the windowsill of this boarding house where I was staying at. In the morning, the canister, it'll be in there along with a ham sandwich. It worked like clockwork."

"Did you ever open the canisters?"

"No sir. I was warned not to. I did try the lid once on one and it didn't budge. Like it was glued on."

"Did this fine gentleman who approached you in the bar indicate what was inside the canisters?"

"Yeah. Sulfuric acid, he said. It was good for the country on account of at a certain time they were gonna dump it onto an important part of a B-17. I'm a riveter on the ass-end of the fuselage, right around where the tail gunner's perch is. Scrunching around, I'm lucky it don't throw out my sacred-iliac."

David's eyebrows raise to the limit. "Good for the country how?"

"You know, all them B-17s crashing on account of metal that got fatigued? Doing it this way, nobody crashes and gets hurt except sometimes when the metal don't fatigue at the right time, and then it's tough shit for the pilots, like if it's over mountains or the water. What they're doing, he said, they're making a statement that we oughta mind our own beeswax and quit sending bombers over there to England."

"How long is the sabotage to continue?"

"As long as the dough's rolling in, it ain't none of *my* beeswax. I get messages."

"You are the salt of the earth."

Hill grins. "All I'm doing, I'm protesting and nobody gets hurt."

"This boarding house. Was it the regular spot?"

"Nah. I was kicked out the next day. For drinking too much and being messy. Like that landlady and everyone else in the world's perfect."

"Then?"

"Then what?"

David stares at him.

"How do the workers get the messages?"

"I get the code by radio and pass it on."

"To Jones and Stormson and Randall?"

"I dunno. I sent out the code I'm given. I dunno who gets it."

"How?"

"I took radio shop in school and know Morse code. The guy, he musta knew that, or I told him in the bar. My memory, it gets fuzzy after a night out, you know. Anyway, he gave me a shortwave radio. It's right outside in my car. My last message from wherever it comes from said that it was the last and they're shutting down. I'm supposed to dump the radio in the bay, but I'm figurin' to hang on to it and sell it off for parts."

David stands. "Gentlemen, can you take charge of my prisoner while I go to the car for handcuffs and formally place him under arrest? I will make a call and have people come for him."

"Prisoner? Arrest?"

"For treason."

"Hey, you lied to me!"

"Not under oath."

"We'll do our duty," Pegleg Paul says.

Herbie says, "We're on the job."

Pegleg Paul says, "I got cast iron pans to bonk him with if he gets antsy."

David is out the door.

Hill bats the Derringer away and is on his feet. "I'm scootin' and you can't stop me."

Harry buries a fist in his gut and says, "Take tomorrow off work. After all your patriotic work, you deserve it."

Lips fluttering and reddening, eyes akimbo, LeRoy Hill resumes his seat.

237

A 1931 Dodge sedan on its last legs is parked behind the shack. The radio is on what remains of the back seat, where the upholstery had been.

As they load the radio into David's car, he asks Harry and Alice, "His story, especially the chain of events, is muddled. Do you believe him?"

Alice says, "I do. I had the world's best lie detector aimed at his nuts."

Harry says, "Me, too. His brain is pickled, but it fits with what Dorothy told us, with the left aileron sabotage decoding being so slick and easy. Then her department suddenly being shut down."

"So, the worst is yet to come," David says.

*****

A 1936 Pontiac with TAXI stenciled on each front door has been parked around the corner. The driver is in uniform: white shirt, tie, jacket, and matching billed hat. The back-seat passenger wears a heavy coat suitable for the weather and a brimmed hat pulled low on her forehead.

When David, Harry, and Alice leave with the radio, the taxi follows.

CHAPTER 45

Seattle.
Sunday, December 28, 1941.

In the Hudson, David asks Harry, "Did you have to hit my prisoner so hard? He may have a rupture."

"He can talk, can't he?" Harry says from the back.

"While gasping incoherently."

"Hire a translator, Dave. And a guy with a rubber hose."

Alice says, "Harry is right, dear. Besides, you squeezed him dry as a bone."

"Mrs. Haymarket, it is standard procedure to interrogate subjects multiple times, to check for inconsistencies and discrepancies."

"Don't coddle him, Mr. Booth. It isn't necessary. He's a traitor and a big baby who, if he feigns an inability to speak, a rubber hose will do wonders for his enunciation. Electrodes on testicles, too."

David raises an eyebrow, then cocks his head and asks Harry, "Do you believe him? The sulfuric acid?"

"I believe he's telling us part of the truth, but it's not the part of the truth he's telling us that will do us any good, which is the truth we have to have, which I don't think he knows."

"Harry."

"I'm saying that he doesn't know what he's taking into the plant. He just knows what he's being *told* he's taking into the plant. And he doesn't give a damn as long as he's being paid. It could be TB germs for all that asshole cares."

Alice says, "Harry is right again, Mr. Booth. That LeRoy creature's brain is whiskey-soaked oatmeal, and he has the morals of a Nazi trollop. But he's all we have without Dewey and that succubus of his."

Succubus. A female demon fooling around with guys in their sleep, Harry knows.

He pictures himself fast asleep, wrestling with Wonder Woman, the real Diana, who's wearing a swastika armband and tearing at his clothes and, guiltily, he banishes that image and says, "The key is sulfuric acid. We gotta have a scientific answer. I know just the person."

"Who?"

"Somebody who oughta be teaching high school chemistry instead of teaching girls about egg whites."

"Egg whites?" David says. "Dorothy and egg whites? Harry, you are speaking in riddles again."

"Egg whites?" Alice says. "Oh. Oh! I get it. Such a modern young lady."

*****

Distracted, David forgets that the streets are icy in spots. He skids sideways when he sees a phone booth beside a Safeway, and bounces over the curb. He recovers, parks, and barely avoids an old man who curses and swings his cane at the car, thumping the rear fender.

Alice says, "Mr. Booth, don't they teach driving at secret agent school?"

Harry smiles. "He's sick of me asking him that."

"Who's he telephoning?"

"His sis."

"Oh, she is so lovely and sweet, Harry. Very smart too. You two lovebirds should be in a dark room, ripping each other's knickers off."

Harry blushes. "Yeah, well, the problem is, she *is* real smart. She knows better than to get hooked up with me."

"She has in the past, hasn't she? Don't fib, young man."

"I'll be gone any day now, too, in the Army Air Corps."

"Harry, all you have to do is sweet-talk her, telling her your best lies, and nature will take its course."

David jumps back into the car and says, "Dorothy and the gals were released early for lack of work again."

"That's a bad sign," Harry says. "A *really* bad sign. The Nazis have a new code, or there's nothing to *de*code."

"I fear that you may be correct. A second fifth column team is at work, using dupes like LeRoy. If they're communicating, it is on a channel unknown to us," David says. "Alice, may I drop you off on the way?"

Wagging a finger, Alice scolds, "Not on your life, mister. It's my life, too, if you don't pay attention to your driving, I'll be a premature corpse. I'm in the middle of the fifth columnist soiree, and I'm loving every minute of it. You'll make good use of my maturity and worldliness, if you have an iota of sense."

Harry claps his hands, applauding.

"Very well, Alice. However, what information Dorothy provides will be in the strictest confidence," David says. "Furthermore, our people are in the Boeing factories, working undercover, too. Other agencies are also represented. I may receive confidential phone calls at home."

"So?" Harry says.

David says nothing, which Harry takes to mean they've found absolutely nothing, no secrets for Dorothy or any G-men to reveal.

*****

Dorothy Booth lays out a tray of the remaining Whitman's Sampler and puts on a fresh pot of coffee while she listens to their story.

"My principal question is how much damage can a large quantity of sulfuric acid do," David says.

"Well, concentrated sulfuric acid, H2SO4, reacts against most metals, but we're largely concerned with aluminum and aluminum alloys, aren't we? Airplanes are made of aluminum. If the contents of these containers have been dumped on B-17 parts individually, we'd have noticed by now. Aluminum and sulfuric acid combine to form aluminum sulfate and hydrogen gas, which bubbles and smells like rotten eggs.

"Damage would be minimal, nothing like eating completely through the aluminum or exploding. If sulfuric acid was in a vacuum container for long, *that* would be noticeable. Hydrogen gas would build up inside and combine with the inner bottle, which is made of steel. The space between the inner and outer is a vacuum."

"And?"

"Remember the Hindenburg? Hydrogen gas is highly explosive," Dorothy says. "Something bad might happen before or during its opening. That's an experiment I don't care to perform."

"No chance of ordinary lunchbox bottles of sulfuric acid causing a disaster?" David asks.

"No. Not on a large scale. As I said, what the saboteurs used to cause premature metal fatigue is completely different, and as far as I know, Boeing security people and outside agents have put an end to it."

"Something else is being brought in," Harry says. "It has to be."

"I agree," Dorothy says. "The metal fatigue business may be a smokescreen to give us a false sense of security. That's my theory, but it isn't shared by everyone."

Harry says, "I'm with you one-hundred percent. How do we find out who, what, and where?"

"Not *we*, Harry," David says.

Harry lifts a shoulder. "I'm speaking as a concerned citizen, Dave. Don't work yourself into a lather."

"What are you and your people doing, David?" Dorothy asks.

"This is top secret, as I told Harry and Alice earlier, but several agencies, ours included, have been in the plant since the aluminum fatigue failures. Dorothy, you being off early today, is that a cause of concern?"

"After what you've told me, yes. We were told that we'd probably be sent home anyhow since it's Sunday."

The coffee pot is bubbling and hissing. She goes to it and brings back steaming mugs, with a cream pitcher and a sugar bowl.

David says, "If an attack is imminent, there should be notification."

"There should be."

Pacing in a small circle, Harry slaps a fist in a palm. "There damn well should."

"Please settle down, Harry. There isn't a thing you can do," Dorothy says.

Harry touches his pants pocket, feels LeRoy Hill's Boeing badge, and smiles.

CHAPTER 46

Seattle.
Monday, December 29, 1941.

In the morning, Lou stops Harry before he leaves their bedroom.

Without making eye contact, he asks, "Are girls supposed to, you know, like, you know, *it*?"

"It. Okay, uh, some like it, some don't. The ones you want to see again, it's good if they like it. If they don't like it, or don't like how you do it but like it in general, they complain of headaches. Headaches that no amount of aspirin will cure. They get one of those kinds of headaches, you don't know where you stand, and they're not going to say it in so many words. I can't count the numbers of girls who complained to me of a headache. Like I was the Typhoid Mary of headaches."

"Julia's mother told her that all men are animals who are just out for what they can get. She told Julia that she just had to put up with it as a housewife. It was her duty."

Harry knows Julia's mom. A battle-axe who looks at Harry like she'd love to shove him in front of a train. Blunt honesty with Lou is the best policy, he thinks.

"You have to understand, Lou, this is Julia's mom talking. I wouldn't fuck her with Adolf Hitler's dick. But Julia seems like a modern gal with a mind of her own."

Lou laughs, amused and relieved. "Julia, you know, yesterday? As

244

I was saying, you know."

"Right."

Lou gulps. "She liked it. Liked it a lot. Even better than I did. All the noise she was making, we were afraid the neighbors would hear. She didn't let me out of bed until after the third time."

Julia Wilson. Noisy. Three times. Sometimes, you never know.

"Tell her not to worry," Harry says, unsuccessfully picturing Julia in the throes of a screaming orgasm. "Not to worry about anything unless she kills a rabbit."

Lou helps Harry find a clipboard holding lined paper in a pile of miscellany from their school days. Not explaining the clipboard to him or his parents, he makes a peanut butter sandwich. With it and a canister of hot coffee in his lunchbox, he runs to the bus stop and waits with Dorothy.

"Harry, what on earth?"

He smiles and shushes her.

She looks at the LeRoy Hill badge he's clipped to his shirt, and the lunchbox with LeRoy Hill's name haphazardly taped on it.

"Harry, do you realize how much trouble you can get into? And the picture on the badge, you look nothing like him."

"I'm sure glad I don't. If somebody asks, Dorothy, I had the world's worst hangover when the picture was snapped."

Dorothy grips his sleeve, pulls him close, and says, "Listen to me, Harry, I got you out of jams in Lisbon. David, too. We all did our share to save humanity from the Nazis' uranium, but this is completely different."

"Different *and* the same. A Nazi is a Nazi."

"Harry, please. Like David says, his and other agencies have infiltrated the plant and are everywhere. They're hunting Dewey, too, with everything they have."

Harry nods. "Mm-hmm."

"I can't help you inside the plant. You're on your own and your goose is cooked if you get caught."

"Somebody has to do something," Harry counters. "Get it done in time."

"Get what done in time for what?"

"In time to stop what they're gonna do."

"I'd feel a whole lot better if we knew."

"Me, too. This is the only way to find out."

Dorothy sighs. "You can't resist, can you? You're told to stay out of something, like David did, and you cannot resist. Wild horses can't drag you away from trouble. Trouble like you've gotten yourself into constantly from the fifth grade on."

"From the *fourth* grade on."

The bus comes and they get on. Sitting side by side, Harry begins penciling letters and numbers on the lined pad.

"What are you doing?" Dorothy says, looking at pure nonsense.

"Sorry. Classified."

Dorothy stares out the window, seeing nothing. Hoping there will be code for them to break today. Wiping a tear, wishing that she didn't care for Harry so much, the big dope.

Harry is looking at his clipboard, wishing he wasn't such a jerk about Dorothy, how if he had half a brain, he'd drop to a knee in the bus aisle and propose marriage right here and now.

As they file off the bus at the main entrance to Boeing's Plant Two, Dorothy says, "Please reconsider."

He blows her a kiss and says, "Why aren't *you* going in? Reconsider?"

She points at a line of women and a WOMEN ONLY sign by another gate. "Because purses are checked and it's considered unacceptable for men to see what's in a lady's purse, her personal items and all."

Harry is puzzling over that one as he goes through the other line, lunch box open. The bored guard has one eye on the WOMEN ONLY gate. Harry doubts if he's seeing what he's supposed to be looking for. Four-hundred-pound Hermann Goering in full uniform could waddle through.

Harry looks upward at guys spraying camouflage paint on the walls, and others on the roof laying webbing for the fake miniature city. Gotta hope it fools the Jap bombers everyone is expecting.

Inside, clipboard in hand, lunchbox in the other, pencil behind his ear, head held high, Harry looks around. The rivet-gun clatter is deafening. He sees young women zooming around on Cushman motor scooters with boxes mounted in front of the handlebars. Pickup and delivery of mail and small parts, he assumes.

I'm a riveter on the ass-end of the fuselage, right around where the tail gunner's perch is. Scrunching around, I'm lucky it don't throw out my sacred-iliac.

Harry finally has a plan, yeah, a tricky half-assed plan that might be better or worse than no plan at all, but nevertheless, a plan. He goes to a row of bombers in various stages of assembly. Fifty of them, at least. They're backed in, so he starts at the rear end of the fuselage line, pencil poised, in deep concentration. Most of the workers are ladies, their hair tied up in bandanas, a safety measure to keep it from being caught in the machinery. He didn't know that they could look so good in working clothes, coveralls and pants and shirts straining at vital points.

Some of the gals are inside the fuselages, riveting away. Others are on ladders, assembling parts on the vertical tails.

"Excuse me, ma'am," he says to a riveter on a ladder. "Anybody not show up for work today?"

A big lady with short hair and sleeves rolled up, she lowers her rivet gun. The way she's holding it, the thing looks too much like a real gun to suit Harry.

"Who are you?"

Clipboard covering his badge, pencil poised, Harry says, "I'm with the manpower assessment evaluation board."

"*Man*power?"

Harry is pretty sure she could take him in a fight, with or without her rivet gun.

"Well, *lady* power, too. Definitely." He flashes a quick smile. "Ladies preferred."

She sweeps the rivet gun around toward the plane, making Harry tense as it goes by him.

"Notice that we're all female? Every one of us. Not one missed day by this crew. Not one."

Harry scribbles and says, "I'll make sure the bosses know."

"Four stations down, there's a bird who shows up when he doesn't, if you know what I mean. He smells like a brewery and when he crawls inside the fuselage, it's not to work, it's to sleep it off."

Harry scans his clipboard. "Hmm, I think I have him check-marked. Guy by the name of LeRoy or Larry Hill or LeRoy or Larry Hoopsma?"

"Using a lot of names to weasel out of the draft, huh?"

"Yeah, that's what my supervisor thinks," Harry says.

"Whatever he goes by, that's him. While you're down there, sonny boy, talk to a sweet young thing named Daisy. Her and a couple other little gals, our foreman is badgering the holy hell out of them. A rat-faced hick named Jimmy Ray, he climbs inside the planes while they're working to check their work, but what he's doing is copping feels. Daisy in particular. She's a living doll who has a small kid and can't afford to lose this job."

"Oh yeah?"

"Yeah. Daisy Myer is her name. A freckled blue-eyed blonde. You can't miss her. The father of her little boy's long gone, and Jimmy Ray knows it."

"Have Daisy and the others complained?"

"They have, but the higher-ups don't do anything. Jimmy Ray tells them that the gals are encouraging him. They're all afraid of him, is what we think. He's a bully, so he gets away with it. Even the bosses on the floor are leery of him. Afraid of what he might do to them after work."

She holds her rivet gun menacingly. "He tries it with me, he'll get this where the sun don't shine."

He learned early on that all bullies were cowards.

Harry backs away and says, "Thanks for the tip."

"You be careful if Jimmy Ray's there."

"It's Jimmy Ray who'd best be careful," Harry says, winking.

She raises her eyebrows in disbelief. Which means Harry will take Jimmy Ray on for certain.

Four stations down, he frowns at his clipboard and looks at an unfinished fuselage section, its aluminum strips are up and down and sideways. Sure looks flimsy.

He asks a pretty lady of thirty or so, "Excuse me, a guy named Hill or Hoopsma, he's not on shift?"

"Nope, and good riddance to *that* lollygagger. Who are you?"

Harry evades her question, saying, "By the way, I hear that there's a foreman named Jimmy Ray who's being mean and dirty to you gals?"

She blanches. "Yes. He sure is. Are you with him?"

"No ma'am, I surely am not."

He holds up the lunchbox. She looks at LeRoy Hill's name and at Harry.

"I don't get it. You're not him."

"I'll forever be thankful of that, ma'am. If I can put the lunch box where LeRoy keeps his, and if you'll watch if anything happens to it, I'll take care of Jimmy Ray for you."

"Do you know him?"

"Nope."

"Ever seen him?"

"Nope."

"How do you know you can?"

Harry smiles.

The lady smiles back. "Give me the lunch box and I'll tell the other gals. This we gotta see. Oh, my God, there he is, he's there three rows down, with the cowboy boots. He'll be here in a sec."

Harry sees him. Lean and rawboned with long sideburns, taller than Harry, five or ten years older, with neck veins sticking out. He notes blubber around his midsection. Saddlebags.

When he's by them in the aisleway, Harry yells, "Hey, Tex."

Jimmy Ray looks at him.

"Yeah you, cowpoke. Come on over here."

Jimmy Ray walks up to Harry, closer than polite social distance, and says, "Who the hell are you to be ordering me around, boy? I don't see no badge."

Harry has pocketed LeRoy's. He says, "I want to have a confidential talk about the young ladies you've been doing bad things to."

Jimmy Ray brushes by Harry and walks between two airplanes, affording partial privacy. He says, "We're gonna have a talk about *your* bad manners, boy, and how you're gonna be sorry—"

Before he can finish his threat, Harry shoves him against a plane and has him by the saddlebags. In too close for Jimmy Ray to throw a punch, Harry says, "I'm gonna do the talking, you fuckin' hillbilly. You are not to touch any of those gals *ever* again."

Jimmy Ray smirks. "You and who else is gonna back that up? Plain and simple, that little blonde in there, she got a kid and never had no husband. She's a whore who spreads her legs when you lick your lips at her, so I can do whatever I fuckin' well please."

Harry is so angry he's seeing spots. He twists the saddlebags and lifts Billy Ray to his toes. "I get one single complaint, I'll be waiting outside the gate. When you get off, you and I are gonna have at it. No holds barred."

Jimmy Ray grimaces.

"After I kick your ass, I'm gonna stomp on your hands and bust your fingers. You won't be grabbing these girls, and you'll have to hire somebody to pick your nose for you."

Harry twists harder. "Hear me?"

Jimmy Ray can only grunt.

"I'll take that as a 'yes sir.' Some call these of yours I'm holding onto as love handles. None of these ladies want your love."

HISTORICAL NOTE: The term "love handles" did not come into use until around 1970, but usage seems to be appropriate here.

Harry releases Jimmy Ray and watches him limp out of sight.

He learned early on that all bullies were cowards.

The ladies in LeRoy's crew and others have been watching.

One says, "You're neater than the Lone Ranger."

"Captain Marvel."

"Superman."

As Harry basks in the glow of the ladies' praise, him leaping off the pages, cape fluttering, fists extended, one of the girls cries out, "Oh my God, I'm so sorry. I missed him!"

"Him?"

"On a Cushman. It's ninety-percent ladies in here, but if they have to expedite something, a guy will jump on."

"What did he look like?"

"I only saw him from the back. Just an ordinary guy."

"My lunch box?"

"He was by it. I don't know."

Harry runs to it, looks inside, and sees a different canister.

A gal peeking around the landing gear yells, "Jimmy Ray's coming with a couple of bulls. Moving like a gimp, but he's keeping up."

"The hillbilly?" Harry asks.

"Yeah, the crybaby," another lady says, laughing.

He gets a long peck on the cheek from the cutie who must be Daisy.

She says, "Go behind us and head to the door leading to the front gate. We'll send them off in the opposite direction."

Blue-eyed, freckled, blonde. If this isn't love at first sight, Harry doesn't know what is. "Thanks."

"Here," she says, handing him a slip of paper.

Harry doesn't have to be asked twice. He strides to the gate as quickly as he can without running, opens his lunch box for the guard, and hops on the first bus he sees. He checks inside the canister and digs out $20 in ones and fives. Twenty bucks a day to sell out his country.

Harry gets off at Burien, a small town south of the city, somewhere he's never been. Harry tosses the LeRoy Hill badge into a ditch along with the clipboard and LeRoy's name he's peeled off the lunch box.

He hops on another bus that takes him somewhere he's never been. And another bus that takes him somewhere else he's never been. And another that by pure dumb luck takes him to Rainier Avenue.

He gets off and starts to walk the three miles home in a freezing drizzle, thinking that the life of a secret agent isn't a bowl of cherries. He has read the slip of paper, though, and decides that his mission has been a stunning success: DAISY MYER, SU-7881.

*****

Harry has been followed all the while by a taxicab.

The driver says, "Do you think he spotted us?"

The back-seat passenger says, "Of course he has, you idiot. Why else all the buses?"

"LeRoy Hill's no good to us now."

"No, he isn't."

"Antonelli knows the score."

"He does. He's trouble."

"Will we have to move the timetable up?"

"Yes, we will. We have plenty."

"We *don't* have plenty."

"I say we do. It's the mission that counts."

"You and that paring knife. Get it off my leg."

"You're going to do what I say?"

"I'm a personal friend of Reichsführer-SS Himmler."

"Calm down. You're lapsing into your accent. Forgetting that you're from a Pittsburgh steel-baron family. You are nothing to Himmler."

"Get that knife off my leg."

"Say please."

"Ow. Please."

"Himmler is paying us well."

"The canisters. The gas. I wasn't informed in Paris."

"Aside from your wounded pride, does that bother you?" She slides the blade back and forth over his pant leg. "Answer me. Does it?"

"No, but I should have been advised at the outset."

"Stop pouting. You know now. We move ahead."

"Why wasn't I informed?"

"Himmler didn't trust you. Chameleons change colors."

"I wouldn't."

"Shut up. You're here to follow orders. *Mine*."

"I don't understand you. You're American, but you're not loyal to them. Or anybody."

"I'm loyal to money."

"That's not all."

"Is that a question?"

"I honestly don't know. I can't figure you out."

"It's not the money alone. Now, for the last time, shut up. We have to get off the road and out of sight, then switch cars. Everybody and his brother is chasing us."

"Antonelli?"

"We watch him. And wait for his next move."

CHAPTER 47

"Harry, you look like a drowned rat," David Booth says.

"A rat drowned in a vat of whiskey," Dorothy Booth says, wrinkling her nose. "I heard stories about a commotion on the factory floor and a spy on the loose. I was worried sick about you."

Harry, occasionally no fool, had no intention of risking pneumonia on a three-mile-Arctic death march. He had stopped for food, coffee, and barhopping en route, in some erratic order. Seated at the Booths' dining-room table, brother and sister listen without interruption until Harry is done with his story.

David beseeches the ceiling and says, "Did I not tell you to stay out of it?"

"Pardon me, Agent Dave, but have all your G-men come up with as much as I did in one short day?"

David's clenched teeth inform Harry that they have not. "We are working methodically in an organized manner."

"Meanwhile, they stick their bombs in a hundred different places and blow everything and everyone to smithereens. Any moment now."

David is shaking his head. "That will not happen. Not, as you say, any second now."

Dorothy has brought Harry a second cup of coffee. "Drink."

Harry drinks and says, "Yeah? How do you know?"

David looks at Dorothy. They look at Harry, who says, "What?"

David says, "This has to remain in the utmost confidence. I could go to prison for five years for revealing this to you."

Harry says, "I could go to prison for one-hundred-and-five years for what I did today. Go ahead. My lips are sealed."

"President Roosevelt is visiting Boeing and other war-related installations in mid-January. This is why we feel we have some breathing room. We have time to throw a net over the entire operation."

"FDR? Here?"

"We believe they are planning their attack to coincide with his visit, that they will set off an explosion while he is on the factory floor pressing the flesh, killing him and others near him."

Harry asks, "You're certain it's about assassinating FDR?"

"Logically."

"Logically is not a *yes*."

"We have exhausted other possibilities. Of course, they can do extensive damage with randomly-placed bombs or sulfuric acid release. However, that would be insignificant compared to a presidential assassination by a single large device."

Harry and logic don't always mesh. He gives up, accepts a third cup of coffee, and joins in diversionary small-talk. Thinking.

HISTORICAL NOTE: President Franklin Delano Roosevelt did visit Boeing Plant No. 2 in 1942, but in September, not January. On September 17, he departed Washington D.C. aboard a train to tour and inspect defense plants and military bases. Stops included Chrysler in Detroit; Fort Lewis, Washington; Bremerton's Puget Sound Naval Shipyard; and the Mare Island Navy Base in Vallejo, California.

On the afternoon of September 22, accompanied by Boeing executives and the Washington State governor, he made a stop at

Boeing's Plant No.2, in the 1941 DeSoto convertible brought along in the train. FDR made time to pause under the wing of a B-17, where workers hurried to meet and greet him.

*****

Harry goes home too late for dinner. Despite drying off at the Booths, Joanne Antonelli notices that her older son has spent too much time out-of-doors in foul weather, risking his death of cold and pneumonia, something that mothers simply know.

She sits him down at the kitchen table and feeds him Campbell's Chicken Noodle soup and saltine crackers. After which, she orders him downstairs, early to bed.

For once, Harry knows better than to argue. He surprises himself by immediately conking out. Awakening hours later, he hears Lou snoring and squints at their alarm clock: 11:42.

There's not a chance in hell he can fall back to sleep. His mind races around and through David's Roosevelt story. The fifth columnists are going to wait two or three weeks to blow up Plant Two, so they can get FDR, too? It makes no sense to him. None. They've already shown their hand in too many ways.

Vice-President Henry Wallace would take over if FDR was assassinated. Wallace is a New Deal Democrat, too, so what's the diff? Is he gonna start a war that's already started? Are we gonna drop more bombs on Germany and the Japs to get even? It's way too late to be backing Neville Chamberlain at Munich, swallowing Hitler's baloney along with him.

David had told him a fairy tale, or he's buying one that his G-men bosses dreamed up.

He has Daisy's note under his pillow. He sniffs it, but no perfume. Daisy, a living doll.

Is it possible to be in love with two women at once?

Harry thinks back and decides, yeah, it's possible. More than once.

Twice, too.

Make that three or four times. Gabrielle in Havana. A sultry café singer in Lisbon. His burglar in Amsterdam. A countess in Budapest.

Dorothy deserves better than him, and has since they met in grade school.

Harry eases out of bed, dresses and creeps upstairs. The telephone has a long cord, which he takes into the bathroom.

SU-7881.

The SU prefix is short for Sunset. The Ballard district, predominantly Scandinavian, where many are fishermen.

He white-knuckles the receiver. This late at night, it's stupid and rude.

Of course, he dials.

One ring and a pick up.

"Is it you?" is the whispered answer.

"Daisy?" Harry whispers.

"Yes. I didn't get your name."

"It isn't LeRoy."

"Oh, we all knew that. You were the Lone Ranger and Superman and everything."

"Harry. Harry Antonelli."

"Harry, why are you whispering?"

"I guess for the same reason you are."

"My mama and my little boy are asleep."

"My folks and brother are asleep, too. Your little boy. What's his name and how old is he?"

"Danny. He's one-and-a-half."

"Are you okay? No repercussions at work?"

"I am. Whatever you did to that horrible Jimmy Ray, he can barely walk straight, and he won't look at me or the other girls. When we laughed out loud at him, he looked the other way, too. His supervisor and the security guys he had hunting for you, they were smiling, too, behind Jimmy Ray's back. Everyone hates him, and

257

they aren't as afraid of him as they had been. What on earth did you say to him? None of us could hear."

"I gave him a lecture on manners and etiquette and the proper treatment of the opposite sex, like Emily Post does."

She giggles. "That was so swell and brave of you. He's a whole lot bigger than you."

"He could be seven feet tall, but he's a bully. All bullies are cowards. That's a known fact. Thanks for helping me get away."

"I didn't want you caught, Harry."

"Me neither."

"You had that slimy drunk, LeRoy Hill's badge. None of us understood that."

"Nobody does."

"Can you tell me how? I'd love to hear the story."

"I can't on the phone."

"Can you come over?"

"At this hour?"

"Yes."

"Absolutely positively."

"Here's my address."

"Wait a minute."

Harry crawls out of the bathroom, fumbles around on the kitchen counter, finds a pencil and a paper napkin, crawls back into the bathroom, and writes it down with a trembling hand.

In sixty seconds, he's down the road in the Booths' Chrysler Airflow. Gunning it.

CHAPTER 48

Seattle.
Sunday, December 29, 1941.

Harry has forgotten that there's a blackout. Residential and street lights, too. Traffic lights are hooded, but working.

By recklessly speeding and ignoring red lights, and thanks to no traffic, he manages somehow to avoid arrest or an accident, crossing through downtown to Ballard.

Daisy Myer's home is a small bungalow with a front porch. Daisy comes out the door, huddled in a long coat, a finger to her lips. She looks even prettier with her long blonde hair down, out of the bandana.

Inside, from what Harry can see in the dark, the living room is small and tidy. It smells of waxes and nosegays. Daisy Myer invites him to sit beside her on the sofa.

"I have to tell you about myself. To get that out of the way before things go any further," Daisy says. "Did Jimmy Ray call me a whore?"

She's like Alice, and Wonder Woman with her lasso: Harry cannot lie to her.

"He did, but I don't believe that for a second. I told him so in a way he won't forget."

"Exactly how? Everybody's dying to know. And don't say how Emily Post would."

"Well, not in so many words, but I got the message out that he won't be able to touch you or any of the other ladies if his fingers are broken."

"He twisted what people there know about me, or what they *think* they know. I was a cheerleader and a homecoming princess. Mama and I were living in Portland, Oregon, then. My boyfriend was a three-sport letterman. We were the perfect couple. Everyone envied and hated us because we were *so* perfect. We were all over the yearbook.

"One thing led to another. When we learned I was expecting, he dropped out of school and skipped town. I haven't a clue where he is now, and I don't care. That's what my own father did to Mama when I was in junior high. When I began showing, I dropped out of school to go away and live with an aunt, if you know what I mean."

To go away and live with an aunt.

Three or four girls in Harry's high school class had gone away to live with an aunt, which meant a home for unwed mothers. The baby's born and given up for adoption. The girl returns home like nothing's happened. A cold and hard business.

"I couldn't give up Danny. I couldn't! Mama is a stenographer, the best and fastest there is. She got a job here in Seattle. When I called her, she came and got us in St. Louis, where my quote-unquote aunt lived. We fought tooth and nail to keep Danny. I don't have a boyfriend, and I don't do those things Jimmy Ray said I do."

"I know you don't," Harry says, meaning it. "If that hillbilly comes near you again or says another word, I'll be really, really happy to…"

"Harry, you're shaking."

"Sorry. That hillbilly, what he did to you with his hands, the things he said."

"I know you would protect me from him, Harry. He knows, too. Please keep your distance from him. If you kill Jimmy Ray, they'll lock you up."

Harry smiles. "I won't kill him. Wouldn't dream of it. But I'll make him wish I had."

"Let's please change the subject. Tell me all about yourself."

Harry does, beginning with football, glossing over Dorothy and his craziest stunts in 1938–1940 Europe, keeping the Lisbon uranium out of it. He speaks of Havana, too, although excluding Gabrielle. He moves on to David and the fake Dewey and the fifth columnists. On that he cannot stop, cannot even punctuate, thoughts joining like a 5,000 word sentence.

"You're hoarse. I'm getting you a glass of water. Or a beer?"

"Beer is the best medicine for the throat."

When Daisy comes back with a cold Rainier, Harry thanks her, takes a long pull, and says, "I shouldn't't've let the cat out of the bag about FDR. We'll both get the firing squad."

"Oh bosh. There's been a rumor about him visiting for days. Everybody on the B-17 fuselage line knows."

Harry smiles. "I'm glad I didn't get a junior G-man badge, but, damn, I'm a solid-gold dumbbell for tossing LeRoy's badge."

"Harry, you can't possibly be thinking of going into the plant again."

"Daisy, something bad is gonna happen soon. I really think the FDR trip is a decoy. The Cushman girls are a clue. That guy on the scooter instead of a lady."

"Guys fill in when the gals call in sick, guys with jobs less important than theirs."

"Yeah, but that one guy did a switcheroo inside my lunch box, thinking it was Leroy's lunchbox and—" Harry digs in his pocket, fishing out five one-dollar bills and three fives. "This was my payoff. There're other Nazis in the plant, too, guys LeRoy knew from Spain who are being paid off."

"You're scaring me," Daisy says.

"That's not my intention. After meeting you, more than ever, I gotta get to those canisters before they blow up."

"After meeting me?"

"Well, yeah."

"Do you know how to disarm bombs?"

"Nope."

Harry's head is in his hands, and Daisy is stroking his back. The last thing in the world he wants to do is cry in front of a girl, but he doesn't know if he can hold out. He has to save Daisy and everyone else, but doesn't have an inkling how.

"Perhaps I can help."

CHAPTER 49

Seattle.
Tuesday, December 30, 1941.

"Mama," Daisy says. "I didn't mean to wake you up. This is who I told you about."

"You two were as quiet as mice. I'm a natural eavesdropper. I'm Emma Myer and I'm very pleased to meet you, Mr. Antonelli."

Emma resembles her daughter twenty-five years in the future. Harry guiltily shunts aside fantasies of strong discipline and being tucked in at bedtime.

"Mama, you said you can help?"

"No, I can't directly help, by drawing a bull's-eye on the criminals and their explosives. But I can assist with logic. Let's move to the kitchen table."

"Your beer is gone, Harry," Daisy says as they take seats.

"Evaporation."

"I'll fix that," Daisy says, getting another out of the fridge for him as Emma Myer sits down with a pencil and sheets of typing paper.

Emma Myer says, "The job I landed when I came to Seattle was with an insurance company. I quit working for them because the pay was too low, and took my chances on my own. I do better as a freelance stenographer. I make more money and I can set my hours, so there's more time to be with Danny, and save on babysitting costs."

Speaking of Danny, a gurgling noise comes from a bedroom.

263

"Mama is the best stenographer in Seattle," Daisy says, getting up.

"I take dictation for a variety of very smart people when there's too much work for their staff employees. University professors, attorneys, business executives. Logical people with deduction processes that I hope rubbed off on me somewhat. Logic. I'm going to try to use it to help you with your problem, Harry. This isn't to say that I'm encouraging you to rush into something blindly and risk your life."

"Logic?" Harry asks. "How so? There are times when logic and I are total strangers. We wouldn't recognize each other if we passed in the street."

Emma says, "Logic is only a word for a thought process that leads to the valid solution to a problem. You may have to discard old ideas to reach the solution."

She draws a rectangle and makes small Xs all over it. "An unknown number of canisters full of explosives are scattered in Plant Two, do you think?"

Harry says, "I'm close to one-hundred percent sure. Scattered, they'd do the most damage. Small amounts of damage in many areas."

"But how do you set them off all at once? If one goes off, everyone's on the alert. Whoever sets off the next one would be noticed."

Harry nods. "Yeah, you'd have to have a lot of guys setting them off or lighting fuses or whatever they'd have to do. A lot more than we know of. And if they weren't placed just so, some might not do much of anything. You know, blow up a bathroom door."

Daisy is back with her son, who's wearing warm pajamas with feet, tucked over her shoulder.

"He's hungry. I'll warm up some baby food. He's growing like a weed."

Emma Myer blows a kiss at her grandson and says, "I agree. Scattered locations aren't logical. You'd have to have that many traitors to set them off all at once. It's not logical that a handful of men run from one to the next to the next. If it's all in one place, it will make a big bang and do much more damage to a critical spot, wherever that may be."

"True," Harry says.

"So, why? What's the point? Damaging aluminum parts on the bombers prevented some from getting to England. We know that from what news leaks out and from what you told Daisy. Setting off a bomb will shut down production temporarily, but not for long. The Flying Fortress is being manufactured in California, too. How logical is this coffee canister business?"

Harry shakes his head.

"How many traitors who passed through the Dorrinsen Arms Hotel do you think there are or were?"

Harry shrugs. "Between seven to ten. A dozen, tops."

"Suppose you are able to identify exactly where you have to go inside the plant, and suppose you get past the guard gate, how far would you get?"

"Before I'm jumped and beaten up by seven to ten security guys? Thirty feet. Maybe."

"This phony Dewey Concannon individual you followed to Boeing and the woman who tried to run you down when Miss Dorothy Booth—is it?—was almost kidnapped."

"An old family friend," Harry says too quickly.

Emma smiles, not buying it, and says, "The first phase of the problem has to be solved from the outside. You can concentrate on a handful of people versus a factory as big as a small town."

Danny is in his highchair, waiting for his food, slapping the tray, looking at Harry.

"Hi," Harry says.

"Da-da," Danny Myer says.

Harry quickly terminates the conversation with a wink and asks Emma, "How do you think we ought to proceed?"

"Fast and get some help outside of Plant Two."

"Yeah. I agree."

"Assemble a team. That darling old Alice Haymarket. Even those hobos, if you have to. They strike me as creative. Like you, they'll approach the problem obliquely. Everyone can play a part. The G-man David Booth? You know him and I don't, so you choose whether to include him. My first thought is that you and him have been at cross-purposes."

"Yeah, Mr. Dave Cross-Purposes."

"Let him in on what you decide to do. He can do it his way, and you can do it your way. Two plans are superior to one."

"Mama," Daisy says. "You're telling Harry to do exactly what he *shouldn't* do, telling him to do what'll get him into big, big trouble."

"I know. Because whatever I say, he'll do it anyway. Nothing I say will stop you, will it, Harry?"

Harry has a drink of beer and says. "Two plans are better than one. As long as at least one of them works."

CHAPTER 50

Seattle.
Tuesday, December 30, 1941.

Harry has been invited to spend the night on the couch. For two reasons, he can't sleep beyond a few winks:

1. The Problem That Must Be Solved Fast.
2. Daisy In Her Bedroom, In Her Bed, Mere Feet Away.

Logic. A thought process that leads to the valid solution of the problem. You may have to discard old ideas to reach the solution.

If the packed-with-explosive-not-hot-coffee jugs can't do much damage on their own, they have to be in one spot, maybe inside a large box or buried inside a B-17, but where, and how much damage can they do anyway? Kill ten people and blow up two airplanes? Terrible as that'd be, it wouldn't hurt the war effort much. Hitler would hardly notice the difference.

If the canisters are gonna be set off like it's the Fourth of July, who gathers them up and takes them where they're gonna be set off, and when?

Where the hell are Concannon and Diana?

The criminal always returns to the scene of the crime.

Who said that, Sherlock Holmes?

How the hell did that just pop into his noggin?

And how logical is it?

Harry thinks of football and *reverse* logic. He's on defense. The

267

halfbacks and both ends are to his left. The play is going that way? Usually, but not every time. Now and then, it's a Statue of Liberty play or a toss to his right to the fullback. Playing right halfback on defense, once in a blue moon, Harry sees something in the quarterback's eyes. The ball carrier is coming to his right when everybody else is buying the fake, going to his left. It's just him and Harry; few things feel better than pancaking a guy in the open field, plastering him so hard that the ball flies out of his hands.

The criminal always returns to the scene of the crime.

The criminal doesn't return because he forgot to steal Grandpa's gold pocket watch.

Where's the last place on earth that anybody would look for Diana and Concannon?

Harry smiles. He's able now to sleep soundly until he hears an alarm go off half an hour later.

Daisy is up feeding Danny. There's light under Emma's door.

Daisy tells Harry that there's a spare toothbrush for him. Harry spruces up as well as he can and tells Daisy that he wants to drive her to work, and that he doesn't want her to actually go to work.

She says, "I'm not completely awake, so I guess I didn't hear you right."

"Is your mother working today?"

"No, she isn't. Mama can take care of Danny all day."

"Please call in sick, Daisy. I don't want you in there today."

"Harry, you're scaring me."

He has his arms around her. "I'm sorry. I don't mean to. The criminal always returns to the scene of the crime. That is a known fact, so humor me, okay? Make the call."

She is hugging him back. "Well, I don't think they'll mind after what happened yesterday, and you haven't been wrong yet."

"Good," he says, taking a slip of paper from his pants pocket. "First, may I use your phone?"

Emma is dressed, pouring a cup of coffee, looking at the wild man her daughter invited over in the middle of the night. He is a mass of coiled springs with a nose that the Seattle Rainiers may have used for batting practice. But Harry fixed the wagon of that monster who was terrorizing her little girl. She smiles, seeing Cupid's arrows flying back and forth between them like a medieval battle fought with longbows.

Daisy could do worse, much, much worse, she thinks. She already has.

"Who died?"

"Good morning to you, too, Alice."

"Horatio Alger Antonelli, thank God."

"Mrs. Haymarket—"

"Don't call me that, you little brat. I've tried to reach you at home. Desperately tried."

"Why?"

"I had a hunch and asked Hughie do some snooping for me. He's my pet bloodhound. He'll roll over and bark and do anything else I ask."

"Alice."

"Well, the evil twins—you know who I am speaking of—have a car in the garage that isn't registered. A cream-colored Studebaker coupe. As elusive as they are, I deduced that they store it in order to have a clean getaway vehicle. *Clean getaway vehicle.* This is how they term it in the detective novels, you know."

"Sherlock Holmes would be proud of you, Alice."

"I insist upon playing detective with you again after this vital mystery clue."

"I can't say no after this."

"I can be at the front desk and ready for action as soon as I powder my nose."

CHAPTER 51

Seattle.
Tuesday, December 30, 1941.

Emma blocks the front door and orders Daisy and Harry to the dining table.

"Breakfast is the most important meal of the day," she says, making toast and scrambled eggs.

Afterward, in the Airflow, Daisy says, "You're going to explain what you said sometime?"

"What?"

"The criminal always returns to the scene of the crime."

"Sherlock Holmes said that first. I think."

"Is it true?"

"Either it is or it isn't. It's the only place to look if you haven't the foggiest where else to look."

"I think I believe what you're saying, even if you may not. It's where you flush that Dewey creature out into the open."

"We can hope."

*****

Alice is at the Dorrinsen Arms' front desk, pointing at her watch and steaming.

"What kept you?"

Harry smiles. "I'm not a girl. I didn't know how long nose powdering takes."

Alice looks at Daisy. "Handsome Harry and his charm. Don't be bewitched by him, dear. He'll have your knickers off before you know it. And you are?"

"Alice, c'mon."

"Daisy Myer, ma'am."

"How on earth did you become involved with this rascal?"

Anxious for this chitchat to end, Harry says, "Let's go. We have to move quickly. There's no telling when they'll come for the car."

Harry fills Alice in as they go to the parking garage on the slick pavement, him on one of her arms, Daisy holding the other.

Inside the garage, Harry says, "Fancy. Like last time, Cadillacs, Packards, Chryslers."

Alice tells Daisy, "My husband Max parked our Duesenberg in here until he passed away."

"I'm so sorry."

"Oh, don't be."

"Save it, Alice. This isn't the time," Harry says, thinking of Agrippina the Younger and Lizzie Hennshaw.

"I could tell you stories about men that would curl your hair, dear."

"C'mon, Alice. Which car?"

"The Studebaker that's up front."

"A thirty-nine model. Backed in, all set for a fast getaway," Harry says. "I'll bring our car right up front, then call Lou, and have him come over and break into it."

The big door starts to slide open. Dewey Concannon the Fourth is pushing it.

"Duck," Harry says. "He's returning to the scene of the crime."

"Which crime?" Alice whispers.

"Pick one, "Harry says.

They're crouched behind the trunk of a Mercedes-Benz convertible and see a taxi drive away. The phony Dewey strides in, spiffy in suit,

271

tie and hat. Clipped on to a lapel is a round Boeing employee badge. He drives out in the Studebaker without pausing to close the garage door, burning rubber so fast that they can smell it.

"Shit," Harry says.

"Your language, young man."

"He must've seen us," Daisy says.

"Whatever, he has to be going to Plant Two," Harry says, scribbling on a slip of paper."Alice, please go back to the hotel and call Dorothy and David. This is his G-man office number."

"Harry, you're leaving me behind?"

Harry isn't listening. The Airflow is two blocks away. He tries the Mercedes door. It's unlocked. A key is in the ignition.

"Hop in quick, Daisy. We're going for a spin."

CHAPTER 52

Seattle.
Tuesday. December 30, 1941.

"We're stealing this car?" Daisy asks.

"No. Not stealing. *Borrowing*. It's an omen."

Daisy laughs, as excited as frightened.

"Tell me, how can it be an omen?"

Harry grinds the gears as he fishtails out of the garage, saying, "We parked two blocks away. Our phony Dewey would be long gone if I had to run for the Airflow. The key's in the ignition, begging us to borrow it. If that's not an omen, I don't know what is."

"Oh, Harry."

"I never thought I'd be behind the wheel of one of these snazzy driving machines," he says.

"It has leather seats, but what else is so special?"

"It's a drophead 540K with a fender-mounted spare and wire wheels. There's a V-8 under the hood that has as many horses as a small plane. My brother Lou talks and talks about all the cars he'd love to drive. This is one, even though it's German."

Daisy grips the dashboard and says, "Please be careful, Harry. The curb you just hit, some of those horses nearly hit an old man."

Harry's attention is on the street ahead, not innocent bystanders. "Do you see him?"

"There, *there*. Two blocks ahead. He's turning left."

They stay on him. It's easy, Harry thinks, fairly sure where he's going. *Too* easy. This is one time when Harry is sorry he guessed correctly.

Dewey pulls over a block from Plant Two's gate. He reaches under the passenger seat and gets out with a black lunch pail.

"This is wrong," Daisy says.

"What is?"

"He's dressed like a boss and bosses don't carry lunchboxes. It's beneath them. They eat lunch in their own cafeteria."

"Well, we know there's no egg salad sandwich in it," Harry says. "Daisy, do you have your Boeing badge?"

"It's in my purse."

"Let's have it."

"No, Harry. You can't be serious."

"There's no way I can get my hands on him before he goes through the gate. I gotta get in there. Please, Daisy, hurry up."

"You can't pass as me!"

"The guards are paying half their attention to the ladies at their gate, and I don't have a lunchbox for them to look into. C'mon."

She hands him her badge and kisses him so passionately that it verges on violent.

"Please be careful."

"Wow. I'll have to be careful after that," Harry says, jumping out of the car, woozy from the smooch.

The guards are bundled up against the cold, paying little attention to Harry, who has no lunchbox to inspect. He makes it inside when he sees Dewey enter the plant. Thousands of square feet, thousands of workers. Gotta close the gap.

He guesses he'll go straight ahead, toward the middle, the best spot to set off a bomb, doing the maximum damage to property and lives. He guesses correctly again, making up ground on his prey.

*****

Dewey is walking faster, head held high with the arrogance of a boss, toward what appears to be a trash bin on wheels or casters, roughly six by six and five feet high, covered by canvas. Signs all around the thing state in red: DO NOT REMOVE. In the hotel garage, he thought he caught a glimpse of movement behind an old Mercedes-Benz. Whether it was his mind playing tricks or not, he has to move fast.

Reichsführer-SS Heinrich Himmler will be so proud. When this is done, he will be a hero of the Reich.

*****

A garbage container. Damn clever. Could've been there for weeks, Harry thinks. Nobody wanting to touch it and get into trouble, or make extra work for themselves.

Dewey opens his lunch box, turns something inside it, closes the box, and drops it in the bin. A thin wisp of smoke curls up and around the canvas.

Legs pumping high as if he's on the kickoff squad, pursuing the returner with the ball, mayhem in his heart, Harry sees a mechanic holding a long wrench, studying whatever he's studying on a blueprint.

Harry veers off, yanks the wrench out of the guy's hand, yelling over the riveting racket, "I'll get this right back to you."

*****

Dewey has reversed course, beelining for the door before the explosion that will alter the course of the war.

Harry Antonelli! Where did he come from? Antonelli is running straight at him. Fifty meters away and closing fast.

Dewey stops, plants his feet, and raises his fists to clobber him fair and square. Antonelli is a ruffian, but he possesses the American's ludicrous belief in fair play. Unlike the Führer, who will destroy this nation and their archaic embrace of chivalry by any means at his disposal.

They will square off in a few seconds. Dewey will land a knockout punch on Antonelli's jaw, then stride past him and out the door to safety.

*****

What the hell's going on, Harry wonders? The phony Dewey has his fists raised like Jack Dempsey at the start of round one.

Harry is remembering Saturdays as a kid, walking to the Columbia City Theatre and shelling out a dime to see Tom Mix and Tarzan. There'd be a cartoon, a newsreel and a serial. He loved the serials! Flash Gordon most of all. They'd end with cliffhangers you'd never think they'd survive, but they did. You had to come back the next Saturday, pay your dime, to see how. Flash on the Planet Mongo dealing with Ming the Merciless. Terry Lee, too, any of them engaging the villain in a fair fight, Marquis of Queensberry rules, no low blows by the good guys, et cetera, no matter how dirty the opponent fought.

This is no Saturday serial. No time to play nice. Not the time for a cliffhanger. This has to be the last reel.

Harry slows and says, "Hey, pal, maybe you and I got off on the wrong foot."

Puzzled, Dewey frowns but keeps his dukes up.

"You'd be smart to join the winning side, Antonelli."

"Yeah?"

"I am a personal friend of Reichsführer-SS Heinrich Himmler," he says, lowering his right hand to his pants pocket. "When the war is won, I can use my influence for your benefit. Dorothy's, too."

The wrench is a two feet long and heavy. That's all Harry knows about its use. The smoke in the bin is curling higher. Dorothy and thousands of others are in the building.

As Dewey's pistol comes out, Harry swings the wrench with both hands and breaks Dewey's left forearm. He swings again, crushing his cheekbone, muffling a scream. Harry hears but doesn't see the pistol strike concrete.

Harry drops the wrench, slings the moaning, semi-conscious saboteur over a shoulder and dumps him into the bin, hoping he'll smother the fuse.

No such luck. The smoke is even thicker.

Harry has drawn a crowd, predominantly women, riveters with their hair in bandanas. He jabs toward the other end of the building, yelling, "What's out there, Rosie?"

"Some small docks and the Duwamish River. The 16th South bridge on the right. What's that smoke about?"

"Workers out there?"

"Not many."

He screams, "C'mon. Help me push this thing and have someone get the doors open."

"Is that a bomb in there?"

"Yeah."

"How big?"

"Too big."

Two gals get behind the bin and they start moving it.

One of Dewey's legs is dangling out.

The gal on Harry's left says, "Who are you, cutie?"

"A secret agent G-man."

"Who's he? The leg? Shouldn't we pull him out of there?"

"He's a Nazi spy."

"Fuck him then," she says, pushing harder and faster.

A gate is rolled up when they get there. They're all out of breath, but have enough left to give the bin a hard shove into the open.

"C'mon! Help me get the gate down. We gotta run for it before it blows!" Harry orders, waving at workers on each side, hanging on the chains.

Half a minute after the stampede, the bin explodes. Harry had expected the side of the building to blow inward, but it doesn't, and the explosion is barely louder than the riveting racket.

The metallic clatter is dying out as the word spreads. Harry goes to the gate and looks through a window. What's left of the trash bin is tipped on its side, shards of canisters scattered everywhere. Dewey is sprawled face up, his face as shriveled and black as a rotten banana peel.

A greenish gas has wafted upward, diffusing. Crows and gulls drop to the ground, like victims in some hideous Biblical prophecy.

One of the ladies faints. Another leans on Harry for support. A man terrified of guns and clowns, he is strong and stolid right now.

Out of breath, David Booth arrives.

"It's gas, not a bomb. What the hell is it?" Harry says.

"I will explain later," David says."

"Is Dorothy out of the building?"

"She is," David says, looking outside. He turns back to Harry, hand on the gate to steady himself. Like me and guns, Harry thinks. Guns and clowns.

"Dewey's lady friend?"

"She will not get far."

"Good. Take it from here, Dave. I've got a car to un-steal."

*****

Harry tells his story to Daisy as they drive back to the Dorrinsen Arms. She snuggles so tightly that he can't shift gears. He stays in whatever gear he's in as the engine roars. It's not his car, and it's German, too.

"Oh my God, Harry. How many workers were in there?"

"Oh, eighteen thousand or so," he says, dreaming up the number.

HISTORICAL NOTE: The exact number of employees inside Plant Two at the specific time and date isn't known, but by war's end in 1945, 30,000 worked there on three shifts, so it was unlikely that Harry was exaggerating by much.

"You saved eighteen thousand lives, Harry?"

He shrugs modestly, changing the subject to Alice Haymarket. "I'm worried, Daisy. She doesn't like to be left out of the action. She's impulsive, and upset that we left her behind."

"I'm worried, too. She is adorable," Daisy says. "You and your Sherlock Holmes."

"Yeah, the last place in the world they'd think Diana is."

"Can you drive faster?"

"Nope. The oil and temp needles are way up. We have to make it back before the engine seizes up."

"I can move over a little so you can shift gears."

"No, no. You're fine where you are."

They do make it, parking the chugging, wheezing Mercedes a block from the Dorrinsen Arms, in front of a five-and-dime. They leave it steaming, emitting the odor of an industrial fire.

Up they go to Alice's floor, bound for 1101.

They find Diana Doe in the hallway, holding Alice close to her, a paring knife in her free hand. Alice is in a woolen jacket, purse on her shoulder, frightened, looking not just old, but ancient.

"Get away. This isn't your concern," Diana says.

"The hell it isn't," Harry says, holding bobby pins.

"She's my ticket out of here. If she hadn't been snooping at my door, I could have waited it out until the fuss died down."

Harry says, "What's your angle, girlie? I figure Dewey was in it because he thinks Hitler is the bee's knees."

"Unless you grew up like I did, you wouldn't understand."

"Lizzie Hennshaw told us how you grew up. Poor as a church mouse and treated as bad as can be. That's rotten, but not as rotten as what you tried to do at Boeing."

Daisy says, "There isn't enough money in the world to make me—"

"You wouldn't understand either."

Harry says, "I gotta tell you. Your partner won't be joining you."

"He's not in my future plans."

"You ever read the funnies? Dick Tracy? Your boy looks like Pruneface. Except skinnier. The poison gas blew up outside. Him and a thousand or so birds were the only victims. The game's over."

"You're lying."

"Turn on the radio, lady. It'll be on the news by now. Any station on the dial."

"Get out of my way or I'll slice the old bat open."

Alice says, wheezing, "Wherever you're taking me, I won't be alive if I can't take my heart medicine now. My nitroglycerin, in my mouth, under my tongue. Otherwise I'll faint, and that will be the end of me and you, too. The cops will make Swiss cheese out of you. Please, for both our sakes, I beg you."

"Make it fast," Diana snaps.

Alice reaches into her purse.

She takes out not her pills but her Derringer.

She twists and sticks it not in her mouth, but Diana's.

She pulls the trigger.

Alice doesn't faint, but Harry does.

CHAPTER 53

Seattle.
Wednesday, December 31, 1941.

In the morning, in the confidentiality of David Booth's Hudson, David tells Harry what he knows thus far about the deadly gas.

"Leave it to Nazi Germany to invent a poison so vile it doesn't even deserve a vowel."

"What's its moniker?"

"Ztrvn."

"Say that again."

"Ztrvn. Zzt-trr-vnn."

"Okay. Gotcha. So what do you know about it?"

"Our agency was informed by British intelligence officers that the Germans were working on a poison gas that will make mustard gas seem like an expensive Parisian perfume in comparison. I must admit, we were taken by surprise by its final development and its use here. We believed it was earmarked for the Soviet Union."

"Your agency, which is…?"

"Ztrvn kills instantly, and its residue will cling to hard and soft surfaces. If you had not thwarted their attack, thousands would have died. Plant Two and everything in it would be contaminated and unusable. For years, if not decades. People would be reluctant to work at other plants. Bomber production would cease to destroy Hitler's war machine."

"Jeez, they'd win the war."

"If not, it would take much longer for us to win."

"So logically, I kind of saved the world again, huh?"

David pauses, then says, "A mild hyperbole, but yes."

"That taken into consideration, when are you and your G-man agency bosses paying me a decent wage?"

"I shall attempt to arrange cash payments, but this, uh, incident is to remain classified."

"Incident? Jesus Christ, Dave. Must've been five or ten thousand dead birds out there, and our friend shrunken like a fucking mummy."

"Harry, please, do not yell and curse in this confined space. Few workers actually looked out the window. They shall be counseled."

Harry shakes his head. "Counseled? Told to zip their lips or else? Just like the Gestapo counsels."

"Harry, it's a choice between that or widespread panic."

As usual, Harry thinks, David has a point. "Okay, but back to the subject of me being paid. I can't wait for approval to go through some supervisor of yours. Don't you agents have a slush fund?'

David doesn't answer.

"Like the packages of dough taken from that post office box."

David smiles and says, "Please advise Mrs. Haymarket not to spend any from the envelope she slipped into her purse."

"She did that?"

"You know good and well she did, Harry. It is counterfeit, every last dollar of it."

"C'mon, Dave. Our Nazis were financing their operation with it and nobody caught on?"

"The Germans are extremely proficient at counterfeiting. The bills look genuine to the casual eye, but our departmental people discovered it, albeit with difficulty. The paper is wrong, the ink, too. Very subtle differences."

Harry says, "Do you know who our fake Dewey really was?"

"No, and I doubt if we will. Even if our allies have his fingerprints on file, we cannot take them accurately from his remains. Every bit of him is shriveled like a walnut."

"How did that zert-fun gas get here?"

"Your hobo pals, bless them, are assisting us in tracking down the rest of their colleagues from Spain who assisted in delivering the poison gas."

"Well, great. Diana?"

"We've drawn an utter blank. She goes by Diana Doe, as in John Doe, but has no identification to support that. Any documentation about her is via men she has known."

"Like Hubert Hennshaw." Harry pauses. "Diana in Bremerton in 1930?"

"Nobody can make a positive identification, or is afraid to. The widow Hennshaw will not, claiming that it is gossip and rumor. She is demanding payment for any information, which is likely useless. Thanks to advanced alcoholism, her memory is unreliable."

Harry doesn't answer, lost in a fantasy of his sadistic, diabolical Wonder Woman, aka Diana Whomever.

David says, "Back to you, Harry. The report of what you did is racing up the chain of command. President Roosevelt himself will be informed. We know that you intend to enlist in the Army Air Corps and enter flight training."

"As soon as I can."

"I can almost guarantee that you'll enter service as a second lieutenant. I am expediting the paperwork to expunge your record, a record that would make Lucky Luciano proud."

"That'd be swell, Dave."

"You will be an officer and a gentleman."

"Gentleman?"

David laughs. "Flyboys are given some flexibility in regard to decorum. I'm sure you will fit right in. Out of curiosity, do you have plans for tonight?"

Harry evades, saying, "How about you and Dorothy?"

"She is going out with Boeing colleagues for a glass or two of bubbly."

"You?"

"A quiet evening at home, avoiding all the drunks driving on slippery roads, while listening to Guy Lombardo on the radio, retiring after hearing him usher in the New Year with his *Auld Lang Syne*. And you?"

Harry is tempted to ask if Dave'll have a lady friend with him, but doesn't. Come to think of it, he's *never* seen Dave with a gal. Could he be…? Nah, not a secret agent.

"Me? A glass or two of bubbly with a couple of friends."

"Happy New Year, Harry."

"Happy New Year, David."

CHAPTER 54

Seattle.
Wednesday, December 31, 1941.

W histling as he walks to the Airflow from the liquor store, Harry has two bottles of sparkling wine in a bag. As he told David, he's bringing in the New Year by having a glass or two (or three or five) of bubbly with friends. The friends: Emma and Daisy Myer.

Daisy has told him that her mother becomes drowsy after a couple of drinks, then "sleeps like a log." She'll have Danny in her room, too, Danny who regularly sleeps through the night.

Harry has great expectations. Thus the whistling.

He sees a black 1940 Ford coupe ahead, idling loudly at the curb in front of a bank. Harry likes the looks of that model Ford. Lou does, too, and has talked about how they're the favorite of young guys who soup up cars. Milling the heads, twin carburetors, dual pipes, and other stuff Harry doesn't understand.

Joe Bobby (Rob) Banks is inside that bank, brandishing his Colt .45, customers and employees jammed into a corner, their hands up, as he orders the tellers to fill his bag with what they have in the drawers.

"Don't be wastin' no time and don't be stingy. It ain't your own personal money," he yells from behind his clown mask. "Don't nobody be no hero neither, unless you want a bullet hole in your head."

Not every word is crystal clear, but they get the drift and know who he is, a killer who has nothing to lose if he kills again.

At the end of the teller windows, Rob Banks snatches the bag from the trembling girl. It's plump with greenbacks. Rob Banks' instincts are on the button again. It's not a Friday, but on New Year's Eve, there's extra dough on hand for folks who're buying food and drink for their parties.

Out he goes with his .45 and bag of cash to Leamy and the hot Ford he swiped two hours ago. Rob comes within an eyelash of bumping into a guy carrying a bag full of bottles. The guy's eyes bug out and he screams like a goldurn banshee as he grabs Rob's arm. The bottles fall, smashing to pieces between them.

They tangle up and land on the sidewalk, Banks on top of the screaming guy. Leamy is watching this and knows the jig's up. It's every man for himself, he thinks, putting the car into gear.

Horatio Alger (Harry) Antonelli's worst nightmare is on top of him, a clown carrying a gun. With every bit of the considerable strength in his arms and legs, he launches Joe Bobby (Rob) Banks upward and streetward.

As Leamy powers into traffic, Rob lands on the Ford's hood, blocking Leamy's vision. He steps on the gas, colliding with an oncoming bus. The impact slams Leamy against the steering wheel, breaking his collarbone, while propelling Rob over the roof and trunk into the path of a coal delivery truck.

Harry has finished off the Killer Klown Gang, but sees none of it, because he's out cold.

ABOUT THE AUTHOR

G ary Alexander is the author of sixteen novels. *Disappeared*, first
in the Buster Hightower series, has been optioned to Universal
Studios.

He's also written 150+ short stories and sold travel articles to six
major dailies.

One story appeared in *Best American Mystery Stories 2010*, and
another in *Mystery Writers of America Presents Ice Cold: Tales of
Intrigue from the Cold War* anthology.

On his last visit to Lisbon in 2015, Alexander walked where Harry
Antonelli had in 1940, although somewhat less recklessly.

His website is www.garyralexander.net.